ABOUT THE TASTY EVERYTHING SERIES

★ ★ ★ ★ ★ **Knight is downright diabolical in her use of humor,** starting us out with a my-drink-choked-me, hilarious opening scene, and it just gets funnier from there. ~ BookAddict

★ ★ ★ ★ ★ I'm passing out over here from that swoon. ~ Southern Chicks Lit

★ ★ ★ ★ ★ Tasty Mango causes belly aching laughing, with **full on tears running down your face from laughing so hard**. ~ Misty Reads Book Blog

★ ★ ★ ★ ★ **This book had me laughing out loud too many times to count.** Thelma of Thelma & Louise Book Blog

★ ★ ★ TASTY CHERRY ★ ★ ★

A hospitality intern at an upscale castle hotel decides to lose her virginity with a stranger before starting her first job, only to discover that the one-night-stand is her new boss.

tasty CHERRY

by JJ Knight

the *USA Today* bestselling author of

Big Pickle ~ Hot Pickle ~ Spicy Pickle
Tasty Mango ~ Tasty Pickle ~ Tasty Cherry
Royal Pickle ~ Royal Rebel ~ Royal Escape
Juicy Pickle ~ Second Chance Santa
The Wedding Confession ~ The Wedding Shake-up
Single Dad on Top ~ The Accidental Harem
Uncaged Love ~ Fight for Her ~ Reckless Attraction

Casey Shay Press
PO Box 160116
Austin, TX 78716
www.jjknight.com

Paperback ISBN: 9781938150708

THE CASTLE HOTEL

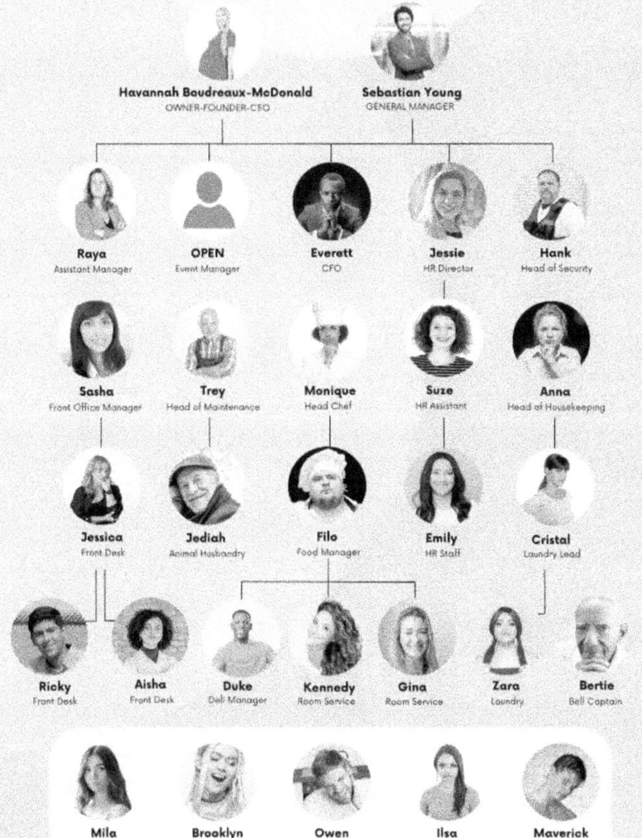

1

MILA

Thank God virginity isn't visible, or mine would definitely be showing.

I dance with my third man of the night, feeling despair that this Colorado bar isn't going to cough up a solution to my problem.

I've simply got to find someone to break into this flower shop.

Cut this grass.

Bust a hyme.

Or if you're kicking it old school: pop this cherry.

At least my current dance partner is in the right range. Male. Twenties. Not scary. And most importantly — interested. That's been hard to come by.

Which is why I'm here. I've been trying all summer to get this V-card cashed in.

Time is running out. I start a new job tomorrow, a live-in situation with five interns. Camille, my best friend from college, has told me to get this taken care of or I'll be the talk of my new coworkers if anyone finds out. My hymen situation is something I'll never live down.

I can hear the nicknames.

Hey, Veek.

Good afternoon, VILF.

How's it hanging, nergin?

Goodntight. Poptart. V-squad. Dusty Murphy.

Maybe I shouldn't have looked on Urban Thesaurus.

But I know Camille is right.

I'm not attached to my status. I've tried to give it up plenty of times over the years. Now, I'm desperate.

I'm a college graduate about to meet potential long-term friends and maybe get a real dating life. But I have this thing I don't want hanging over my head. It makes me feel awkward and weird, like I can't do a casual hookup. And trust me, I'm totally fine with a casual hookup!

But first-time sex will feel too big, too important to whatever guy it ends up being.

Or, it will be the subject of ridicule.

I don't want that scene.

I want to be saucy, experienced, ready for what happens next.

So, I need this situation handled, like Christian Grey did for Anastasia.

I want someone to manage it for me.

Maybe it'll be this man leading me around the dance floor. He's the best chance I've had all night. He reminds me of Jack Black. Shaggy hair, huge smile. His attention is riveting.

Better than the other two. The first one was polite and danced us across the floor as smoothly as an ice skater.

But he was easily sixty.

Still, I would have done him, except he thanked me kindly and left me at the stool where he found me.

Then came the one with a chipmunk-packed lower cheek full of snuff. I haven't seen anyone doing dip in a hot minute, as I didn't run in those circles in Texas. When he leaned in like he might kiss me with that mouthful of carcinogenic spit-mush, I took off for the bathroom.

This third partner seems game. He's definitely touchy feely. That's a good sign, right?

Except his hands are roving *everywhere.*

As one song turns into two, he starts grabbing me more aggressively. He squeezes my butt. Then, he moves up to my waist. Then he's got one of my boobs! Right here on the dance floor!

I can't help but look at the drinkers scattered about the tables, wondering if this is some test for the new girl in town. Can the Texas girl handle a Colorado man?

I shy away, but he lets go of the boob to draw me even closer. Both of his hands grasp a buttcheek so he can rock me against what might be a very impressive part of his anatomy.

Or is it socks?

Something about the shape doesn't seem quite right. But what do I know? The only male parts I've seen have been on screen (yes, I paused that unforgettable cameo on *Sex/Life.* Maybe a few times).

But this is simultaneously too big and too soft. It moves, not side to side, but front to back, like it's squishy. I picture my favorite pickle stress toy, and I can't hold it together.

I press my lips hard, bite my cheek. Anything not to laugh.

This situation is ridiculous.

I'm ridiculous for doing this.

Time to throw in the towel.

I'll have to save myself for The One. Fair enough, universe, I get it. I'll have to hope for someone discreet. Who maybe cares about me.

Not sock-man.

Is this song ever going to end?

As the dance drags on, he pulls me even closer to him, until I'm practically attached to his crotch. Yeah, I'm done with this.

"I should hit the little girls' room," I tell him.

But he grunts and hangs on.

Surely he can't hold me hostage right here in the middle of a bar.

I try to wriggle away, but his arms are like a vise.

"Hey," I say. "Let go."

And that's when someone finally steps in.

"That's enough, Carl."

The man is tall, with a mass of black wavy hair and a close-trimmed beard. He knows Carl's name, but they don't seem like friends.

Carl doesn't want to let me go, but the man pushes between us and twirls me out of the brute's arms.

We two-step away from the scowling, broody Carl, who stalks right out the door.

I'm saved.

This man smells so good that I want to drown in him. Woodsy, masculine, with an undertone of something crisp, like citrus.

He has total command of our steps, and when he draws me close, there's nothing gross or seedy about it. We fit together like one person, gliding across the floor in easy time with the music.

Sorry, universe, I've changed my mind again.

This man could totally be the one.

Or does he have a girlfriend sitting somewhere who told him to come save me?

We keep dancing, and as I survey the bar while we circle, there aren't any unattended ladies sitting around.

Could he be for me?

Surely not. He's gorgeous, older than me, and well dressed. In my experience, men like this don't go for frumpy, curvy girls like me. It's not that I don't deserve them. I do. But I'm never anyone's first pick. That's the facts. I have years of evidence to demonstrably prove I'm never the center of anyone's attention.

And yet, here is this one, holding me close as we circle the floor.

The song switches, and mystery man seems perfectly content to keep dancing. The woman on stage sings the opening line to "Cherry" by Lana Del Rey.

Really? Cherry?

But she's right, I am falling to pieces right here. We make a turn, and when his hand tightens its grip and lifts over my head, I know what to do, even though I've never been a good dancer. I turn beneath his arm in a slow spin, only to end up right back in his arms.

I'm completely entranced. No movie has ever been as good as this. No romance story.

This song has a different beat, so we don't two-step, but something closer to a waltz. I feel like I'm in *Bridgerton*, or Giselle in *Enchanted*. I don't need the big ball gown, the ceremony, the glitz.

A Colorado honky-took with sawdust on the floor and neon signs on the walls does just as good. I'm a taxidermy princess, a dive bar debutante.

Works for me.

"Cherry" ends, and he leans in. "You want something to drink?"

I nod. We sit at a booth in the corner, and the waitress brings us two blackberry ciders. "On the house for getting Carl to leave."

We laugh and clink our cans. The cider is cold and sweet, and I feel high. How is this working so perfectly?

"I'm Sebastian," he says. "Sorry about Carl."

"Mila," I tell him. "And thanks."

It's so easy from there. We grin at each other. We talk about random, unimportant things. TV shows. Favorite musicians. We compare concerts attended, movies seen, memes shared. We don't have a lot in common, but there's an age gap at play.

I peg him at thirty-something to my twenty-two. I don't mind. That's even better if I'm trying to find someone who knows what he's doing.

But how do I go from this to what I need to get done?

What's normal? How do I have a one-night stand where we never exchange information, and he never knows why I had a stranger take away my status as a *crotch noob?*

I can't mess this up now that we've gotten this far.

"Did you drive here?" he asks.

Oh, God, we're transitioning.

"I did. I'm at a hotel about a mile away." Here goes nothing. "Want to see my room?"

My face burns hot. I think I said exactly the same thing to my first boyfriend in sixth grade.

But Sebastian simply runs his fingers over the back of my hand. "I'd like that."

And the way I shiver tells me this is it. If he's a one-night-stand kind of guy, then I will, at last, be the girl.

2

SEBASTIAN

I follow Mila to the hotel I've driven by a thousand times between work and home. I'm a Boulder native, and I know every nook and cranny of our small city.

She's waiting for me outside of her car when I get out of mine.

"Hey," she says.

I'm not one to waste time, so I pull her to me. The air outside is brisk. Her mouth is cool, but not for long.

I kiss her slowly and thoroughly as a test. I want to know she's really down for this before we go inside.

Her hands go around my neck. She's eager and responsive. Everything revs up. This is happening. I snatch her up in my arms, cradled to my chest.

She lets out a whoop, then laughs. "Are you sweeping me off my feet?"

"I hope so."

I carry her across the parking lot, but when we get to

the lobby doors, she presses on my chest as a signal to set her down.

Even so, the two of us practically race across the empty lobby to the elevator. No one's at the desk, so I kiss her again while we wait.

When the doors open, we stumble inside, laughing as we fall into the side wall. The doors close, but nothing happens, and we laugh again when we realize no one pushed a button.

"Ever done it in an elevator?" I whisper in her ear.

She laughs again. "Maybe next time."

Next time. I like the sound of that.

She pushes the button for the third floor.

We kiss all the way to her door and almost fall in again when it pops open with her key card.

I'm not sure I've undressed this quickly with anyone in my life. We drop our jackets, kick off our shoes. I pull her sweater over her head and one of her earrings flies off. We laugh about that, too.

I've never had an encounter so easygoing, so carefree.

We tumble onto the bed at the underwear stage, and now she's mine to explore. I take my time, kissing along her skin as I remove the rest of her clothes.

Every inch of her is delicious, smooth, and soft. I explore all of her with my hands, then my mouth, moving down her belly to lick every inch.

She's wildly responsive, as if everything is new. I love every sound she makes, and how her fingers thread through my hair.

She likes watching me work, and my eyes meet hers

right as she loses it, crying out unintelligible things. I keep going until I know she's done, before nipping the inside of her thigh.

Then she's pulling me up, pressing me near her. I rush to get a condom on.

I don't think anything's amiss until I'm inside and her expression shifts. It's a surprise, like maybe I'm bigger than she expected.

I can go with that.

Then the moment passes. I figure her as one of those who likes it best when she's the star of the show. Penetration isn't her favorite part.

That's not unusual. I push her hair away from her face as the long, dark strands spill over the white pillow.

She watches me, quiet this time, with a pleased smile. Her hands press into my back, and we move together. I'm ready to work her again, and reach down to bring on another round, but she takes my hand and kisses my knuckles.

I understand and hold onto her, letting go of my tightly held control. I haven't unleashed like this in ages. Everything about this night has been unexpected and perfect.

When I'm spent and can focus again, she pushes my hair back the way I had hers.

"I liked that," she says. "I like you."

I grin at her. "I like you, too. And I haven't forgotten about that raincheck on the elevator."

Her smile drops for a second, but then she says, "Nor should you."

I slip out of her. We've left the lights on, and I see

the condom is coming out red. "I think we might have gotten your monthly started," I tell her. There had been no sign of it earlier.

She looks down, and every muscle in her body tenses. "You don't think that when you were down there…God." She seems panicked. "When your mouth was, that there was…Oh, no."

"It's fine. Woman things happen." I pull away, but she grabs my arms.

Her eyes flash wildly, as if she has to explain this to me. "I'm not on my period. I thought it was an old wives' tale about the blood. I'm twenty-two. It shouldn't have been like this."

I don't know what she means. "What old wives' tale?" Then it hits me. "Were you…a virgin?"

She sucks in a breath. "I'm sorry I didn't tell you. I didn't want to freak you out. I ruined it, didn't I? I'm sorry. God. This is why it took so long. I'm so awkward. And nobody's choice. I know what I am." She lets out a strangled groan. "This is the worst."

"Don't think that." I snatch a tissue from the box by the bed to quickly handle the condom. Then I draw her against me. "You are *my* choice. It's all right. You're all right."

I slide us down on the bed and draw the rumpled covers over our bodies.

She gulps in what sounds like a sob. "I'm sorry I didn't tell you. I didn't want to ruin it."

"It's okay. You didn't ruin anything." I draw her head to my shoulder. "Shhh."

I wait until her breathing slows and I'm sure she's not crying.

Then my thoughts whir.

Hell of a thing. I've never had sex with a virgin. Not even when I was one.

What would make her do that? Pick up a stranger?

God, it could have been *Carl*.

But I'm not asking questions tonight. I'll stay here.

We can talk about it in the morning.

I just hold her close.

3

MILA

I wake up with a start.

I lie perfectly still in the unfamiliar bed, staring at the ceiling in the dark.

Everything's wrong. The feel of the sheets. The scratchiness of the bedspread. The smells. What was that sound? Panic rises.

I peer across the room, trying to make things out.

It's a TV on a dresser.

Right. I'm at a hotel. I checked in here yesterday.

Then I went to a bar.

Then I came back with a man.

Oh, God.

I lift the sheet, staring down at my body.

Yep, I'm naked.

And sore.

Not a lot, but it's a weird feeling, like I did some screwball Pilates and sprained a muscle I never use.

I guess, probably, that's about the truth of it.

But, I did it.

I did it!

No more V status.

No more worries.

It's done.

I let out a long, slow breath.

It's really done.

I start to get up, then I realize something else.

He's here.

I carefully turn my head.

His dark wavy hair is stark against the pillow. Muscled shoulders lead to a honed back that disappears into the dark of the covers.

His breathing is quiet and even. He's asleep.

Sebastian.

He shifts next to me, and I hold my breath until he goes still again.

This can't be.

There can't be breakfast. Or conversation.

Definitely no elevator raincheck.

He needs to remain a stranger.

He knows what I am. What I was.

That was the whole point!

New town. New status. New me.

I don't want to get to know the person who holds my secret. I can't meet his friends. I can't be his girlfriend. I can't tell our grandchildren, *Oh, it all started in a bar then I had him take my virginity hours after we met.*

I have to get out of here.

But this is *my* hotel room. My purse is on the dresser, the contents spilled because I was in a rush. Well, *we* were in a rush.

Clothes are scattered on the floor. My earring is on the floor somewhere from when it flew off.

Pale blue light filters through the gap in the curtains. Dawn is coming.

I slide toward the edge of the bed, slowly and carefully, to avoid disturbing him.

I hit a cold patch on the sheets and the violent shiver that erupts across my body makes my leg jump so hard I almost kick him.

I grit my teeth and make it out of the bed, holding my pillow in front of my body in case he wakes up. Somehow I can't bear for him to see me naked, cold, and sticky. I slip into the bathroom and, afraid to run the water, do my best to clean up with a dry hand towel.

How do I get him out of here?

I will have to be the one to leave.

I sneak through the room and gather my underwear, bra, and clothes. I dress quietly, holding my shoes in my hand. Then I pick up the room key and, as carefully as possible, open the door and step into the hall.

When I get down to the lobby, I curl up in a chair in the back corner, hidden behind a potted tree.

I try to relax. He will give up eventually. Then my life can go on normally.

Today is my first day at the Castle Hotel. The big moment I worked for by getting a degree in hospitality and tourism, applying for this incredible internship. Getting selected out of thousands of candidates.

It's my dream.

And I fixed the one detail that had me worried. I got it over with.

I'm so relieved.

And look who he was. So handsome and careful. So much more amazing than all the other attempts that ended in disaster. I've been trying to get this done all summer back in Houston.

I shake my head, just thinking about them.

Once, the guy actually threw up on me as we were leaving the bar.

Twice, my chosen man found someone else to hit on before we made it to the door.

And more times than I care to count, I chickened out. One time, I crawled through the window of an apartment bathroom, landing in a cluster of prickly bushes.

Another time, when I was following the guy home in my car, I made a frantic U-turn and zoomed away.

But last night was different.

Sebastian had saved me. Gotten me away from Carl. Shown me I could dance. That I could be somebody's choice.

I stare out across the parking lot at his shiny SUV sitting next to my car.

Maybe I should give him a shot.

I live here. Maybe we could date.

But then I remember his expression when he realized there was blood. And sure, he'd been cuddly and sweet.

But he *knows*.

I don't want anyone to know. To judge me.

That was the whole point!

Besides, I was too distraught, too weird. I messed it all up.

It doesn't matter. He's too perfect. There has to be a catch. A girlfriend. A wife. Maybe he's a con man, looking for vulnerable woman.

I have a new life starting in mere hours.

He'll come down eventually and pass right through.

I will hide and wait.

And then, this whole thing will be history.

It won't matter if Sebastian would have been a good fit or not. If fate wants to put us together again, I will have to let it do its thing.

But for now, I'm moving forward.

Mission accomplished.

4

SEBASTIAN

I didn't expect to wake to an empty bed. It's Mila's hotel room, after all.

The clock reads eight a.m. That's late for me.

But she's not here, and there's no sound whatsoever in the room.

I flip back the covers, reveling in the bracing chill. I love Colorado, and the arrival of fall is my favorite time of the year. The colors on the mountains. The ease of hiking and working outside in the brisk air.

It's the best.

The curtains slide easily, and I peer out at the foothills. We're on the mountain side of the hotel, otherwise we'd be looking over the highway. I tap the chilly window with three fingers in honor of the view. It's gorgeous, and I wish my partner in crime was here with me.

I don't know much about her other than she's not from around here. That hint of a drawl says southern girl to me, even though it's not heavy. And she's in a hotel, so either she's new in town or passing through.

I'm hoping the former.

But there was that one issue.

She'd been a virgin. And that wasn't expected. She'd danced with multiple men, including Carl with the roving hands. He was known for it, and Smiley has kicked him out of the bar more than once for manhandling the ladies.

But nothing about how she behaved at Smiley's screamed innocent. Or how she asked me to her room. The way we raced to the bed.

I would have done things differently if I'd known.

Maybe I wouldn't have done it at all. Taken time get to know her first. Get a few dates down.

I was at the bar to meet my friend Isaiah, but he got held up. I was about to leave when I realized that the young woman who had caught my eye earlier was trying to extricate herself from Carl.

He was rutting on her like a buck in heat, and I'd had about enough of it.

But when I got my turn on the dance floor, she was luscious and easy to lead. The feel of her in my arms was like homecoming. She fit.

So, when she asked me to leave with her, I was all in.

Everything about her was a revelation. She responded like I was the greatest lover to grace her bed.

Then I realized I was the only one who'd ever been there.

And now she's gone.

I turn from the window. Not *gone* gone. Her suitcase

is still on the floor, and her purse is sideways on the dresser, the contents spread out.

Including her phone.

Did she run for a coffee?

I smile. Now that would be a great way to start the day.

The shower beckons, so I take a quick rinse while I wait for her to return. But when I step out, she's still not back.

Nor when I dress. Or when I sit on the edge of the bed with the dregs of my phone charge. I have no way to contact her.

I pace the room, wondering if I should simply leave.

An hour passes. Did she get lost?

Then I spot her keys in the mass of items by her purse.

She wouldn't leave without those.

Or her wallet.

Where did she go?

I'm not one to go through a woman's things, so I don't pull out her ID or search for clues. I locate my shoes, tie the laces and do the only thing I can.

I leave, skulking through the lobby and across the parking lot, no wiser about what happened to Mila.

I might never know.

When I get home, Alfalfa, my big, clumsy black Labrador, bounds to the door. My sister Arya sits on the sofa, sipping coffee in a hoodie and sweatpants. "Walk of shame?"

I shrug, rubbing both of Alfalfa's ears at the same time. "Been a while. I was due."

"I take it you're over that she-devil for real, then?" She sits up. "It wasn't her, right? She didn't come back and win you over? I'm not giving up my bedroom."

I release Alfalfa, who trots beside me as I move to a chair facing her. "No. Someone passing through. I stayed in her hotel room."

"Whew. I didn't want to have to move. Again."

Arya lived with me before I dated Haley, and during that eighteen-month stretch, she ended up moving out. I own a house on the edge of Boulder, not far from Smiley's bar. Arya is a painter, a free spirit, often unemployed. Currently, she teaches an art class for toddlers, which pays approximately one half of the gas bill.

It's fine. It's just been me and her since Mom followed her dream to return to India. Arya and I wanted to stay in Boulder, although we go see her for Diwali and always try to make her birthday.

Dad still exists, but mainly as a phone call around Christmas. We haven't seen him in person since Arya was two.

I promised Mom I would watch out for my sister. Never let the real world get her down.

But she couch surfed for over a year, and I let it happen. Haley ran my life, right up until she ran out of it.

I won't make that mistake again.

Which is why it's probably a good thing Mila was a one-nighter. She was cute. Passionate. The perfect bounce-back.

But the virginity thing is huge. I feel responsible,

even though she was absolutely an equal partner in the whole thing.

"Hey, you're doing it again." Arya reaches out a foot in a thick gray sock — one of *my* socks — to kick my shin. "Earth to Sebastian."

I shake off thoughts of Mila. "Sorry. Weird night."

"Ooooh. Was she into alternative stuff? Domination? Anal?"

I stand up. "I need coffee before I can discuss anal with my sister."

Alfalfa follows me into the kitchen.

"Don't let that dog lie to you!" Arya calls. "I fed her. She'll pretend I didn't, but I did."

Right on cue, Alfalfa heads to her empty bowl and looks up at me with plaintive brown eyes.

I pour a cup of coffee. Arya made extra for me, probably before she realized I wasn't home. I'm glad to have it. I sorely need a pick-me-up.

Alfalfa sticks her paw in the bowl and starts rolling it around like a prisoner running a metal cup along the bars.

I sip the steaming brew. "Don't bother, Alfie. I'm on to you."

She plunks down next to the bowl and watches me.

"Poor mistreated doggo." I shake my head.

But as I stand in my quiet kitchen, the wind sending leaves skittering across the deck, I can't take my mind off Mila.

Her long dark hair. Her laugh. The way we moved together on the dance floor. Then later, how we moved together on the hotel bed.

Maybe it's good she was only passing through. I might never know her motivations.

I have to accept it as an unsolvable mystery, like why my dad left, or why Mom felt compelled to return to her homeland once we were grown.

Arya pops into the kitchen. "Don't you have somewhere to be soon?" She eyes my outfit from yesterday. "You should change. You're rumpled."

She's right. I head upstairs and change out of my jeans and the soft blue pullover I can picture Mila lifting over my head.

Time to be the boss, even on a Sunday afternoon.

Because today all the new hospitality hires will arrive at the Castle Hotel to move into their new quarters, and I need to be there to welcome them. I'm their general manager. Their new boss. Time to set the tone.

Mila will have to be relegated to my past. A single night. A consequential night. A memorable night.

But I'll probably never see her again.

5

MILA

When Sebastian finally leaves, I head up to my room.

It still smells of him.

I sit on the edge of the bed and breathe it in. Stuff happened here. Big things. Monumental life-changing moments.

But there are more to come. Way more. A new job. New coworkers. Hopefully, new friends.

I need to shower, get myself together, pack whatever I dragged out of my suitcase.

And get to my new job at one of the best hospitality workplaces in the country. The Castle Hotel, nestled in the mountains of Boulder, Colorado.

But first, I text Camille.

Me: Did it. Cherry busted.

Camille: What! Really?

Me: Went to a bar. Found a guy. Super cute. Thirty-something.

Camille: An old! Was he experienced?

Me: Quite. He only noticed at the end.

Camille: Did you tell him?

I hesitate. I consider lying to avoid the embarrassment, but this is Camille, my best friend.

Me: Yes.

Camille: What did he do?

Me: Just cuddled up and fell asleep.

Camille: Adorbs! Are you going to see him again?

Me: Of course not! That was the whole point.

Camille: Right. Too bad, if he's a hottie old. You could call him daddy.

Me: Grrrrl!

Camille: Break a leg on the first day! Cherry's already broken!

This makes me laugh, and the high feeling lasts all through the prep and the drive to the Castle Hotel.

When I arrive at the narrow road to the immense property after turning off the highway, my heart nearly skips a beat.

It's so beautiful, so majestic, all gray stone and turrets with flags flying. The mountains rise behind it. You can almost imagine you are living in some other era.

It has everything. Two towers. Themed wings. Multiple restaurants. Hiking expeditions. There's even a gorgeous waterfall and each night, one lucky couple gets to stay nearby in a glamping tent. It's quickly becoming one of the most popular marriage proposal destinations in the world.

It's a dream, and for the briefest moment, I imagine Sebastian down on one knee, the sun on his wind-blown hair, holding up a ring.

Ha. Hilarious. Time to move on, Mila.

The parking lot isn't packed. It's early September, the slow season for travel since families are starting school and most people took a vacation during summer.

Even so, a few guests have pulled into the circle drive, bell hops loading their suitcases onto rolling carts. The immense front doors, made of heavy wood and two stories tall, are straight out of a movie set. In fact, I heard that three upcoming holiday specials are going to be filmed here. That will be exciting.

A thrill darts through me. I'm so lucky! Everything is working out perfectly.

I follow the signs to a service road around the back side, where staff members park. The lot is so full that I end up with a slot in the far corner.

I debate how much to haul inside since I don't know exactly where I'm going. I choose a rolling carryon and a shoulder bag and start the trek to the back door.

I was probably not as practical as I should have been for moving in, thinking I should dress to impress. My black heels, wide-legged silk pants, and loose cashmere sweater are a stark contrast to the hoodies and jeans of two people who exit the back door and head for the lot.

Maybe they're current staff getting off shift. There are only five of us in the new crew. These two could be anything. Line cooks. Room service. Housekeeping.

They don't spare me so much as a glance as they rush by.

I head for the door they exited, but when I get there, it's locked. There's a scanner affixed to the wall. I'm guessing I'll eventually have a badge for it. But there is no way to buzz in or an intercom to use.

Should I knock?

A large door farther down is clearly meant for deliveries. It has a red buzzer. I start to head for it when this one opens.

A gorgeous blonde woman in jeans and a white puffy vest steps out, then seems startled I'm right there. "Oh!"

"Hi," I say. "I'm Mila. Is it okay if I pop in this door? I'm part of the new hospitality staff."

Her face lights up, and I swear if this woman was on a big screen, everyone would flock to see her looking exactly like this. I feel a little star-struck, even though she's super casual in frayed jeans and Converse.

"That's so great! I'm Brooklyn! It's my first day, too." She holds out a hand, but while she's focused on me, the door closes behind her. "Oh, crap. We don't get our badges until the staff meeting. I only got in because the cleaning staff was coming off shift when I arrived."

We both stare at the door. "Surely someone will come out in a minute," I say.

She frowns at the scanner. "I guess we shouldn't unload until after the meeting."

"Did you meet any of the new bosses?" I'm over the moon to finally meet the owner, Havannah Boudreaux-McDonald. She is legendary in hospitality circles since she opened her landmark castle. But she's also seven months pregnant with her second child, which is why she's expanded the leadership staff. It's taking quite a few people to replace all the roles she has always managed by herself.

Brooklyn steps away from the door. "Well, the assistant manager is there. Raya. Tall, brownish-blonde hair."

"Yes, she did my interview." We had them via Zoom.

"Mine, too." She frowns. "And Anna, the head of housekeeping, was in there. Eep."

"Something wrong with her?"

Brooklyn makes a slashing motion near her throat. "I'd avoid her at all costs. She yelled at two people in the three minutes I was near her."

"Hopefully, we won't have much to do with her."

"Well." Brooklyn twists a flyway bit of her honey hair. "That's the thing. Raya said we will take rotations through most of the departments."

"Oh, right. They did mention that. Are we going to clean rooms?"

Brooklyn shrugs. "I have no idea. But we'll probably have to do some shifts in housekeeping."

"I'm warned."

The door clicks, and we turn to see a guy our age coming out. He's in khaki pants and a navy sweater. "Hey," he says. "Going in?"

"She is," Brooklyn says. "I'm headed to get more stuff out of my car."

"New hire?" he asks. "Because I'm part of the new hospitality crew."

"So are we!" Brooklyn says. "This is…" She trails off. "I think I talked too much and didn't get your name!"

"I'm Mila," I say. "I'm from Houston but went to school at the University of North Texas."

He grins, although he keeps cutting his eyes to Brooklyn. I don't blame him. It's hard not to. "I'm Owen. Oklahoma State."

"Oh, then we can't be friends," I say with a laugh.

"What?" Brooklyn says. "Was there a war between Texas and Oklahoma?"

"Only in football," Owen says. "Where did you go to school?"

"Florida State." Brooklyn blushes, and I wonder what that means, unless it has to do with Owen. I'm the worst at spotting people who are interested in each other, as Camille likes to point out.

This makes me think of last night again, and the flush on my cheeks probably means I'm red-faced too.

Owen lets go of the door.

"Oh no," Brooklyn lunges for the handle.

But before she can catch it, it slams shut. Now all three of us are locked out.

"They should give us our badges," Owen says. A gust of wind ruffles his sandy hair, and Brooklyn is definitely paying attention.

Camille was right. There will be hooking up.

"I think I'll go get a load to be ready when someone opens it again," Brooklyn says.

"I'll go with you." Owen meets my gaze. "If you get in before we're back, have pity on us."

I laugh. "If I get in."

The two of them take off across the lot.

I stare at the door. Presumably, someone else will come out soon.

I wait, the chilly wind blowing my hair all around. I'm going to look a fright. I turn to watch Brooklyn and Owen walk through the parking lot.

The handle turns, and I whip back around.

But when the door opens, all the blood that warmed my cheeks a moment ago drains out of my face.

It can't be.

No way.

A dark head of wavy hair on top of a tall, beautifully put together man emerges from the door. "I heard there were stranded people out here."

Then he sees me.

"Whoa," he says.

I can't say a word.

Because right in front of me is the man I slept with last night. The one person who knows how recently I changed my virginity status.

And on his badge, hanging in front of a charcoal button-down shirt that covers a chest I remember all too well, are the words that absolutely spell my doom.

Sebastian Young.

General Manager.

Castle Hotel.

6

SEBASTIAN

Mila stares up at me like I've grown two heads. The utter shock on her features makes me grin. Her hair blows wildly, and I can picture it spread across the white hotel pillow.

"We meet again," I say, sliding aside so she can walk by.

She passes me to enter the hallway, her rolling suitcase bumping over my polished shoes.

She's flustered. I glance down at the scrape across the top of my shiny toe.

She gasps. "Oh, no. Did I do that?" She drops to her knees, licking her thumb to wipe the mark.

"It's fine, Mila. Don't worry about it. It's just a shoe."

She looks up at me, her hair a wild tangle on her shoulders. Those big brown eyes about kill me. And those lips. I want to kiss them right now.

"If you're checking in, the front is where guests

enter. Did you decide to transfer here from the other hotel?"

Mila stands abruptly. "Oh, God. Yes. I mean no. Oh, God."

She's really out of sorts.

"Hey," I say. "It's okay that you took off this morning. I get it. Things happened kind of fast. But for what it's worth, I have no regrets."

She opens her mouth like she might say something, then doesn't. She stares at my ID card like it's bearing secrets.

I hold it out. "Sebastian Young. I don't think we got to last names or workplaces." I take the rolling handle of her bag. "I can help you to the front and get you checked in. Maybe we could even have dinner tonight? The restaurant here is good, or I would love to show you some of my favorites around Boulder."

She watches me, her mouth opening and closing again.

Okay, something's wrong.

"I apologize. You clearly had second thoughts this morning, and here I am pressuring you." I turn away, pulling her bag. "Let me get you to the front desk."

I head down the hall, turning to see if she follows.

She seems dumbstruck for a moment, looking to the left and right. Then she shoulders her other bag and moves forward.

"I can take that one too, if you like."

She shakes her head.

We're deep in the bowels of the hotel, and it takes a

few minutes to traverse the halls to make it to the back door to the lobby.

The desk is empty of guests at the moment. I roll her suitcase to the long mahogany counter. "Aisha, this is Mila. She's checking in. Take good care of her."

"Yes, sir," Aisha says.

I turn to Mila. "I'm easy to ask for here. Any employee can page me. Just ask. I would like to see you again, but I understand if that's impossible." I want to plead my case, but now we're in front of employees, and clearly she's not that into me.

She watches me. She's said nothing since her initial expression of shock.

Time for goodbye, then. I shouldn't say too much in front of Aisha, anyway. Aisha is a talker. "It was very nice to have met you…and everything. I won't soon forget it." I give her a nod and turn away.

You win some, you lose some. Damn. This one smarts.

I hurry back to the employee corridor to resume my duties. Funny how Mila got confused about where to go. The path for the guests versus the employees is clearly marked.

And what an odd coincidence. First that hotel, then this one. Meeting me, then finding me here.

Or was it? She couldn't have known I'd be here. I didn't tell her where I worked. It hadn't come up.

She seemed thoroughly shocked. I shake off the weird feeling about our second encounter as I approach the offices again. My assistant manager, Raya, is speaking to Maverick, and it doesn't look to be going well.

But not too many things make Raya happy. Subordination does. And getting her way. She's not an easy coworker, but she gets the job done. She was livid when Havannah hired me over promoting her. But it was the right call. Senior management isn't only about being tough, but also a keen listener.

Raya is not good at that.

And her tone is a familiar one.

She crosses her arms over her chest. "Maverick, we made clear that our hospitality hires would be doing all types of shifts."

"And I bet you're sticking me with maintenance right off the bat." His posture in jeans and a white T-shirt is defiant. "Let me guess, the women are cooking and cleaning?"

Raya looks to me in exasperation. "This one is yours," she says. "You handle him."

She stalks down the hall to her office, her heels clopping on the polished floor.

Yeah, she does that, too. Ditches the dirty work and leaves it for me.

I approach Maverick. "Everybody will do all the shifts. Nothing is gender specific."

He shrugs. "She stuck in my craw, that's all."

Raya didn't like that I hired Maverick as a favor to my father's former best friend, who has been family to Arya and me since we were kids. Maverick is his nephew, a classic underachiever with a chip on his shoulder. He barely graduated UC Boulder. His GPA wasn't exactly inspiring, but then, neither was mine.

"So, should I switch it up? You can make sandwiches in the deli, shovel donkey dung in the barn, wash sheets, or stock deliveries."

"This is a shit job," he says. "I have a fucking college degree."

I shrug. "Then take that degree and get a spot somewhere else. We had close to a thousand applicants for these intern spots."

He leans against the wall, tilting his chin to the ceiling. He's tough, but smart, and he knows he's got something good here. Besides, his student loans have to be killing him, and even the interns get paid well here, plus free room and board.

"Tell me why this is important again?" he asks.

Good. He's listening now. "You have to troubleshoot fast at a job like this. If you don't know how housekeeping runs the rooms, then you don't know if you can really check in a bus full of tourists inside of an hour when they arrive before they're supposed to. If you don't know how to fix a thermostat, you're probably not going to be able to handle an upset guest who wants to warm up after a cold hike."

"We have staff for all that."

"We do. But hotel management deals in problems and promises. You have to solve the problem and make the promise you can deliver. Until you know what everyone here really does, you can't do that."

He pushes away from the wall. "I'm going to get my shit."

I watch him head for the back door. That one will be hard to manage, that's for sure. But I stole one of Raya's prized spots, so I have to handle it.

Raya leans out of her office. She was listening. "You're going to regret that one."

"Maybe."

She shuffles through a stack of ID badges. "The interns keep getting locked out, so I'm going to give these out now rather than at the meeting." She untangles Maverick's and passes it to me. "I'll pass out the rest."

"Are they all here?" I spot the name "Brooklyn Henry" on the top ID.

"This one is." She taps Brooklyn's ID. "And this one." The next one reads "Owen Thomas." She's about to show me the next one when someone knocks at the back door.

Raya hurries to open it. "And there they are."

A tall blonde woman and a friendly-looking man enter, both hauling massive suitcases.

"Hi," the woman says.

"Hello, recruits," I say. "Let me get you some carts."

Raya closes the back door and detangles the ID badges again. "Good luck getting Bertie to let any go."

I pull my cell phone out to text him. "He'll have to. I'm the boss."

Raya's laugh is hollow. "You are indeed."

While the interns put on their badges, I tap out the message, already wondering if I can get Bertie to tell me if he assisted a certain dark-haired woman to her room.

I have to see her again. There has to be a way.

7

MILA

I stare at the woman at the front desk. Aisha.

She's going to be a coworker. I can't exactly lie. She'll remember.

"You know, give me a minute," I tell her.

She nods, and I grab my suitcase and roll it to the far corner of the lobby by the front window to sit down.

What do I do?

Sebastian is the general manager! I can't work here! We did things! He already asked me out *again*!

Oh, God. This is the absolute worst-case scenario. Why didn't I pop my cherry in some other town? Boulder isn't that big, only a hundred thousand people.

And by the time you break it down to men, single ones, in the right age range, sure, the likelihood that the man I picked might work at this hotel, which is a major employer in this area, was probably higher than I should have risked.

But the general manager? Really, universe? The big

boss? The one who I definitely, positively cannot see again?

Except I can see him. All of him. The muscles of his chest. The plane of his belly. And below. Yes, I can picture every inch of *that*.

"Can I help you?"

I nearly jump off the cushion. A kindly elderly man with deep black skin and gentle eyes stands beside me in a crisp red Castle Hotel uniform. A gold pin on his chest reads "Bertie: Bell Captain."

"Oh, no. I'm fine," I say. But my insides quake. I've been noticed by two staffers.

I have to make a decision. Am I going to leave? Or fight for this job? Clearly, Sebastian doesn't realize I'm one of the new interns. He led me to the lobby.

But he'll know soon. We're supposed to meet him and Havannah in less than an hour.

What do I do?

"You seem a mite lost," Bertie says. He sits beside me.

Something about his kindness melts me a little. "I might be."

"Are you waiting on someone?"

I hesitate. What to say? "I'm not sure I should be here."

"And why is that?"

"I wasn't expecting there to be someone I know. Now I'm not sure what to do."

The quiet stretches a moment. I'm probably going to bail. Just leave. Go home, I guess. I was there all summer, waiting for this job to start. I can go back, tail between my legs. Try to find something else. Hotels are usually hiring.

So why not say something to Bertie?

I face him. "Have you ever done something really impulsive, thinking no one would ever know about it, and then the very person who knows your biggest secret ends up being right in front of you?"

His face shifts, his lips twisting as he considers this. "Well, one time, I ate one of my wife June's award-winning cupcakes, not realizing each one was different and she would not have a chocolate-filled one for a competition."

"What did you do?"

"Blamed it on the dog."

I huffed out a laugh. "Did it work?"

"Yes, except I forgot how chocolate is dangerous for dogs, so June packed up poor Peanut to take to the vet to induce vomiting."

"Did you confess then?"

Bertie shakes his head. "No."

"You let that poor dog go through that?"

He lifts his hands. "Now, now. I didn't. I volunteered to take the dog."

I let out a laugh. "And of course you didn't go."

"Of course not."

"What did you do?"

"I took the dog to the park and confessed my sins to the sunflowers."

"Did June ever find out?"

"I didn't think so, but then about twenty years later—"

"Twenty!"

He nods. "Twenty years later, I go in the kitchen where she's baking cupcakes with our granddaughter, and if it don't beat all, that angelic little girl turned right around and said to me, "Grandpap, Grandmom said to make sure you don't eat any cupcakes and blame it on the dog.""

"Oh no!"

"Oh, yes. My beautiful wife didn't even look up, kept right on stirring that batter. Turns out everybody in the family knew that story."

I drop my hands in my lap. "So, you're saying this truth will get out?"

"I say secrets are like greased pigs, hard to hang onto."

"Should I run away then?"

"Depends on if what you want is bigger than the secret. Choose wisely. Life is long. Secrets are short, even if you think they are forever."

I sigh. I do want to work here. "I guess I'll face this thing."

"What can I do for you?"

"Take me to Sebastian Young."

Bertie's smile tells me he already knew I was over here brooding over Sebastian. "I had a feeling it might be about him."

"Did he mention me?"

"He sure did. Texted me to bring some carts for the interns moving in today. Then asked me to look after a young dark-haired lady named Mila who was at the front desk to get her room."

"Oh."

"But there wasn't any Mila who checked in. Or any Mila on the guest list."

Oh, dear. "I bet not."

"But you know what list came up with a Mila?"

I stare at my hands.

"Now, I'm not privy to what happened between you and Mr. Young. That's not for me to know. But I know he's a fair man. A man who listens. So you're in good hands."

I definitely was last night.

"Thank you, Bertie."

"How about you get started on that intern work, and you and I push some carts to the back hall? Sound okay?"

I nod.

Might as well get this over with.

8

SEBASTIAN

Since we're missing two of the new interns, Raya asks me to show the three that are here how to get to the staff wing.

I lead Maverick, Owen, and Brooklyn through the maze of back halls, their suitcases rolling silently alongside them. The carts haven't materialized. I should text Bertie again.

Only a small portion of our staff lives on site, but we offer it as a temporary option to new hires from other cities since Boulder is notoriously difficult for renters.

When Havannah got pregnant and knew we would need more leadership staff, it was her idea to set aside five of the small apartments for the best and brightest new graduates from colleges all over the nation. She wanted them close and young and hungry for advancement.

We haven't announced it yet, but she's looking for someone as passionate as her to take over the event management, the crown jewel of what our hotel offers.

From the infamous Haunted Ball to *Bridgerton* fetes and murder mystery nights, she keeps the hotel busy, even in the off season.

There are secret suites behind hidden staircases that not even all the staff knows about, an entire princess wing with party suites for special birthdays, and the haunted wing as well. The specialized rooms in the castle have an entirely separate process for booking, since they are in high demand.

It's a fun place to work. Havannah is great. These new interns don't know how good they're about to have it.

"I'm never going to find my way out of here again," Brooklyn groans as we make yet another turn. "I feel like a rat in a maze."

"You'll figure it out. There is a system." I point to the corner where the hall splits. "At the top there, you'll see letters and numbers. That one says 'SW-1' for 'Staff wing one.'"

"How many staff wings are there?" Owen asks.

"Two," I tell him.

"Men's and women's?" Maverick asks.

"Nope. All mixed." I stride ahead of them. "We've made it to your block of rooms." I pause in front of SW175. "Maverick, this one should be yours. Use your ID card."

Maverick steps forward with all the swagger of a man who thinks highly of himself. I think he's showing off for Brooklyn, but she's not paying him much attention. He holds his ID in front of the infrared lock and it pops open.

"Sweet," he says, pulling his suitcase through the door. "Catch ya later."

"The staff meeting starts in fifteen minutes," I tell him. "It might take that long to find your way back."

He doesn't answer, just allows the door to close behind him.

Uncle Roger is about to owe me big time for this.

"Brooklyn, I think you're next." We head to another door.

She walks up, leaning over to use the card hanging around her neck.

Owen can't stop staring at her, taking in the back of her jeans. There might be a cockfight between him and Maverick over her. I may have to keep watch over this group more closely than the usual new hires. We've never had five young unattached interns arrive at the same time before, much less living on the same hall.

"Got it!" She lets out a squeal as the door unlatches. "This is exciting!"

"Do you want me to wait for you and make sure you can get back?" I ask.

"I'll do it," Owen says. "I'm good with halls, and directions, and stuff."

"Cool," Brooklyn says. "I'm not. Meet you right here in ten?"

Owen's face lights up. "Absolutely."

Yeah, real close watch. Maverick's about to be behind the eight-ball on this, and I have a feeling he'll take it out on Owen.

I turn to the other side of the hall. "Yours is over here."

He's pleased that he's so close to Brooklyn. When his door clicks open, I tell him, "Ask anyone for directions if you get lost. It's a big place, but the staff knows you're here."

"Will do. Thank you, Mr. Young, sir."

"Call me Sebastian." I give him a wave. "See you soon."

I have a few minutes before I have to be back at the offices. I wonder which wing of the hotel Mila is staying on. It's going to take some willpower to avoid looking up her room. I left things in her hands. She can ask for me.

It feels unlikely.

Even so, I decide to stop by the lobby to check on Bertie under the guise of needing the carts. See what he knows.

But when I get there, he's not around, and neither is Aisha. Jessica is manning the front desk alone. There's no one in the lobby. We're in the lull between check-out and check-in.

"Hello, Mr. Young," Jessica says. "How are the interns?"

"I took three of them to the staff wing." Since there is no one here to casually ask about Mila, I decide to head back to the offices. I can't make a big show of seeking out Aisha or Bertie over this. It will be too obvious.

Jessica is fairly new, but both Aisha and Bertie have been here long enough to know about Haley, and the effect of that relationship on my sister, and that I haven't seen anyone since. They'll clue in if I seem interested in someone new.

I push through the staff exit to the back hall. Once the meeting is over, I'll ponder my options. I could send Mila a complimentary basket like we do the VIPs. Or a cookie tray. Or…

Just stop, Sebastian. She's temporary anyway. Two hotels equal not being local.

But there is that matter of her virginity.

Maybe that's what I really want to know about. Why me? Why now? Why a stranger?

Of course, I have access to her phone number if I want it. Her address. Anything. But I won't abuse my privileges here. If Mila wants to be left alone, I'll simply have to accept it.

Raya steps outside her office when I return. "Oh good. Do you think we have time to send the last two to their rooms before we meet, or should they leave their things on the carts and move in after? I gave them their badges."

"The other interns will be on their way back," I say. "But it doesn't matter. We can make small talk while we wait."

"They'll need someone to show them the way," Raya says. "And if you go, you can scoop up the others if they're lost."

"Sounds like a plan."

The two carts sit by the back door, already partially piled with suitcases and boxes. I'm sure the other three have a lot more to bring in as well.

But that means Bertie was here. I missed him. Damn. I really wanted to get an idea from him if Mila seemed upset, or off in any way.

One of the bags on the second cart looks familiar. I pass Raya to look at it more closely.

That's odd. It's exactly like the one Mila was carrying.

The one I saw on the floor of her hotel room.

And isn't that her rolling case? I distinctly remember the bright pink tie.

I stare at it, my brain trying to solve this unexpected puzzle, when the door opens.

The first young woman is petite, dark-haired, and Hispanic. She seems surprised to see me so close, but quickly drops two boxes on a cart.

And behind her, sporting one of the white intern badges, is a face I absolutely recognize. Eyes I stared into. A mouth I kissed. A lot.

Mila.

9

MILA

Oh, God.

Here we are again.

I can tell by his expression that this is a shock. I had hoped that maybe he saw the last two badges Raya was holding before she passed them over. She said Sebastian had gone to show the other three interns their rooms, so he had been right there with the ID cards.

But no, he's figuring it out right now. Right in front of me.

His eyes hold mine for a moment. "Hey."

I manage to swallow and echo back a quiet, "Hey."

Ilsa, the intern from California who walked in with me, jerks her head our way, looking from Sebastian to me. Something in our tone has tipped her off.

I can't do anything about that. I don't know what he's going to say or do.

But he grins, like this is the best thing ever. Like maybe he's the fox, and he's spotted me in the henhouse. "You're an intern."

My throat feels tight, and my voice is barely a squeak. "I am."

Ilsa busies herself with her bags, but I can feel her attention. This is not good. I'm tempted to run.

Sebastian rocks back on his heels. "You didn't mention this earlier."

Ilsa is stock-still. I tilt my head in her direction.

Sebastian clears his throat. "Right. Welcome aboard. It's good to see a friendly face." He extends a hand, and I shake it. "And who is this?"

Ilsa straightens to greet him. "Ilsa Lopez."

Sebastian gives her a nod. "Excellent. Do you have more to load?"

"I do," I say.

"I do, too." Ilsa's eyes cut back to me.

"Why don't you two keep at it? I'm going to check on the other three to see if they're finding their way back. Raya will watch over your things."

"Will I?" Raya calls.

Sebastian's jaw clench is almost imperceptible, but I catch it. "I'll call a bellboy. In fact, maybe we'll have them move these young women's carts to their rooms during the meeting."

"Much better plan," Raya says.

I grunt as I lift my bag onto the cart. When I push out the door, Ilsa follows close behind.

"So you know him?" Her legs move swiftly to keep up with me.

"We met once."

"Where?"

Why is she being so nosy? I don't even know her.

"Here in town."

"Were you already hired?"

I really don't like her questions. "Yes. I bumped into him yesterday in town, that's all."

"He didn't bring you on?"

Why does she care? "No."

This mollifies her, and we separate for different parts of the parking lot.

When I get to my car, though, I sit in the driver's seat, willing my heart to slow down.

Sebastian seemed awfully pleased I'm an intern. Did I sleep with a scoundrel? Will he dangle the job in exchange for sexual favors?

Or is he faking me out, all broad smiles but ready to kick me out? He's the general manager. The big boss. Nobody is higher than him at the hotel other than the owner, Havannah.

I glance in my rear-view mirror at all the boxes. The studio apartments here come furnished with a complete kitchen, but I have all my books, my clothes, my electronics. If he's going to ask me to leave, maybe I shouldn't bother unloading anything else.

I close my eyes. Bertie said he was a good guy, but he doesn't know what happened between me and Sebastian.

Seeing him again has filled me with yearning. I just got started on discovering what all the fuss was about.

I can picture him, rising from the edge of the bed, kissing his way up my thigh. And after that, the things he did. I've never felt anything like that.

He doesn't have to pressure me for anything.

I want to do it again.

I won't bleed this time. I won't be so naïve or uncertain.

A buzz comes alive in my belly. Thinking about it makes me a little crazy. And he was so happy to see me before he knew. He asked me to dinner.

Will he still try? Is that even possible? I'm sure there's something in the HR documents about this. Most big companies have a policy.

Dating him in any capacity would be a huge mistake. If we broke up, that could be the end of my job. I'd be stuck starting over at the bottom of some crummy chain hotel, worse off than if I had no experience at all since I couldn't use this as a reference.

A movement in my rear-view mirror catches my attention. It's Ilsa, already heading back into the castle.

I lunge out of the seat, open the back door, and pull out one more small box. There's nothing to be done but to see this through. Maybe I can find a moment to ask him what he plans to do about me before I move in completely.

When I return to the hall, it's empty. I set down my box and check my phone. Five past the hour. I'm late.

The door to the kitchens is propped open. Amazing smells waft out as several chefs in white uniforms bustle about the stainless-steel counters.

On the opposite side, another open door leads to a room filled with washers and dryers. This team, all in light blue, folds towels and sheets on a long white table.

A young man, probably only a teen, steps out, bright in his red uniform against the white room. "I'm watching the carts. You want me to roll it to your room yet?"

"Not yet," I tell him. "I have more."

He shrugs and turns back to his conversation with a blue-haired woman folding hand towels. "Come on, Cristal, go out with me."

"You wish," she says. "Not just anybody gets a shot at a piece of this."

I walk down the hall, past the door marked "Head of Housekeeping," and another marked, "Assistant Manager." That's Raya, who interviewed us.

There's two more for the CFO and head of maintenance.

Then I hear voices.

Ahead is a staff room with double doors, both propped open. I pause and smooth my pants and sweater, then lift my chin and enter.

Sebastian and Raya stand at the front. The other four interns are seated in the front row. I hurry to sit next to them, choosing the end next to Brooklyn rather than Ilsa. There's only one intern I haven't met, and he appraises me with a long, penetrating gaze like he's undressing me and making a judgment. His legs are kicked out, and he's sitting low on the chair like he's comfortable at home.

Raya is talking. "Today is for unpacking and exploring. Each of you will get five meals a week comped in the dining room. There is a significant discount for anything else you do, including room service. All this is coded into your ID."

Sebastian speaks up. "But tonight, room service is on

us. Order something, settle in, and we'll get started with orientation in the morning."

I avoid looking him in the eye, instead fiddling with the edge of my sweater.

"We have plenty of paperwork for you to fill out," Raya says, turning to retrieve a stack of clipboards from the table behind her. "Let's get started on that while we wait for Havannah to come."

Owen raises a hand.

"Yes, Owen?" Raya asks.

"Is it the standard practice here to call everyone by first names?"

Sebastian nods. "We do. Havannah thinks of us as family."

He raises his hand again and the other male intern sighs loudly.

"What address do we use on these forms?"

"Good question," Sebastian says. "The hotel address is at the top of the privacy form. Use that. There is no need for a room number. Your name is good enough for your mail to get to you through our internal sorting."

Raya passes each of us a clipboard, and she and Sebastian talk quietly as the five of us get to work.

It's all the usual things. Tax forms. Privacy agreements. Then the hotel policies. I glance up at Sebastian and Raya, then flip through the code of ethics. I pause when I spot "fraternization."

Here we go.

No relationship between members of the hotel staff shall be permitted if there is the potential for preferential treatment or disruption of work tasks. Romantic partners must have no more than one level in the chain of command separating them to avoid the abuse of authority or the appearance of abuse.

All relationships between employees in the same department but at different levels in the organizational chart should be reported to human resources for evaluation. Failure to follow these policies will result in disciplinary action, including possible termination.

My face feels hot. Sebastian is a thousand levels above an intern. He could get fired. Or more likely, I will get fired. Anything between us is dead in the water if I'm going to work here.

I draw in a slow, easy breath to calm myself.

The other interns have plowed through the policy document, initialing all the way. I quickly flip back and start scribbling M.S. M.S. M.S. I hesitate at the fraternization clause, then again, M.S.

Now to copy my new address, or hopefully my new address, onto the tax documents.

The man with an attitude finishes first, smacking the clipboard against his thigh and looking around. He notices me, then shakes his head, eyes resting on Brooklyn instead.

I'm used to it. Frumpy girl. Average girl. Not the chosen one.

Except with Sebastian.

He made me feel like the most beautiful woman in the room.

I sneak a peek at him. He's talking with Raya.

Ilsa finishes her paperwork, carefully clipping the pen beneath the clamp on the board and turning it sideways in her lap. She sits ramrod straight, her ankles crossed, her long black hair curling over one shoulder.

I resume my initials, then glance over the privacy statement and nondisclosures. I scrawl my signatures, and by the time I've double checked everything, we're all done.

Raya collects the clipboards.

Sebastian rubs his hands together. "Tomorrow, we will meet here, and each of you will be assigned your first rotation. You will spend time with each crew, and we'll be assessing your strengths and interests for your long-term placement."

"What are the rotations?" Brooklyn asks.

The male intern clasps his hands behind his head like he has no need for formality here. "Some of them suck."

Everyone turns to him, except Raya, who looks to Sebastian.

He grins. "You might not fully enjoy some of the tasks, but it's good to get a feel for everyone's job here. Havannah firmly believes that the only way to know how to improve a segment of the hotel's operation is to see exactly what happens in each of these roles."

"Did I hear my name?"

Everyone sits up straighter as a blonde woman with a decent belly bump strides into the room. She wears all-white boots, pants, and a sweater. She doesn't have an ID badge, but she doesn't need to.

This is Havannah Boudreaux-McDonald, the owner.

Brooklyn and I exchange an excited glance. She's why we're here.

Havannah pauses to look at us. "I'm so thrilled to

see you. I dreamed up this internship when I first learned about this little one." She pats her belly.

I try to squelch my awe, but I'm sure it's all over my face. I catch Sebastian looking at me with a knowing smile. He's pleased with my excitement. I glance away.

"I have a surprise for you all that will surely help with motivation as you fight your way through some of the harder weeks ahead." She glances at Sebastian. "And yes, I'm talking about the custodial shift."

He laughs and nods at her.

"I'm very pleased to announce that I've created a new position at the hotel. It's a role I've done since we opened, but if my second baby is even half as wild as the first, I'm going to have my hands full. So, in six months, one of you five will be named the event manager here at the Castle Hotel. It's a fun job. You'll love it." She meets each one of our gazes. "I just know I'm looking at this person right now. I'll be training you myself once we choose. I can't wait to see who it will be."

My heart hammers. She's going to have one of us be the event manager? We get to come up with the amazing balls and parties, as well as handle the weddings and conferences?

Havannah gestures to the door. "I'm having catering bring in some drinks and snacks, so let's get to know each other."

The servers must have been waiting in the corridor, as they immediately come in and set trays on the long table lining the side wall.

We all stand to greet her, and I spot the fifth intern's

name on his badge. Maverick. Figures. That's a hellion name if I've ever heard one.

Brooklyn approaches me, her cheeks pink with excitement. "Can you imagine it? Event manager? During our first year?"

I nod. "Now that's a dream job."

"It sure is."

Maverick has already jumped in to meet Havannah with no hesitation. I steal a glance at Sebastian right as he looks my way. I immediately turn aside. We have to cut that out.

"I'm so nervous," Brooklyn says. "Please stay with me when we meet her, so I won't screw up."

"I will." But even as I say it, my anxiety gives way to despair. I already have a friend here with Brooklyn. Havannah is magical. And my dream job is possibly six months away.

But I had to go and accidentally sleep with the boss.

10

SEBASTIAN

I'm in a pickle bigger than any of the cucumbers they sell in the hotel deli.

Mila is ten feet from me in the hotel conference room, and she's at the rock bottom of the company hierarchy. She's an intern. Ten years younger than me. And I control whether she works here another day.

But all I can think about is her naked body under mine.

"Sebastian? What do you think?" Raya's been talking the whole time, and I've completely lost the thread of the conversation.

I'm good at the smile-and-nod when Raya's around. She's a complainer, and I'm not here for the angst.

"I think we should get a snack," I say.

She huffs in annoyance. "Go on, then. You've never seen a buffet you haven't plundered."

If only she knew what else in this room I've plundered.

I head for the serving table, allowing myself only the

barest of glances in Mila's direction. She's talking to Havannah. She looks nervous and excited. Havannah is patiently nodding, a bemused expression on her face.

Maverick stands in front of the buffet dishes, looking over the spread. "This is better than I expected." He adds a prime rib slider to the pile on his plate. "Lobster mac. Steak on a stick."

"Skewers," I say before I can catch myself.

Maverick aims one at my face. "It's a stick, ain't it?"

"It is." I pick up a plate and take a couple of them myself.

He sticks the skewer in his mouth and pulls off all the meat and baked brie in one big bite.

He knows better than to act like a buffoon. He's smart and can read a room.

He's pushing my buttons.

I have news for him. My buttons all got mashed years ago. You don't become the head manager of a hotel like this without having a dozen people trying to tweak you every day.

Raya, though, she's going to increasingly resent me bringing him on if he keeps this up. And then if she finds out about Mila…

This whole intern program has gotten more complicated than it should have.

Might as well eat. I fill my plate with cheese and crudités and smoked salmon on crostini. Havannah had Chef Monique pull out all stops for these interns. But, knowing her, she'll be watching for how they react to unusual cuisine. Events will encompass culinary styles across many cultures. Interns who act like Maverick might not be trusted with taking event details for food they find unusual.

I take a bite of the crostini and feel my head swoon with the sharp flavors.

"Not a fan of the hot cheese," Maverick says, wiping his mouth with the back of his hand.

"It's not for everybody." I pass him a napkin. Okay, so maybe there's a button or two that has some life to it, given that Raya is ready to pull the "I told you so" card from across the room. She hasn't missed a thing.

Maverick wipes his face with all the panache of a toddler. "You're fussed that I call it like I see it?"

I shrug. "I'm fussed that you seem intent on blowing an opportunity graciously dropped into your lap."

He shoves half of a slider in his gullet and sniffs as he chews. He does at least take a moment to swallow before he says, "The way I see it, I don't stand a snowflake's chance in hell of becoming event manager, not with all the estrogen in the room."

"Don't be sexist." I turn my back to Raya, so she can't see my face as I get stern. "You can decide to lowball your experience here, but there are some things nobody is going to stand for, and I will not get in the way of you getting kicked out on your ass if you cross the line."

He frowns at that.

"So cool it with your act. I know you're smarter than that. You were raised by good people. Knock it off."

And I'm done with him for one day.

Button mashed.

I head over to Owen, careful to skirt Mila and the

sunny blonde Brooklyn, who are headed to the buffet. The other new intern, Ilsa, is speaking with Havannah.

Owen has a dreamy expression, no doubt inspired by the food.

"It's good, right?" I say.

"Ungodly." He turns his plate around in his hands, as if not sure where to dive in next.

"When you're done, we have some carts ready to help you transport your things."

"I already have it all in my room," Owen says. "I just had the two suitcases I came with."

That's not much. "You're from Oklahoma, right?"

"Born and bred. I don't have a car here, so I only brought what I could manage on the bus."

"We can arrange to have more shipped if you need it."

He shrugs. "I don't need much else." He takes a bite from his plate, which is stacked high. He got one of everything. He seems to be forcing himself to slow down.

He has a friendly, golden retriever look to him. Shaggy brown hair, lean. He wears khakis and a sweater, but they've seen better days. His shoes, too, are worn, brown loafers scuffed at the toe.

He'll be eager to impress, I bet. He probably bootstrapped his way through college and made the most of every opportunity he got.

"Did you intern in college?" I ask.

He picks up a skewer. "I worked at a nice hotel in Norman."

"Did you see things that could use improving?"

He gulps the bite he shoveled in while I asked the question. "Everywhere. The front desk was inefficient. They were understaffed in housekeeping and room service. Everyone was run ragged all the time."

"And this was a good hotel?"

"It's considered upscale for the area, but the definition of that varies based on where you are." He glances around the staff room. "This place is unbelievable."

"It's got a lot of character. We don't try to run it like a Ritz-Carlton or Four Seasons. We have a lot of families. We want to keep it Boulder friendly."

"But you have one of the most sought-after secret suites in the world," he says.

So he knows about it. Word is getting out.

"We do. You can only book it by talking directly to me. How did you hear of it?" I came on board only a year after the castle opened, and I personally know every person who was officially told about the secret suite since then.

"I wasn't sure until now." His eyes are mischievous.

He got me. "I'm glad you're on our team, then. A nondisclosure was part of your paperwork."

"Will any of us get to see the suite that is more rumor than fact?"

"The event manager will, for sure. Otherwise, it takes permission from Havannah to reveal its location."

"Dang."

Havannah approaches. "I haven't met this young man yet."

Owen stands a little taller. "Hello, ma'am."

"Oh, please. It's Havannah. You must be our Oklahoma representative."

"I am."

I leave them to it, turning around to find someone else to chat up.

"Oh!" Mila cries out in surprise as the edge of my plate bumps the side of her head. And...there's Monique's special dip in her hair, her dark strands streaked with white.

And that's sending off all the dirty thoughts.

"I'm sorry," I say. "I should look where I'm going."

Brooklyn bites her lip, trying not to laugh. She sets her plate on a chair and wipes at Mila's hair with a napkin.

Mila avoids looking at me as Brooklyn works.

"It's not bad," Brooklyn says. "And you smell like an herb garden."

Mila's eyebrows draw together. "Thanks for the help."

Brooklyn heads for the trash can at the end of the buffet, leaving me and Mila alone.

"I'm so sorry," I say. "This has been quite the introduction, hasn't it?"

Mila touches her hair. "It's probably karma for hiding behind a potted plant."

"This morning?" She must have been in the lobby. I didn't look.

Her eyes cut left and right. "This is no place to talk about it."

She's right. "We should probably have a word later."

"I guess." She quickly switches topics as Brooklyn returns. "When will we find out our first rotation?"

"In the morning. We'll meet back here and give out assignments."

"Will all the interns be split?" Brooklyn asks.

"For some shifts, there is only one intern due to the work. The deli and the sandwich cart can't handle a lot of extra people, for example. But sometimes, all five of you will help out, like during the donkey rotation. Jed is expecting some foals soon, and we'll be sending you all out to help."

"We get to take care of baby donkeys!" Brooklyn's eyes light up.

"We thought it would be fun," I say. "And it prevents us from having to pull anyone off the maintenance crew."

"This is the best!" Brooklyn says.

Mila is quiet, staring at her plate. I can see I'm making her uncomfortable.

"Feel absolutely free to call on me if you run into any trouble."

"Thank you, Sebastian!" Brooklyn says.

This is a disaster. I head to the bussing bin and drop in my plate. A night that was so perfect has morphed into a day from hell. I can't seem to do anything right with Mila.

I turn to the room to see if I can simply escape. Everyone is occupied.

I won't go home yet, though. I need to talk to Mila, and we should be careful about how we do it. I can't go to her room, not with all five of the new hires on the same hall.

I'll send a note. Maybe we can meet off site.

Of all the dumb scrapes I've gotten into in my thirty-two years, this one takes the cake.

11

MILA

The five of us leave the meeting together. Ilsa and I push our carts. The bellhop got called away before he could move them.

We wander an endless maze of halls, and after fifteen minutes, Owen, who is leading us, comes to an abrupt halt.

"What?" Brooklyn asks.

"I think I'm lost," Owen says.

Everyone groans.

"I'm out," Maverick says. "I can jog the castle and find my way back in no time. See ya." He takes off in a run.

Owen turns to us, hands extended, his shaggy hair falling in his eye. "I thought I knew what I was doing."

"We can figure this out," Brooklyn says. "Sebastian said there are codes on the corners." She walks ahead. "There, I see a turn."

Owen hurries to catch up with her, Ilsa and I trundling along behind our carts.

When we get there, Owen and Brooklyn are puzzling out the letters at the top of the wall. BH-1.

"Bathhouse one?" Brooklyn says.

"There's no bathhouse here," Ilsa grumbles.

"Barbie hall?" Owen ventures.

"No," Brooklyn says. "The only themed wings are princess and haunted."

"Besides," Ilsa says, "we're in the guts, not the public area."

I snap my fingers. "Banquet hall one. There's a banquet hall with an outside entrance, so that guests can park in the side lot and not have to go through the lobby. I think we're on the west side service entrance."

"Well, that's fine," Ilsa says. "But where is the staff wing from here?"

I pull up an aerial of the castle on my phone and angle it at them. "If we've gone all the way to the west side, then we went too far."

"We definitely walked a lot less last time." Brooklyn heads back the way we came.

Ilsa sighs. "Let's check every turn on the way back."

Owen takes the lead again. "There's a turn."

This one has a sign reading SW-2.

"Yes! Staff wing two!" Brooklyn practically glows. "At the end of this hall will be the turn to staff wing one."

"They put us at the ass-end of the castle," Ilsa mutters.

We keep moving, and eventually we spot the sign for SW-1.

"We made it!" Brooklyn says. "By next week, we're going to laugh at how hard we thought this was today."

"Can't wait." Ilsa's voice is deadpan as she approaches a door and scans her card. Then she disappears inside her room without another word.

The three of us exchange glances.

"She's a real peach," Brooklyn says.

My belly turns over. Of course, the mean one would be the one who saw how Sebastian reacted to me. "Maybe she's nervous."

"And what about that Maverick?" Owen asks. "He's already pissed off both Raya and Sebastian."

"Yeah, I can't figure him out." Brooklyn turns to her door. "You two want to have dinner together later? We can figure out our free room service."

I hesitate. I might have to meet Sebastian.

"Totally," Owen says. He practically has heart eyes over the possibility of time with Brooklyn.

I'll leave him to it.

"I have a lot to move," I say. "I grossly over-packed."

"Okay!" Brooklyn says. "Owen, looks like it'll be you and me. Seven?"

"On the dot."

I hate to miss it. "I'll knock if I'm feeling up for it," I say.

"Let's exchange numbers real quick," Brooklyn says. "That way we can save each other if the hallways try to eat us again."

"Good idea," Owen says.

We take a moment in the middle of the hall to type

each other's names and numbers into our phones. Then Brooklyn and Owen disappear into their rooms.

I approach the door that matches the number on the printout Raya set on my cart. SW181. It looks like I'm the farthest down, although there are several more doors before the hall ends with an exit to the outside. I'll walk out later and see if there is a closer end of the parking lot for when I bring the rest of my things.

If I get to bring the rest of my things.

My stomach goes hot.

What a mess.

The door pops open with my key card. I push it wide, hearing a crunch of paper. It's a folded note, trapped between the carpeting and the bottom edge.

I leave my cart to scoop it up. Even though it could be anything — welcome papers, something from house-keeping — I already know it's from Sebastian.

The cart is still in the hall, but even so, I walk inside the room to set the note on the back of the pale gray sofa. I stare at it a moment. No, I will wait.

First things first.

I drag the cart into the room. Maybe I'll unload it and return it before I read the note.

Maybe I'll even unpack.

But what if he wants me to leave?

I glance around the small apartment. The main room has a sofa and TV, a small dinette by a big window, and a kitchen. I open a few cabinets, noting the organized white dishes and shiny pans.

A door off the kitchen leads to a bedroom and a typical hotel bathroom. The cabinet below the sink is loaded with toilet paper, and two clean sets of bath and hand towels are on a silver rack by the white shower curtain.

Not a lot of personality, but definitely bright and clean.

I head back to the living room. The white paper stands out on the textured cushion. I let out a long breath. Time to see what he said.

My hands tremble as I unfold the creased page. It's hotel stationery, with the crisp logo of the Castle Hotel in bright red at the top.

His handwriting is spidery but clear.

M—

There is nowhere easy to meet on site until you know your way around. Can you find your way back to Smiley's bar? There is a cute Italian place across the road. I'll be there from 7-8.

—S

I glance at the clock. It's after four.

Three hours to kill until then, and I probably shouldn't unpack.

But by the time I know my fate, it will be dark, and in the morning, I start work.

I remember what Bertie said. I'm in good hands.

Probably Sebastian wants to see where we stand. Surely he won't kick me out. He was so friendly and easygoing.

Other than when he dunked my hair in dip.

I grab the end and give it a sniff.

Uggh. Sour cream and herbs.

I know what I'm doing before I go to dinner.

Washing my hair.

12

SEBASTIAN

Sitting alone at a table at Sicily's is nerve-wracking.

It's a good place, quiet, with only maybe twenty tables. It's my sister's favorite restaurant, so I know half the waiters. Two of them watch me with a mixture of bemusement and concern as I turn my water glass round and round.

At seven-fifteen, Bethany brings me a plate of bruschetta. "On the house."

"Thanks."

She hesitates. "She'll come."

How does she know it's a she?

Maybe they think it's my sister, even though we always come together.

Maybe it's obvious I'm waiting for someone else.

I'm not even clear on what I want to happen.

I can't take this intern opportunity away from Mila. But I don't know her very well. Maybe she's an over-sharer. Maybe she'll tell her coworkers about us.

Probably not. She seemed very anxious that Ilsa was watching us. She'll be discreet.

A thrill zips through me. Discreet enough that we can keep seeing each other?

Then she's here. I jump up. "Mila!"

She slides into a chair. "Sebastian."

At least she's not calling me Mr. Young.

Although imagining her saying it wearing nothing but her employee badge gets me thinking about our night together.

I'm completely out of control here. Something about her is my kryptonite.

As I sit back down, Bethany returns with a second glass of water. "Ready for menus? Something else to drink?"

"Can you do dinner?" I ask Mila. I can't take anything for granted.

She glances around. "Should we?"

Bethany's eyebrows lift. Yeah. This sounds sordid.

"She's in the middle of unpacking," I tell Bethany. "She just moved to Boulder."

"Well, welcome," Bethany says. "I'll bring some menus."

Mila doesn't argue and hangs her purse on her chair. She's staying.

"You find it all right?" I ask.

"Not a problem." She glances out the window at the neon yellow sign for Smiley's bar. "I guess we were meeting about this time last night."

I clink my water glass against hers. "Here's to our twenty-four-hour anniversary."

She smiles at that, and I sit back in my chair. This is going to be fine.

But then she surprises me. "Are you going to ask me to leave the intern program?"

I shoot forward against the edge of the table. "No! Of course not!"

Bethany appears again to set the menus down, so I wait until she's gone to finish. "That's what we're here to figure out."

Mila fiddles with the corner of the menu. "Okay."

"There is a fraternization clause."

She doesn't meet my gaze. "I saw it. No more than one level separating us on the chain of command."

"Yeah. You can date other interns. And you could date other full-time base-level employees. But not any supervisors."

"And certainly not the general manager." She flattens her hand on the menu, as if she's trying to stop fidgeting.

I want to reach across the table and take her fingers in mine, but I know I can't. We're miles from that.

"What happened before today doesn't count," I say. "We couldn't have known."

"She presses the heel of her hand to her forehead. "We were too busy doing other things."

"We were. Delightful things." And then, there is the other question. About it being her first time. That one will have to wait.

She peers at me from behind her hand. "Was it? Delightful?"

I give in and reach across the table to graze the

fingers resting by her glass. "Completely. I haven't dated anyone in almost two years. And there you were. Funny. Beautiful. Smart."

She squeezes my hand. "And now I'm your minion."

The warmth of her hand fills me with hope that we can work this out. I hold her tight. "I think it will be okay. We can see each other away from the hotel. Honestly, you and I aren't going to run into each other all that much. You'll be in the kitchens, the service halls, the laundry."

"Doing grunt work."

"At first. I think you have ten weeks of basic rotations. Raya's in charge of that, but I sat in on the meetings as she and Havannah put this together. After the rotations, you will all be given more responsibility in the areas you are excelling at."

"What if I excel at folding towels?"

I grin at her. She's so funny. "No intern will remain in the trenches. You have a degree in hospitality. You'll move to more permanent roles. Human resources, possibly. Maybe the front desk team. Or assistant to the concierge. I expect someone will end up as a management team floater to handle pop-up problems, particularly in the off hours. You will each have some say in where you go."

"I see. When we get into those roles, will I be closer to you in the chain of command?"

I let out a long gust of air. "No. To be in range, you have to be the assistant manager, like Raya, or the head of a department or the CFO."

"Or the event manager?"

"Actually, yes. That's in range."

"So if I win this thing, we could date."

"Absolutely."

"But otherwise, I could get fired if we're found out."

She's worried. I don't blame her. "Raya has that power, but we could likely get it undone with Havannah stepping in." I don't add that this would probably cause a hostile work environment, particularly with Raya. And anyone who felt like Mila got preferential treatment.

Mila must go on a similar train of thought because she says, "If I win the big job, though, and our relationship became public, there would always be a suspicion around me being chosen, wouldn't there?"

"Possibly."

She lets go of my hand. "It was only a one-night thing. I think we can move on. Do you?"

Damn. I was hoping it wouldn't go this way. "I like you a lot, Mila."

She frowns.

I'm pressuring her. I can't do that. Not under any circumstance. "But yes, we're adults. We had a great night. We'll remember it fondly and move on."

I think of Maverick. If he makes a move on her, I'll bust his ass.

Yeah, this is all a terrible idea. You should never work side by side with kryptonite.

Mila pushes the menu away. "I think that's for the best. Thank you for giving me a chance to stay."

"You don't want dinner?" There I go again.

"I better not." She gives me a wry grin. "I don't want to get any more attached to you than I already have."

Was she? My gut pangs.

I'm dying to ask my question before she goes. This might be our last completely private conversation. "Can you tell me why you chose me? For your…first?"

She slowly slides the strap of her bag from the chair to her shoulder, as if giving herself time to consider how to answer. "I didn't think someone like me could attract someone like you. You were funny and friendly. I wanted to do it with someone like you. That's all."

Someone *like* me. Not necessarily me.

"But you couldn't face it the next morning, so you hid behind a potted plant?"

She shrugs. "Yeah, basically. I was ready to start my new life."

I stack the two menus to prove I won't try to convince her to stay. "I won't get in the way of that."

She grips the strap of her purse. "Thank you. Really. Thank you."

Then she's out the door.

I sit there, feeling far more wrecked than I should for losing someone I barely knew twenty-four hours.

Bethany eventually returns, her concerned expression back. "Do you want anything to eat?"

I consider the empty chair. "Sure. I'll call my sister over. Go ahead and put in for our usuals."

"Absolutely."

I pull out my phone to text Arya. She had no idea I was going to meet the woman from my walk of shame.

Me: I'm at Sicily's. Already ordered your favorite.
Arya: Are you serious? On my way!!!!!!!!!!
Her exuberant punctuation makes me smile.
I have to salvage this day somehow.

13

MILA

I can stay.

    I can stay!

The realization that my mistake isn't going to cost me after all sustains me all the way through a hurried unpacking, ordering my first food from the castle — more of those prime rib sliders — and texting pictures of my new place to Camille and my parents.

I decide not to bother Brooklyn and Owen, eating my free food while watching my free premium television stations, and constantly looking around at my own little space in the castle, in awe of where I am.

The next morning, I put on one of the three uniforms that were hanging in my closet. Black pants, white shirt, and black vest, all made according to the measurements they had us send in. I hang my ID badge around my neck and head to the meeting room.

Already the halls are making more sense. Staff wing one, staff wing two, main service hall, past the ballroom, and to the offices.

Raya is inside, talking to Ilsa, who has her thick black hair neatly piled high. Brooklyn, too, has her hair pulled back. I finger my curling mass, worrying I should have done the same.

Brooklyn comes over. "The guys are late," she says. "There's coffee and pastries. Get the chocolate one. Swoon worthy."

I pour a cup of coffee. "Should I put my hair up?" I ask.

"It depends on your rotation."

"Did we find them out?"

"Not yet. I wanted to be prepared." Brooklyn pulls an elastic band from her wrist. "Here. I'll do yours."

She's a good six inches taller than me, so she has no trouble gathering my hair and twisting it around. She fusses with it a second, then takes a quick shot of me with her phone. She turns the screen to show me. "Good?"

Geez. She's made an elegant updo with nothing but a hair tie. "It looks great."

Owen stumbles in, looking tired. "Hey, everyone."

"Trouble sleeping?" Brooklyn asks.

"I always have to get used to a new place." He aims straight for the coffee.

Brooklyn steps close to me to whisper, "I wonder how late Maverick will be."

I glance at the clock. It's two minutes past the hour.

Raya walks toward us. "Grab some food. We will provide coffee and pastries today and lunch on Friday due to our meetings. Other than that, you're on your own. There's a small shop for basics off the lobby, or you can drive or bus to the closest grocery store about two miles up the highway. It's a pretty far walk, though, since it's almost half a mile up the long drive to get to the main road."

"Who has cars?" Brooklyn asks. "Most of us arrived in rentals."

"I do," I say.

Ilsa doesn't answer.

"I can take us all for a run one evening, if you want." I might as well extend the offer to Ilsa, even though I'm not sure how close we'll get. She has an iron shell around her.

"Excellent," Raya says. "Mila, thank you for being a team player. Grab your plates, and we can review today's plan."

We're all settled at a long white table when Maverick finally wanders in. He nods at us before heading toward the coffee.

"I have a saying," Raya calls out. "Early is on time. On time is late."

"He's neither of those," Brooklyn whispers.

Maverick shrugs as he fills a white ceramic mug. "Sounds like I'm going to be late a lot."

Brooklyn shakes her head. I'm sure we're thinking the same thing. How is he even here? There were hundreds of applicants for these spots.

He takes his time choosing pastries, at one point saying, "I hope nobody's staring at my butt."

Raya looks like her head is going to pop off. She grips her pen so hard, I'm surprised it doesn't snap. Her face and neck are bright pink.

Brooklyn, Owen, and I exchange uneasy glances. Ilsa sits ramrod straight, attentive, as if her perfect professionalism will rub off on Maverick.

Finally, he sidles over to the table, setting down his plate and cup, and turning his chair around backwards to straddle it. "Carry on."

Raya's voice is hard-edged. "Maverick, you have three strikes before I fire you. Consider today's tardiness a warning. I'm assigning you to the dish room today. Consider every broken dish a strike."

He's made an enemy for sure. I wonder what his game is. He clearly doesn't want to be here.

He takes a big bite of a flaky croissant, then dusts his hands of the particles. "Here's what I know," he says, aiming his words at her like they're darts. "I'm not easily fired. You know why. Also, I'm really good when I decide to do something. We'll see what I decide today."

Brooklyn and I glance at each other again. What does he mean, he's not easily fired? Is he part of Havannah's family or something?

I silently pray I'm not put on a shift with him. He's clearly going to be like the classmate in the group project who drags everyone else down.

Raya stares at him in disbelief. "Maverick, I'm not sure I'm interested in being in your presence any longer." She picks up her cell phone and taps a quick message. "Henry from the dish room is on his way to escort you to your assignment."

Maverick shrugs and takes another bite of his croissant.

Raya turns to the rest of us. "Most shifts last a whole

week, but a few are only one or two days. Today, the rest of you will go in pairs. Brooklyn and Mila, you will be at the front desk to learn check-in procedures. Owen and Ilsa, we will start you with room service. There's a system that moves an order to fulfillment."

She taps on her phone. "Kennedy will come from room service, and Aisha will arrive from the front desk."

Aisha. Oh, no. She's the one who saw me with Sebastian yesterday. And it feels like the lobby is where I'm most likely to run into him.

I wish I were with room service. Or even the dish room. Folding towels sounds good, too.

Raya continues. "Next Monday, we will bring a certification team on site to administer the tests for food management. We want everyone in the program to be certified for all areas in case you need to pitch in. We have set aside Friday afternoon for a review. If you're worried about passing, I recommend you study the materials over the weekend."

Owen raises his hand. "If we have national certification, do we still need to do Colorado?"

"Yes," she says. "Just to keep things neat and square. That way, we know everyone is up to date and when you need to renew."

He nods.

Maverick has stopped eating his pastry, scowling into his coffee. He probably resents having to redo work he's already done. Many hospitality programs require certification. It's like Raya says, sometimes you have to pitch in, or if your certified food manager doesn't show, you serve as the required one in the kitchen.

Not that I expect it would happen here. Probably everyone is certified.

A middle-aged Hispanic man in the same black pants and white shirt as us, but with a white apron rather than a vest, steps into the room.

"Ah, there's Henry," Raya says. "Maverick, he'll take you to your station. If all goes well today, we'll find another rotation for you tomorrow."

His chair scoots back with a squeal. He stands up and leaves with Henry, not bothering to pick up his plate or cup.

Raya stares at it a moment, as if trying to compose herself. "If you all want to get ready, I'm sure Aisha and Kennedy will be here shortly." She touches her tablet, and the screen lights up.

We stand and pick up our plates. Both Owen and Ilsa, who were seated on either side of Maverick, reach for his leftovers to clear.

"I've got this," Owen says cordially.

But Ilsa grabs them. "No, I have it," she hisses.

Brooklyn and I share a confused look. What's going on here?

Owen shrugs, moving toward the end of the serving table where a plastic bin waits for our dishes.

Ilsa hovers over Maverick's until Raya looks up, then makes a big show of stacking the extras.

"Oh, thank you for that, Ilsa," Raya says.

So that's why.

I head to the table to set my dishes in the bin. Brooklyn leans in. "So we have a slacker and a suck up among us."

I nod.

A woman with wild red hair dashes in, a headset cocked back on her curls. "Morning is crazy. Who are my interns?"

"Those two," Raya says, pointing to Ilsa and Owen.

"Let's go," she says. "I left Gina alone with the buzz board!"

The three of them hurry out.

Brooklyn and I wait by the door. Raya seems preoccupied, and I for one don't want to rile her any more than Maverick already did. She's a tough nut, for sure, and I wonder how she'd take the news that I slept with her boss and he proposed a secret relationship away from the hotel.

Thank goodness I had the presence of mind to turn that down, even though I didn't want to.

Aisha arrives and can't quite hide her look of surprise when she sees me. "You're one of the interns?"

I nod. "There was a mix-up." I feel Brooklyn turn to me, but I don't look at her. I hope she doesn't ask about it. I'm not ready for questions.

"Well, let's go. Jessica is handling the desk and Sebastian has stepped in, but it's almost check-out time, and it will only get busier from here."

I try not to let my step falter as I follow her down the hall, her black pouf of hair swaying as she hurries.

We are dressed like her in our black pants and vests. The only difference is the red swatch of fabric in the tiny pocket on her chest. Ours are empty. I wonder if that's how people will know we are interns.

"What are your names?" she asks.

"I'm Brooklyn."

"Mila."

"Got it. Blonde Brooklyn, Meet-again Mila. I use alliteration to remember names."

Ooooh, I wish she hadn't said that.

"You two already met?" Brooklyn asks.

"Just briefly in the lobby yesterday," I say.

But she's curious. I don't want her to be curious!

I count all the people who know Sebastian and I interacted before we should have met. Aisha, Bertie, Ilsa. I hope it can stay limited to that.

When we arrive in the lobby, there is a line of families at the desk. Bertie directs bellboys with carts, the doorman is answering questions, and Sebastian and a mid-fifties woman work behind the desk.

The woman is concentrating hard, but Sebastian is all smiles, as if every person who walks up is making his day.

"That's Jessica," Aisha says. "I'm going to have to jump in. Watch from behind the desk, and if we can use you, we'll direct you."

We weave through the kids and suitcases and circle the desk. Aisha opens a third station, and the families surge forward.

Sebastian turns to us, and my heart speeds up as our eyes meet.

"Hello!" he says. "Why don't you two help everyone with the lines? Chat them up. Keep it organized. It will settle down in about half an hour, then ramp up again around eleven when the last wave comes through."

Brooklyn and I head back into the fray. She immediately starts directing people into three lines. I should do something, but I'm trying to catch my breath from seeing Sebastian in his element.

For a moment, I remember his smile in the bar, our lively conversation. And of course later, in the hotel, his body hovering over mine. He was so happy that night.

I was, too.

"Excuse me, can you call us a taxi?" a man asks me. "We're going to be cutting it close to get to the airport."

"Of course," I tell him. "I'll be right back."

But as I head to Bertie to ask him the procedures for calling a taxi, my gaze keeps sliding back to Sebastian, charming his way through the line, making more than one woman twirl her hair as she looks at him.

And I wonder if saying no to him is something I can stick to.

14

SEBASTIAN

By the time we get a solid break from check-outs, I feel certain every lobby guest and employee has figured out that I have it bad for one of our new interns. I can't stop looking at her.

She notices me, too. I catch her glances as she and Brooklyn help families until there are none left.

Jessica lets out a long, "Whew! That was a Monday!"

"Mondays are always special," Aisha says.

"How about I take the interns through the offices behind the desk?" Jessica asks.

"Perfect," I say. Get Mila out of my view. She's far too distracting.

The three of them take off, and Aisha and I remain at the desk. I plan to head somewhere else in the hotel, but I feel her gaze on me. Aisha misses nothing.

Might as well head this off. "You have something you want to ask me?"

"Are you and Mila a thing?" Aisha examines her

long, sparkly black nails like she didn't just drop a hefty accusation.

I better get this right or Mila will be the subject of speculation from here on out. "I met Mila randomly without realizing she was about to become an intern here. I had nothing to do with the intern hiring, so I wasn't aware she was part of our crew when I mistakenly brought her to the lobby." All true.

"How well did you know her?"

"Not at all." That's mostly true, if we don't count the way I know exactly how her back arches when she orgasms.

"Not at all, huh?"

Focus, Sebastian. "It's my understanding she only arrived in Boulder on Saturday. We ran into each other in town. When I saw her again here, I assumed she was simply checking in for her vacation."

"Well, that's boring."

Now, that's what I wanted to hear. "I'm not really involved with the interns."

"You're not, huh?" Aisha leans on the desk and drums her nails on the surface. "I heard you brought in someone of your own, a hot number with an attitude to match. Maverick, I think? I haven't seen him yet. Raya sent him to wash dishes."

Did she? "I'm hoping we can turn him around with our professionalism."

A woman and her husband come out of the elevator and head our way. "Lead by example," I tell her as I leave the desk.

Aisha shakes her head at me, but greets the guests

with a friendly smile and begins their check-out procedure.

I've been in the lobby more than I normally would, and that's going to get noticed. Bertie stands by the door, arm propped on the handle of a cart, grinning at me.

Yeah, he knows, too.

I'm going to have to stay very clear of Mila if I want to quash rumors.

Time to do paperwork. Or something. Whatever gets me away from the front desk.

I head to the small office Raya and I use when we need to address problems with guests away from the lobby.

It's a cozy spot meant to be calming, with cool blues and greens on the walls and a lighted aquarium. It's functional, too, with a computer and intercom system that hooks into every area of the hotel. Because we don't do actual work here, it's always tidy.

I sit in the leather office chair. I have to get a grip on this distraction with Mila. How long is she going to be at the front desk? It's the one rotation that keeps her near me.

The computer beeps to life with a quick passcode. Raya surely added their schedules to the network.

I dig around and finally find the intern plan. Maverick was supposed to go to HR today. He must have really made her mad to switch him to the dish room.

Owen and Ilsa are with room service. Maybe I'll go check on them to spread my intern interest around.

According to the schedule, all this week's rounds last

until Friday at noon, with Friday afternoon reserved for a review session for their Colorado food management testing on Monday.

Maybe she'll move Maverick back to HR tomorrow if he behaves. The dish room was never a rotation, just a general kitchen tour. The chefs don't want non-cooks in the main kitchen any more than necessary, although the interns will rotate through scheduling and ordering under the food service umbrella. They will also do a brief rotation as hosts, seating people in the restaurant, as well as helping with banquets.

Raya is going to make Maverick serve appetizers on trays. I can feel it.

Maybe I should check on him, too. Clue him in that he has to fly right or she'll make him want to quit.

I shut down the scheduler when I hear voices. It's Jessica, showing Brooklyn and Mila the small break room where the front desk clerks can take a moment between waves.

Maybe they've already seen this office. I should sit tight until they pass.

But no, Jessica pops in, stopping short when she sees me. "Oh! You're in here! The door was open!"

"It's fine. I was heading out." I stand to leave, but Mila and Brooklyn crowd the door.

They all move inside as I awkwardly try to squeeze past. My arm brushes against Mila's. Everything ignites. I forget all my determination to stay away from her. I want to grab her hand and take off with her.

Jessica gestures toward me. "Sebastian or Raya will meet with guests here if there's a complex problem or if the guests get too feisty to stay in the lobby. Sebastian, you want to tell them about the security involved?"

I was about to make my escape, but I turn around. Mila and Brooklyn move farther into the office.

"Sure. There are multiple places you can call for security if there's a problem that is escalating. There's a button by each kiosk at the front desk. There's another inside the door you passed through to get to these offices. And there are several in this room, since this is where we bring people who are behaving angrily or erratically." I move aside the hanging vines of an ivy plant to reveal a red button. "This is one. There is another beneath the desk."

"I haven't seen any security," Brooklyn says. "Where are they?"

"Everywhere," I say. "In the lobby during the day, we have one in plain clothes. That is usually Hank or Jared during the week, Lonnie or Mitchell on the weekends. We don't like a big show of security when guests arrive, although there is always someone in uniform patrolling the parking lots. And there are others in uniform walking the castle. They are the ones who will arrive at a button push. We make very deliberate decisions surrounding when we show a uniform, and when we're trying to simply de-escalate without presenting an authority figure."

"They don't talk about this stuff in hospitality school," Brooklyn says.

"It's different for every hotel," I tell her. "And it can vary here depending on the type of events happening."

"I heard a rogue princess came to one of the haunted balls," Brooklyn says.

I rock back on my heels. "That definitely happened. That was an all-hands-on-deck security situation."

"Wild." Brooklyn grins at Mila.

I catch Mila watching me and heat surges through my body.

I better get out of here before I do something dumb.

"I'm going to check on the interns in room service," I tell them. "Jessica, show these two how to work the system when it's slow. Have them give it a go when there isn't a line and the right sort of guest comes up."

"Will do, boss!"

I give them all a salute, then take off down the hall before yet another member of the Castle Hotel staff recognizes that I'm losing my mind over one of our new interns.

15

MILA

I should be focused on my new job.

I should be giving Jessica all my attention as she shows me and Brooklyn how to sign into the hotel check-in system and search for guests.

But I haven't missed how Sebastian looks at me. Surely everyone else can see it, too.

"We're going to get a small rush after lunch of the people who paid for late check-out," Jessica says, and I force my attention back to her. "We won't have you try the system then, but when it slows down. Our job comes in waves."

Aisha slides over. "Yeah, there are the early birds around eight, the wild rush in the hour before the eleven o'clock deadline, then another group at one."

"When do you all eat lunch?" Brooklyn asks right as her stomach lets out a loud growl. She presses her hand to her belly. "Asking for a friend."

We all laugh.

"Normally we take turns around now," Aisha says.

"If you're alone on the desk, you wear a headset so you can call for backup if there's a rush." She opens a drawer and pulls it out. "You can easily summon a floater, or Raya or Sebastian."

Jessica takes the headset. "How about you take Brooklyn around to see her lunch options, and I'll stay here with Mila?"

"Cool beanio," Aisha says. "I recommend bringing your lunch, but there's a sandwich cart as well as the deli. I wouldn't go for any of the restaurants. They take too long."

"How many restaurants are there?" Brooklyn asks.

"Three. The bistro is that way." Jessica points across the lobby. "It's a sit-down place mainly for burgers and pizza, family friendly, you know. Then there's the primary restaurant that has the breakfast buffet in the morning." She points to the back of the lobby. "Right there."

"The deli is the third, right?" I ask. I studied the options before coming.

"No, I wasn't counting that. There is a private restaurant in the main tower," Aisha says. "It's super fancy. Regular employees aren't even allowed in there unless that's your area. It has its own security."

"I hear eating there is over a thousand," Jessica says.

"Dang," Brooklyn says. "And of course I want to see it right now."

Aisha shrugs. "You all will probably be allowed."

"You're not?" Brooklyn asks.

"I told my man he better take me there for my birthday this year." Aisha examines her nails.

"Is he going to?" Brooklyn asks.

"He says he'll have to eat Mickey D's for a month to save up." Aisha laughs. "He better."

"I hope we get to see the secret restaurant," Brooklyn says. "Don't you, Mila?"

"Definitely," I say. "There are lots of secret things at this hotel."

"You know about the secret suite, right?" Aisha asks. "We can't talk about it with anyone who hasn't signed a nondisclosure, but the front desk does get asked about it, so we're told what to say. There was a blogger who tried to write about it, but Havannah got it taken down. She likes it to be a rumor."

"Have you seen it?" Jessica asks Aisha.

"No way. I don't even know what wing it's in. Everyone is so hush-hush about it. I hear only two people from housekeeping and a couple from maintenance even know where it is."

The words pop out of my mouth before I can think of the wisdom of saying them. "I bet Sebastian knows."

Everyone turns to me. "You got an in with the big boss to find out?" Aisha asks. "You knew him before."

Oh, no. I should have kept my mouth shut. *And* I should have gotten my story straight with Sebastian before anyone could ask me. "Not really." The less said, the better.

"I bet you've got a lot to say about our Mr. Sebastian." Aisha has caught a whiff of secrets. Her eyes have gotten bright. "Do tell."

The three of them look at me. Why is this happening? I don't want to be the subject of rumors!

"How long have you known him?" Brooklyn asks.

Aisha leans her elbows on the counter. "Yeah, how long?"

"I only just got here," I say, my mouth dry. "I drove in Saturday. I didn't know a soul in Boulder before that."

"So, did you meet him on Saturday?" Brooklyn asks.

Everything flashes hot. "Do we have to talk about this?"

Now everyone is super interested. I should have played it so much cooler, but I'm no good at that.

"I saw him looking at her," Aisha says. "He said y'all met before you got here. He didn't know you were an intern."

He told Aisha that?

I want to be sick. This is not happening. I press my hand to my belly.

But then, I'm saved.

Bertie walks up. "If you don't mind, I'd like to show the interns the holding area for suitcases. It already came up this morning when they were working the lines."

Aisha frowns. "Bertie, we were just getting somewhere! Besides, I'm taking Brooklyn around for lunch. Her stomach sounds like it's about to go on attack."

"Then I'll take this one," he says, pointing to me. "We'll be back shortly."

Aisha sighs. "Come on then," she says to Brooklyn. "Let's go."

I follow Bertie to a room off to the side of the entrance.

"Thank you," I tell him.

"The rumors are flying," he says. "Keep your chin up."

I don't want rumors flying!

Bertie opens the door to a large room filled with racks, a few suitcases neatly stacked on them. "Aisha asks a lot of questions."

"You don't miss much, do you?"

"Not really." He heads to a desk near the back wall. "Sebastian didn't tell her much of anything, so don't let her fool you into saying more than you want her to know."

"What did he say?"

"I wasn't specifically listening in," Bertie starts, but I wave him off.

"I'm not judging you. Tell me what you know."

He grins and his eyes flash bright. "He said he met you in town, and that when he saw you here, he thought you were vacationing. That's all Aisha knows. She thought that information was boring and moved on."

I let out a long breath. "So I nearly said too much."

He pats my shoulder. "She's a tricky one. Lovely girl, but very tricky."

"I'm warned."

He raises his arm to gesture to the room. "This is my domain. You can always duck in here if you need a moment. Mostly, it's just me and the luggage."

"Do a lot of guests leave their suitcases here?"

"Certainly. Check-in isn't until three, so if they want to go on a hike or head into Boulder, they'll leave their luggage with us."

"That makes sense."

"Looking up a bag is as easy as logging in for check-in. The bin number for which luggage is theirs is right here." He taps the numbers beneath each cubby on the wall. "If we get overloaded, we revert to the tags." He points to a clear box attached to the wall, filled to the brim with luggage tags.

"I'll know for when the next guest asks."

"You can always ask old Bertie if you need."

"Thank you. Especially for watching out for me."

He leads me back out to the lobby, where Jessica is waiting on a family. "We all need a little looking after here and there."

"You think these rumors about Sebastian will go away?"

His lips tighten. "That'll be up to the two of you. If you keep looking at each other the way you are now, then there's going to be no end to the talk."

I know exactly what he means.

The trouble is, I don't know how to stop.

16

SEBASTIAN

When I get home in the evening, I feel exhausted from the day in a way that isn't usual.

I sit on the sofa, a beer bottle in hand, trying to shake my unease.

Arya comes in with an armful of slippery plastic packages, leaving a trail of them behind her.

"You're molting," I tell her.

Alfalfa sniffs at the packets, then flops on his bed by the fireplace.

"I know. I have to prep the craft for tomorrow's class." She dumps the packages on the coffee table and retraces her steps, picking up the ones she dropped.

I lean forward and turn one around. Inside is a piece of thick paper covered in rainbows with dots of dry paint that the kids will spread with wet brushes. I remember doing similar art when we were young.

"Need help?" I ask her.

"No, I want to put a couple of stickers in each packet." She adds to her stack. "Why the dark circles under your eyes? Trouble sleeping?"

"Long day."

"How did it go with Walk of Shame Girl?" I told Arya about Mila at the restaurant last night.

"Rough. I think everybody knows something happened between us."

Arya pries open a packet and drops two smiley cloud stickers into it before sealing it shut again. "It's a big hotel. How did you even see her?"

"Raya assigned her to the front desk, and you know how Mondays are. A big exodus. We all ended up working closely for hours."

"Yikes. Did you talk?"

"Not alone. I escaped as soon as I could."

She opens another packet. "And that stressed you out?"

"That and Maverick."

"Oh. Him."

Arya is not a fan of Maverick. He was the bane of her existence growing up when Uncle Roger would bring his nephew to barbecues and birthday parties. She's only a year older than him, and he gave her hell.

"He seems determined to get fired. Rude and late." I run the back of my hand over my eyes. "Raya made him wash dishes today."

This makes her smile. "How did he take that?"

"He charmed the pants off the ladies and made friends with all the men. He asked to go back tomorrow."

Now she frowns. "He's always been like that."

"He's something."

"And you invited him into your livelihood. Doesn't he reflect badly on you?"

I chug a long pull of beer. "Nobody's saying it, at least not yet. Raya's annoyed, and he's already the talk of the other employees."

"Everyone will love him by Friday, other than any rivals or authority figures. That's how he operates."

She's right. "We'll see how it goes. I only promised Uncle Roger to give him a shot, not to put up with any nonsense."

"Sounds like he's going to push boundaries with Raya. Not that it's hard." She works faster now, finding her rhythm in opening the packets and stuffing them with stickers.

I set down my bottle to help her. "Raya will take it to Havannah, no doubt. It's only a matter of when."

"Will Havannah call you in?"

"Probably, but not in a troubled way, more in a 'what should we do about this?'"

"He'll charm her. He's strategic."

"Probably so."

We work in companionable silence until all the packets are filled. She peels the backing off an extra cloud and sticks it to my nose. "Put on a happy face."

I laugh, taking the sticker off my nose and pushing it on her forehead. "You're the happy one."

"I'm loving that you have such good work gossip these days. Should I heat up our leftovers from the other night?"

"It's my turn to cook."

"I made too much King Ranch Casserole, though. Remember?"

"Right. Okay. That sounds good."

She trots off for the kitchen, and I stare up at the ceiling, grateful not to have to cook while I'm so distracted. I can picture Mila in the bed, her dark hair spread all over the white pillow. That moment of surprise. The warm softness of her body when I fell asleep holding her in my arms.

Surely it was more than what she said, just one night.

I know it was.

I have to convince her.

The next morning, when Brooklyn and Mila arrive at the front desk, it's quieter. Tuesday isn't a popular check-out day, and Jessica and Aisha have it under control.

"I don't think the two of you got to see much of the hotel yesterday," I say. "How about I take you on my rounds?"

"That sounds fun," Brooklyn says.

Mila watches me warily, as if she thinks I'm up to something.

I am undaunted. "Let's head to the princess wing. There's lots of empty rooms, and you should know about some of our spectacular offerings." I hold out my arm to gesture to the wing, which has a castle facade over the entrance.

Brooklyn lets out a squeal. "I love a princess theme!"

We head past the luggage room to pass through the castle door. Bertie gives Mila a salute. She smiles back, and I wonder if they've become friends.

I want to know everything about her. What did she do last night after her shift? Did she hang out with the other interns?

Did Maverick put a move on her?

I can't think about that.

Just inside the princess wing is the Pickle deli. We pause outside of it, but it hasn't opened yet. "This is a great place to get food," I tell them. "Staff gets forty percent off everything with their ID, so make use of it."

"I got a burger from the bistro last night," Brooklyn says. "It was so good."

"I went to the sandwich cart," Mila says. "I can't wait until we have time to shop for groceries."

"We should do that tonight," Brooklyn says. "We can get the gang together."

I feel jealous of their easy plans. It's not my place to join staff members for casual things. It's not that I can't, but I'd put a pall over any lightheartedness. Nobody wants to get drunk with the boss.

"Let's head into the wing. There are two floors of princess rooms. The suites are at the far end, as part of the tower. There are twelve additional floors in the tower."

"Are the rooms circular?" Brooklyn asks.

"Some are," I say "Let's go look at them."

Brooklyn lets out a squeal. "I want to see every room." She lowers her voice. "I heard there is a sex dungeon in the haunted wing."

I laugh, taking great care not to look at Mila. "There are two."

Brooklyn lets out another squeal. "Can we see them?"

"Both are currently occupied," I say. "They usually are. But we can sneak in one day when housekeeping is clearing them between occupants."

"Do people stay there long?" Brooklyn asks, running her fingers along the sparkling pink wainscoting on the lower third of the walls. The kids do that, too.

"We have people who reserve them for an entire month at a time." I don't mention that sometimes there are group gatherings. They sometimes hire a bartender from the haunted bar, and they've gotten an eyeful more than once. We're careful who we allow to work those events. They have to be discreet.

I hear all about it, of course.

I once got called to the dungeon by the night manager with an SOS on our headsets. I almost sent security, but then decided it might be better to go myself.

I had stayed on site later than I planned, feeling some concern about the tourists who had disclosed they were having a sex party in the dungeon. It's allowed, but to pass the security of the suite area, every member has to show ID at the front desk. You can't simply walk into that wing. It's restricted. It also helps us keep tabs on how many people are attending to avoid breaking fire codes.

When I arrived, two naked women were tied to the wall. All manner of things were being done to them. At least four couples were making use of the various apparatuses. Nobody seemed deterred by my arrival.

Jeff, the night manager, was handcuffed to a T-bar over the oversized round bed. His shirt was unbuttoned. Apparently he'd said something that made them think he wanted to join, and he hadn't figured out how to get out of it.

I told the others, with some difficulty due to a language barrier, that he had to get back to work.

They were disappointed but let him go.

That was definitely a night.

We arrive at the tower. I flash my ID at the security door.

"Do ours work here?" Brooklyn asks.

"Not as interns. Depending on where you end up assigned, it might get added. The towers and secure areas have designated staff, from managers all the way down to housekeeping and room service."

"Wow," Brooklyn says.

"It's not unusual," I tell her. "People who pay for secure floors don't want just anyone to access their rooms, even among the employees."

The next space is circular with four doors, three for the rooms and one for the stairwell, plus a narrow elevator taking up a big chunk of space. It has silk on the walls, and a huge crystal chandelier hangs above us.

I pull up my phone to hook into the application that runs housekeeping to ensure that the room we enter is empty. Only one of them has a family inside.

I pop open the door to the room next to the elevator.

About seventy-five percent of the princess rooms are

pink, but this particular one is pale blue. It's set up as a Cinderella room, and a huge mural with the pumpkin chariot is painted on the back wall. The space that is the door on the pumpkin is actually a short door to a tiny balcony overlooking the side garden. All the rooms with this view have this feature, since they aren't on the mountain side.

"It's beautiful," Brooklyn says, her voice breathy. She turns in circles in the open space.

"All the princess rooms in the tower have themes. Havannah did her research. There are lots of Belles, several Cinderellas, and Moana is also quite popular."

"What does she do when a new princess comes along?" Brooklyn asks.

"We will devote a couple of the rooms of the regular wing to that. I expect, as the hotel ages, some of the tower rooms will get redecorated to newer princesses. The big suites have multiple themes."

"Can we see one?" Brooklyn asks. "How many princess suites are there?"

Mila speaks up. "Most of the floors have a suite and one or two regular rooms, but the top floor is completely open with a large suite and a party room."

She's done her homework. "That's right."

"Is the top floor occupied?" Brooklyn asks.

"It is. In the other tower, of course, is the private restaurant."

"Do we get to see that?" Brooklyn asks.

"That's a tour Raya has planned," I tell her.

I watch Mila take in the space, hoping she's impressed. I'm not sure why it matters to me. I'm only the manager, and I had nothing to do with the hotel's design or interior decorating.

But I want her to like it. To be proud to be here.

I want everything about her time at the Castle Hotel to be perfect.

And hopefully soon that will include me.

17

MILA

I swear I did not just think about having sex with my boss in a princess bed.

But it's big and heart-shaped. I know it's meant to be cute for the kids, but I can picture him on it. Me on it.

Is this what it's like? After you've done it once, you want to do it over and over again?

Heat rises from my belly.

Sebastian's phone buzzes. He frowns. "You're in luck. We got a call from the party suite at the top of the tower. They need a manager."

Brooklyn and I silently squee at each other. We get to do real hotel stuff!

We head to the elevator, and Sebastian calls it with his ID. "Yours won't work on this elevator," he tells us.

"Awwww," Brooklyn whines.

"In due time."

The doors slide open, and Brooklyn and I both gape at the interior. A thousand tiny mirrors are mounted to the walls, almost as if you're stepping inside a disco ball.

A happy voice says, "Please scan your room card. The elevator will magically take you to the correct floor!" Then in a slightly more serious tone, "If anyone in your party is affected by blinking lights, press any button for a silent, easy ride." And back to the bright tone. "Let's party like a princess!"

"Yes, let's!" Brooklyn begins dancing as the music fills the space and a cascade of stars flash from a projector near the ceiling.

The whole room becomes a disco in colored lights and mirrors.

Sebastian grins at Brooklyn and scans his card.

The lights shut off.

"Awwww," Brooklyn says.

The voice says, "Welcome, staff member. Please choose a floor."

Sebastian presses the 12.

"We can't get the music back?" Brooklyn asks.

He laughs. "Only on a guest ID."

"Bummer."

We zip up three floors, where we're stopped.

When the doors open, a little girl dressed like Jasmine holds the hand of an older, almost-teen brother. "This is it," he tells her. "The last time I'm going to do this."

The girl looks up at us. "I like the dance party."

"We're going up," Sebastian says.

"We have a friend on the tenth floor," the boy says. "We shared cards so Tiffany could go up and down all she wanted."

Sebastian nods.

"Where's the dance party?" Tiffany asks.

"Scan your card and it will start," Sebastian says, his voice kind.

Something in me uncurls.

When the boy scans the key card, the voice says, "If anyone in your party is affected by blinking lights, press any button for a silent, easy ride."

"Don't press any buttons!" Tiffany yells. She turns to Sebastian. "He killed the party yesterday."

"I wanted to test it!"

Then the lights and music begin. Tiffany starts to dance.

Brooklyn apparently can't help herself, and starts swinging her arms with her.

"That's right!" Tiffany yells. "I got a princess friend!"

"You bet you do!" Brooklyn shouts.

Sebastian's gaze meets mine. He's all smiles.

I wish I was self-confident enough to dance with them, but I'm not nearly so bold as Brooklyn.

The two of them bop all the way to the tenth floor.

"Let's go down again!" Tiffany cries.

Her brother pulls her out of the elevator. "They have to keep going up."

"Awwww."

When the door closes, the party music starts back up. It doesn't seem to know who got off, the guests or the staff.

"Yeah!" Brooklyn shouts, but she barely gets her dance on when we arrive at twelve.

But the doors won't open.

"What's wrong?" I ask.

"This is a secure suite," Sebastians says. "You have to scan your way out of the elevator on the top floor since it opens straight into the party space. You both ready?"

We nod.

He scans his ID and new music penetrates the moment a gap appears, loud and bouncy. A woman dressed as Snow White is leading a clapping line of seven dwarves. They aren't particularly short, probably other women, but they have masks on and their costumes are lumpy, so it's hard to tell.

A dozen little girls, probably four or five, wave their arms on a small dance floor. Several mothers sit at circular tables scattered through the suite. There's a sitting area with two sofas and a television, a bathroom, then a long hall that leads to bedrooms.

Brooklyn looks ready to party again, but Sebastian gives both of us a serious look, so she plays it straight.

As soon as we step out, a mother with a crying girl on her hip hurries our way.

"It's about time you got here," she says.

"How can I help?" Sebastian asks.

"Look at her." She swivels to show the crying girl. "It's her party and she's miserable!"

Brooklyn and I exchange a glance. And how is this our problem?

But Sebastian is not fazed. He leans into the girl. "What's your name?"

She sniffs. "Gina."

"Happy birthday, Gina," he says. "How old are you?"

She holds up five fingers.

"Five. That's a good age."

Gina watches him with set, solemn eyes.

"It's those dwarves," the mother says. "Referred to us by your hotel, I might add."

"What's the problem?" Sebastian asks.

"He's too grumpy!" Gina wails. "He's scary!"

I work hard to bite back a smile, and I see Brooklyn is, too.

"He's what?" Sebastian says, with outrage. "Nobody should be grumpy at a party!"

Snow White dances close, her teeth gritted in a forced smile. "The face is permanent!" Then she dances by.

I look beyond them at the dwarves. It's true. The dwarves all wear full-face masks with hats and hair attached. There's no way to change an expression. Dopey dances up to Gina, swinging his head back and forth, but she buries her face in her mother's shoulder.

The mother swings her away from us. "I want them out of here. I want a full refund. I want my daughter to stop crying!"

Dang. It's not the hotel's fault her kid hates the costumes.

But Sebastian nods. "Absolutely." He taps Gina on the arm. "Gina? Come down and pick who gets to stay."

Interesting.

Gina wiggles away from her mother, who sets her on the floor.

She walks up to the dancing dwarves.

"Stop the bloody music!" the mother calls.

The man behind a DJ setup in the far corner lowers the volume until it is barely audible.

Sebastian turns around, his arms upraised. "The birthday girl is going to pick which characters get to stay extra-long!"

Huh. That's a nice spin on it.

Snow White looks doubtful, but she holds her practiced smile.

"Line up the dwarves!" Sebastian calls.

The seven of them stand across the dance floor. Doc is first. He clasps his hands like he's begging. "Can I stay, please, birthday princess? Your Highness?" He gets down on his knees in a silly bow and falls over on his back like he lost his balance.

Gina giggles. "You stay."

Then Dopey comes up, clumsy and tripping over his feet. "What about me, Princess Gina?" He takes her hand and kisses it, or at least lifts it to his painted lips.

"Yes!"

Each of the dwarves ask to stay until we get to Grumpy. He crosses his arms and huffs, turning away. Then he slowly turns around, does a silly tap dance with his feet, then huffs and turns away again.

Gina laughs and claps her hands. "Again!"

He does another dance, this one even sillier, and Gina collapses on the floor in giggles. "More, more, more!"

The mother bends next to her. "I thought you wanted him gone?"

"No, Mama! Grumpy is silly!"

Grumpy lies on the floor next to Gina, kicking his legs in the air. She mimics him.

The mother stands. "Well, all right. I guess she is five, after all."

"Can we help with anything else?" Sebastian asks.

"We could use another server," the mother says, even though the two that are already here are simply standing behind the counter of a kitchenette on the back wall.

"Done," Sebastian says. He passes her a card. "Call me directly if you think of anything you need."

She holds the card. "Thank you." She seems mollified.

"Happy birthday, Princess Gina!" he calls as he herds us back to the elevator.

When the doors close, Brooklyn says. "She's a piece of work."

Sebastian shrugs. "Most people are."

I think about him all the way back to the ground floor and to the front desk, where he calls the kitchen to send someone up to assist the party.

He loves what he does. That's plain.

And he's good at it.

He's good at everything.

I'm still thinking about him when I try to fall asleep that night.

Sebastian smiling. Him with the little girl.

Standing in front of a heart bed.

Any bed.

The thing about only ever having had sex one time is that you *have* had it.

And you want to have it again.

I regret pushing Sebastian's hand away when he was over me that one night we had. I want to see what he would have done.

Can you really have two orgasms in one encounter?

I bet you can with Sebastian.

Yeah, I'm feeling it.

He doesn't live on site at the castle like we do, and he went off shift at five.

It's a good thing. I'd be sneaking down corridors, trying to find him.

Because as I get to know him better, as I see him interact with the employees, fun and easygoing but competent and self-assured, I like him more and more.

And he hasn't stopped looking at me

I think that maybe, possibly, he feels exactly the same.

I turn on my belly, holding onto every detail from that one night. If I could go back, I would do things differently. I'd tell him. I'd let him take care of me. I'd savor it.

When I finally fall asleep, my dreams are torrid. Sebastian in the princess room, ripping off the ball-gown. Me, holding the metal rails overlooking the flower garden, naked, him behind me.

I wake up sweaty and desperate for him.

What have I done?

I wash my hair in cooler water than usual, for the first time understanding why people take cold showers. To calm their thoughts. Bring themselves down.

I pick up a cup of coffee at the cart near the lobby and head to the front desk, bracing myself for seeing him after the night of sexy thoughts and dreams.

He's there, perfect in his suit jacket and vest, smiling for an elderly couple who are checking out.

Now I get why people bite their fists. I fight the urge to do it myself.

The couple steps away, and he catches my gaze. I don't know what he sees there, but his eyebrows lift. I think he got some subliminal message. Is that what happens between partners? They can convey a need with a look, a tilt of their head, a lift of their eyebrow?

I force my gaze away. It's Jessica's day off, and a young man works beside Aisha. He smiles at me, then his gaze is clearly drawn to something behind me.

I turn. It's Brooklyn, her hair down for the first time since I've known her, the cascade of blonde curling in beachy waves over the shoulders of her black vest. She's ungodly beautiful, and every man in the lobby is staring at her.

I cut my eyes to Sebastian. Okay, every man but him. He's busily tapping on his computer. He looks up, spots Brooklyn, and says, "There's our other intern. You two come back here and meet Ricky. He's another front desk employee." Then he's back to the screen.

Is he immune?

I'm not sure even I am.

Brooklyn doesn't seem to notice or care about the

fuss she's causing in the room. She hooks her arm through mine so that we walk behind the desk together.

"Interns Mila and Brook, reporting for duty," she says cheerily.

Aisha turns to her. "Did you get laid or something?"

"Hey now," Brooklyn says, but she blushes.

That gets Aisha's attention. "Who's the lucky guy? You haven't left this place. Maverick? Owen?" She leans in close to us. "A guest?"

The way she says it makes me think that it's not okay to have one-offs with visitors. I should have read the employee policies more closely.

Not that it matters. I won't be seducing random men who check in.

"No," Brooklyn says. "A lady doesn't tell."

The other front desk worker is clearly wildly interested in our conversation. He keeps turning his head to listen.

Aisha notices. "That's Ricky. He doesn't kiss and tell either, because he has nothing to tell!"

Ricky's cheeks get two bright spots of pink. He can't be much older than us, boyish and probably shy. His shock of thick, black hair tries to fall in his eyes, and he nervously pushes it aside.

"Ricky speaks Spanish, so he's helpful if you get a family who needs him," Sebastian says. "He can also do sign language in English and Spanish."

"Impressive!" Brooklyn says, and Ricky's face goes pink again.

Aisha rolls her eyes. "He's too easy to tease. You won't be able to help yourself."

Another woman arrives from the back hall. She's mid-forties, with straight hair that hugs her face. Her dark eyes take in the group. "To your stations!" she cries, clapping her hands together. "Go through the morning checks." She notices me and Brooklyn. "These must be the interns."

Sebastian logs out of his station. "Brooklyn, Mila, this is Sasha, the front office manager. She works Wednesday to Sunday. Raya or I help out on her days off."

"This is a lot of people back here," Sasha says. "Sebastian, take one of your interns on your rounds or find something for one of them to do."

She's bossy. She might be more hardcore than Raya.

Brooklyn and I turn to Sebastian to see who he'll pick.

I'm reminded of that scene in *Grey's Anatomy* when Meredith tells Derek to "Pick me."

Didn't that show also start with Meredith accidentally sleeping with her attending physician?

I groan inwardly. I'm a story cliché.

"Mila, come on," Sebastian says. "We'll take a tour of security."

"Surprise, surprise," Aisha says.

Brooklyn elbows her.

Sebastian ignores the dig. "Brooklyn, I'll be back for you shortly. Aisha, make sure she reviews how to log in and do check-in and check-out. We're going to have the interns try it alone today."

"They better know what they're doing," Sasha says. "Show me."

Sebastian tilts his head toward the back. "Let's go meet Hank. He'll be going on shift soon."

And as we head into the hall behind the front desk, I have to seriously work to suppress my smile.

He picked me.

18

SEBASTIAN

I should have chosen Brooklyn first, and I know it.

But it's quiet at this hour. The first rush of check-outs hasn't begun. The staff in this part of the hotel is minimal. It's almost like being alone.

We walk past the break room. "Did Jessica show you security yesterday?"

"It was locked up."

"It usually is. There's an office for the guards back here, along with a holding room, should we need it. There's a buzzer, though. You can get their attention quickly."

Our steps are muffled in the carpeted hall. I scan us into a small room with multiple desks. Hank sits at one of them, beneath the security monitors that flash black and white feeds of the various cameras on site.

"Hank, this is Mila, one of the new interns. I'll try to bring each of them around."

Hank stands, looking like any tourist in jeans and a

polo shirt. He's the incognito guard today. He extends a hand. "Nice to meet you, Mila."

"Is Jeff around?" I ask. "He's on duty today, right?"

"I saw him leaving for his parking lot rounds." Hank jingles the keys in his pocket. "How many new interns did we get?"

"Five," I say. "Two are on front desk this week. The others will rotate through."

"The boldest and brightest from all over. I like it." He glances at the clock. "Time to head to the lobby." He tips his ball cap at Mila. "Nice to meet you."

Then we're alone in the office.

Only a handful of people have a badge that will let them back here. Havannah, Raya, me, and security. Even maintenance and housekeeping have to be let in.

"The holding area is through here," I tell her.

I scan us through a door in the back wall to another simple room with a table and a few cushioned chairs. "It's rare we use it," I say, "but sometimes we have a guest who destroys a room, or waves a weapon around, or even hurts somebody. We keep them here until the police arrive."

She looks around. "When was the last time anyone was in here?"

"Early summer. It's not used often."

Her eyebrows lift.

"I didn't bring you here for anything illicit. I mean. I wouldn't suggest——" Why am I a tongue-twisted schoolboy around her?

"Sebastian, it's fine. I get it." She walks through the room, brushing her fingers along the backs of the chairs.

"It's been harder than I thought, working with you. Do you think it's going to be a problem?"

Now that's a question. "I think we can handle it."

She grasps the back of a cushioned office chair. "Are we, though? I don't feel like I'm handling anything. Bertie said we have to stop looking at each other the way we are or everyone is going to figure it out."

"Bertie knows?"

Her gaze skitters away. "Not details. But he knows something happened."

"I showed a lot of interest in you before I realized you were an intern. Bertie's observant."

She grips the back of the chair like it's the only thing holding her up. "I like it here. I don't want to get fired."

My footsteps are quick as I move closer. "You won't. I won't let that happen. Aisha talks about everyone. She thinks everyone's hooking up. Nobody takes her gossip seriously."

"Okay."

"I know how I'm looking at you," I tell her. "I'll try to do better. It's just hard."

That gets her attention. Her dark eyes meet mine. "Is it?"

"Completely. I'm ridiculously attracted to you. I want it all. My job for me. Your internship for you. And you. For me."

She shakes her head. "I don't get men like you."

That takes me aback. "What do you mean? What's there to get?"

"No, that's not what I mean. I don't get to *have* you. I'm never the choice."

She said this before, in the hotel. "Why wouldn't you be?"

She lets go of the chair to stand directly in front of me, arms crossed. "You think I held onto my V-card on purpose?"

"Lots of people have reasons to wait."

"Nobody wanted it!"

Something about her saying this makes me feel feral, like a wolf protecting a den. "I did."

I draw her to me, my mouth covering hers. I know I shouldn't. I absolutely should not. But I want her to know that she shouldn't feel that way. Not in the least. That she's perfect. Everything I want to get to know.

Everything I want in my bed. Again.

She melts into me, and I pull her body tightly against mine. She's so luscious in my arms. I want to touch everything. Do everything.

My fingers tangle in her hair. A hotel full of rooms. We could be in any of them. I want to break in each and every one.

I linger on her mouth, making up for all the times I've had to hold myself away from her. I want to kiss her for hours, for days.

She breaks away, gasping.

I hold her shoulders so she will look at me. "Don't let anyone make you think you're not beautiful, sexy, and perfect. You are all those things. Plus smart. And talented. Look where you landed, all on your own."

Her face is pained. "But if I do this with you, if we're together, then they will think I'm just a chick who sleeps with the boss to win."

Fuck.

I release her.

"Okay." I run my hand through my hair. "You're right. We can't do this if that matters to you."

"I need to think about it," she says. "You're a lot. You're more than I bargained for."

Hope sparks in my chest. "So, this could happen?"

"Maybe. Give me some time."

"Can I kiss you again since I have to wait?"

She lets out a shaky laugh. "I would love that. I love your kisses."

I want to do so much more than kiss her. When I pull her against me this time, I make sure she knows it. I lift her by the thighs to wrap those Castle Hotel pant legs around my waist. I slip my hand beneath that official vest, and snake my way to her skin until my thumb slips beneath her bra.

Her breathing speeds up, but I keep my mouth on hers. I kiss her and kiss her and kiss her until she finally breaks free, laughing. "Set me down, you brute!"

I kiss her again before I let her feet down to the floor.

She shakes her head. "I get it. You want me. You want to keep doing this forever." She brushes her hand against my cheek. "Give me until the weekend. I'll come to you. I promise. I want to. I just found out what all the fuss was about."

My whole body feels alight at her words.

She wants this.

And no one has ever had her but me.

Fuck. It's an intoxicating mix.

Even though we're alone, I lean close to her ear to say, "Please know that when I get you, I'm going to do wild and unspeakable things to you for hours."

She takes in a sharp breath. "Understood."

I step away, eager for time to pass, for the weekend to come. "Let's get you back to your training."

"And you can show my beautiful blonde coworker this security room." Her voice is teasing.

But I'm serious as I pull her against me one more time. "I can't picture anyone in this room with me but you. And I promise you, if you'll let me, I'll make you cry out like you did that first night in every room of this hotel. And there are hundreds. Hundreds and hundreds of rooms, of beds, of sofas, of tables." I lean in close to her ear. "I know which days the sex dungeon is open."

I can feel her heart race, which sets off mine.

"Okay," she says.

And then we hurry out of the security office, straightening our clothes.

Full of anticipation.

19

MILA

By Friday, I'm ready for my internship to move to another part of the hotel. Brooklyn and I are masters at check-in, check-out, room transfers, and have started to get a good understanding of the problems that crop up in the day-to-day operation of the hotel.

People complain about noise. About towels. About temperature. Aisha and Jessica have a running bet on how many people will need to be shown how to work the thermostat controls each day. I've become an expert at it, since Brooklyn and I started getting sent to handle room problems. And there are many.

Sasha replaced Sebastian at the front desk, so he was around less. It was a relief not to have to worry about people watching us together, and the probing questions finally stopped.

"I feel like the front desk has to be the most useful station for us," Brooklyn says as we head to the meeting room at lunchtime.

"We learned a lot," I say. "I think we saw everything that can go wrong with a guest."

She bumps my shoulder with hers. "Except when a sex party goes sideways. Notice how we never even saw anyone checking into the super-secret suites. They're not in the normal database at all. I looked."

"I did, too!" I bump her back.

"We're such naughty, naughty interns."

We laugh as we buzz into the back hall. Raya is providing sandwiches for us as we do the review for the food manager certification on Monday.

It's the first time all the interns will be together since Monday, although I know that Owen and Brooklyn have had dinner together most nights. Something's going on there, although Brooklyn insists they're just friends.

We laugh as we pass through the service door to the employee hall.

"I wonder how Maverick did with the dish room," Brooklyn says, but then she stops short.

I almost run into her. "You okay?"

She makes a strangled sound, like someone's choking her.

"Brooklyn?" I spot Maverick in the hall, wildly making out with Kennedy, the redhead from room service. He has his hands all over her, up in her hair, touching the skin exposed at her waist.

He looks up at Brookyln's garbled cry and spots her, his eyes raking over her body. Gross. He's literally got his hands all over Kennedy, and he's ogling Brooklyn?

Then he kisses Kennedy again!

Brooklyn dashes into the meeting space. I take a second to glare at Maverick. What an ass.

No one else is inside the room, and lunch is already set up on the side table. Brooklyn stands in the middle of the rows of chairs, her head down, her shoulders shaking.

What's going on?

"Brooklyn?" I come up beside her and tap her shoulder. "Are you okay?"

She turns away from me, her entire upper body quivering. Is she crying?

"Brooklyn? What happened?"

I look back at the door. What was going on with Maverick that seeing him kiss Kennedy would upset her this much?

Was he all over Kennedy in the hall on purpose, wanting to be seen? I might have thought he wanted to tweak Raya again, but was it actually Brooklyn he was showing off for?

Brooklyn doesn't move or speak.

"The others are going to be here any minute," I say. "Do you want me to make excuses for you? I'm sure you can be gone while we eat. I'll make a sandwich for you."

She blows out a long breath. "I can't give him the satisfaction."

"Maverick?"

She turns, and I see her whole face is red. She's not crying much, like she's more mad than sad, even though her eyes are wet. "I slept with him, Mila. Twice."

"With Maverick?"

"Yes, Maverick."

"I thought you were into Owen."

She throws up her hands. "Owen is nice! Owen is great! But Maverick is…"

"A slime ball. What the hell was that out there?"

"Him getting me back for saying I wouldn't have sex with him if he was going to flirt with every woman in the castle."

Oh. One of those. "And you *like* him?"

"I thought so! And now he's having sex with the redhead."

"Maybe. He might have been using her to get to you."

"He already had me!" She paces around the rows of chairs. "I knew better. But he was so hot. And so sexy. And knew all the right things to say." She shakes a fist at the ceiling. "He's a snake charmer! How did I fall for another one of those!"

"When did this happen?"

She whirls around. "Monday night. Then Wednesday night. Last night I said no more."

"You had time for this?"

"Yeah, he's like that. Knocks on your door, wham, bam, thank you, ma'am."

Maverick must be good to have gotten Brooklyn that fast.

But then, I slept with Sebastian within two hours of meeting him.

"You want me to punch him for you?" I ask.

This makes Brooklyn laugh. "Maybe!"

Owen and Ilsa enter the room, and Brooklyn whips in the opposite direction, swiping at her eyes.

"What's wrong with her?" Ilsa asks, heading straight for the food like she doesn't care about the answer.

"Brooklyn?" Owen's voice is full of concern.

"We're good," I tell him. "Just a frustrating morning."

"I get that." Owen shoves his hands in his pockets. "Room service is no picnic. They complain about everything."

"I bet." Did they see Maverick? Was he still out there? I casually move close enough to the door to peek out. The hall is empty. Huh. And he didn't come to the meeting room. Were they going to continue somewhere? No, I don't want to think about it.

Brooklyn seems to have it together as she turns back around. "We should eat!" she says brightly.

"I'm on it," Owen says, passing both of us plates.

All four of us are considering the sandwich choices when Sebastian leans through the door. "I need an intern for a haunted suite!"

"Isn't that the sex dungeon?" Owen asks.

Sebastian grins at all of us. "It might be! Who wants to come?"

I don't volunteer. He shouldn't choose me. It will be too obvious.

"Me, me, me!" Brooklyn says.

"But I want to go," Owen says.

Ilsa turns with her plate. "I'm the only one of us mature enough to enter that space professionally, and you all know it."

Owen and Brooklyn wave their hands in the air like they want a magician to choose them to go onstage.

But then Sebastian does exactly the wrong thing. "Mila, let's go. Come see what all the fuss is about."

"Awww, she didn't even volunteer." Owen loads sandwiches on his plate in consolation.

I spot Brooklyn biting her lip as I return my plate to the stack. She knows.

Ilsa's eyes narrow, like she also suspects something.

When we get in the hall, Raya approaches us in the corridor.

"Are you stealing my intern?" she asks.

"Mila has been on the front desk dealing with problems all week. I thought she should experience one of the more delicate situations."

Raya's face scrunches. "One of the suites?"

He nods. "Thought I should bring a woman with me."

"Okay." She looks at me. "Be discreet."

"Absolutely." Now my curiosity is huge.

We cut through the kitchen to a service hall that follows the back side of the haunted wing. There's a door to the old-fashioned Wild West-style haunted saloon, where the bartender wears a period costume.

Then a long service corridor connects to the secure section of the haunted wing, where the suites are. I've never been this far, and my belly buzzes with excitement that I might see the sex dungeon.

Sebastian scans us into a small private lobby with a secondary elevator. There's a security desk here, but it's currently unmanned.

"Do you have a guard posted here?"

"Only if there's a party," Sebastian says, leading us

through another secure door into a short hall. "We also check in guests who don't want to come through the main entrance."

"Like who?"

"Celebrities. Public figures. Billionaires."

"Am I about to meet a billionaire?"

He grins. "Tempted?"

"Nope."

We grin at each other as we approach a room with the sign "Suite of the Dead."

"This isn't the sex dungeon," he says. "It's just a playroom." He draws in a deep breath. "But it does have some, well, *features*. The woman who contacted us can't come to the door, but she managed to call the front desk requesting help. She's handcuffed to the wall."

"Handcuffed to a wall? Was she kidnapped?"

"No. More like…wanted to be."

"Oh."

"You ready?"

I'm not sure how you get ready to encounter someone handcuffed to a wall, but I nod.

He unlocks the door. "Hello? It's the manager and a female assistant. Is there one of us you prefer?"

A high, strained voice comes from deep inside the darkened interior. "I'd like the girl, if that's okay."

He nods at me. "I had a feeling. Come right back if there's anything you can't handle."

Oh, wow. Okay.

I push the door wider and slide through the gap, mostly closing it but not letting it latch.

"Hello?" Blackout curtains cover the windows. I can barely see.

"I'm back here," the voice says.

"Should I turn on the light?"

"Probably. Please don't laugh."

Laugh. That sounds like this is embarrassing, but not horrifying.

"I promise."

I feel around by the door until I find a switch and slide it on.

It's a nice room, all ruby-red with black accents. There's a mini kitchen and a bar.

The bed is empty, and so is a strange chair shaped like a triangle with a ledge.

Oh, that's a sex chair. They must have to clean the heck out of that thing between guests.

I do not envy housekeeping.

The door to the bathroom is open. I flip on that light, but there's no one in the ruby crystal interior. It's opulent and sexy and stirring just to be here.

There's another door, also slightly ajar. I push it open. "Are you in here?"

"Yes."

The light in this room is blood-red, and occasionally, lightning strikes from a strobe in the corner. A subtle rainstorm is piped in, with thunder cracking at random intervals.

I finally make out the form of a woman by the back wall. She's stark naked, and her legs are spread with a bar between them.

One arm is in the air, handcuffed to the wall.

The other waves at me.

I hurry over. "Are you okay? Injured? Did someone leave you here?"

She laughs. "I was a bad, bad girl, and this is what happens when you're a sub who doesn't obey. But he left hours ago, and I think something might have happened. Or else he really is done with me."

I examine the handcuff, my gaze rocketing away from her flowing breasts and the spread legs. "Is there a key?"

"He probably has it on him. But it's a hotel-issue. I assume there's a spare somewhere?"

"I'll find out." I glance down at the bar on her legs. "What about that?"

"Same problem."

"Hotel-issue?"

She nods.

"Okay, so one, possibly two spare keys. Can I make you more comfortable while I find them?"

"Something to cover myself, maybe? And my cell phone. It's by the bed in the other room. Thankfully there was a hotel phone I got to."

I spot the boxy phone, the receiver still off. I don't know how she stretched to reach it, but she must have called the front desk with it.

I hurry to the other room to gather the bedspread and retrieve her phone. "Here you go." I hand her the phone and slide the cover over her.

"Thank you so much. Now I don't have to flip out that housekeeping or maintenance is going to stumble onto me."

"I'm so sorry."

"I'm grateful I had a free hand." She waves off my concern. "He's not a monster. This is how we have fun. Let me call him. I hope he's just lost."

But before she can even bring the phone to her ear, the door slams open.

"You better not be free," a voice booms.

I turn, expecting some big brute of a man, burly and muscled and probably with a twirly mustache.

But he's maybe a hundred and forty pounds soaking wet, with skinny arms and a clean-shaven face. "Who are you?" he asks.

Sebastian appears behind him. "She's my assistant, checking on your…person. Do you have the keys?"

"Of course I have the keys." He stares down at her. "You called the front desk?"

"I thought you might be lost."

He jerks the covers off her. "You are going to be punished for that."

Sebastian whirls around and retreats to the other room.

I want to help her, but the woman's expression is all on the man. "Hurry, while we have an audience."

Oh. No, thanks.

I race for the door as the man selects a strap from the wall. By the time I hear the first smack, and the woman's happy cry, Sebastian and I are out in the hall.

"That was more than I expected," he says. "Was she okay?"

"She sounded more than okay," I say with a shaky laugh. "People like interesting things."

"Are you upset? Sometimes this job comes with a side of trauma. It's not for everyone."

I shake my head. "That wasn't traumatizing. It was a little—" I can't say it. It's too farfetched for someone who has only had sex one time.

But he knows. "Hot?"

"Does that make me weird?"

He shakes his head. "Not at all."

Everything in my body starts to stir. "I'm not used to this."

His gaze is rapt on my face. "It's all new to you, isn't it?"

"I think you of all people know exactly what my experience level is."

"You're okay, though?"

I press my hand to my chest. "My heart is jumpy." I take his hand. "Here, feel it." I want his hands on me. I'm desperate for it. I shakily take his hand and press it where mine was.

"I feel it," he says, his voice gruff.

"And my cheeks are hot."

"A little pink, too." His interest is intense, and it's making me feel like I might erupt. "I'm listening if you want to keep talking about it."

I do. I really do. I feel painfully alive. "There's more. I...I want..." I glance around.

He steps close. "We're in a secure area. Pretty private."

I swallow. "I feel like there's a fire down below. It's hot and heavy and desperate for someone to touch it." I suck in a breath. "And talking about it makes it so much worse."

"Desire can be intense."

"And you're right here," I say.

He lets out a long, slow breath like he's trying to control himself. "I am."

I detect the slightest tremor in his hand, still on my chest. "I want to get crazy."

He doesn't waste time, but snatches me forward to fit his mouth over mine. Fire licks through me. I want the kiss and the closeness of his body. But I want so much more.

I press against him, desperate to quench this need. My breathing is heavy. "Can we touch?"

He slides his hands over my vest to cup my breast. My whole body burns. I don't care where we are. We're alone. There are only two rooms in this secure hall. But maybe we can use the other one. "Is the other room taken?"

"It is," he says. "I checked them in yesterday."

"Damn it." I reach around his back to press him close to me. "I feel like I'm going to combust."

He presses his face into my hair. "What do you want, Mila?"

I take his hand and press it between my legs. "Make it stop," I whisper.

Then his hand slips inside my waistband and snakes down.

He holds me close as he slides multiple fingers inside me.

I respond so fast, my head spins. He flutters inside

me, and I hang onto his suit jacket like I might fall through the earth.

I can't kiss him. I need all my concentration to go where he's working me.

My hand clutches at his shoulder. It's so wild, so hot, so intense.

Tension builds. I want to feel every part of what's happening. I close my eyes. My body feels tight, like I'm spiraling inward.

Then everything tightens down. "Oh my god," I cry before he covers my mouth with his. I breathe against his lips. I pulse against his fingers again and again. I can barely stand. He holds me up, an arm around my waist.

There is lightning in my body. Wave after wave moves around his fingers, pulsing outward. I gasp, trying to figure out which way is up, not sure how I've managed to stay on my feet.

Only when my legs are working again does he slide his hand out. I press against the wall, feeling both spent and exhilarated at the same time.

"Did we do that?" I asked.

"We did." He slides his finger into his mouth, closing his eyes as he tastes me on his skin. "Just like I remember."

Holy shit.

I flash hot again. Already? What is happening to me?

It must be what made Brooklyn sleep with Maverick —twice. And what made Kennedy make out with him in the hall by the offices where anyone could see.

This is dangerous stuff. A drug. It's everything. I'm figuring out what everybody else already knew.

And I want more.

"At five o'clock it's officially the weekend," I tell him. "Are we going off site or should we break in all the empty rooms?"

He closes his eyes as if thinking of the night ahead. "All of the above."

20

SEBASTIAN

After I drop Mila off at the study session with the other interns, I'm done for as far as concentration.

I do some rounds, check on the restaurants, security, and the front desk. Then I sit in my primary office near the kitchen, still able to smell Mila on my fingers.

This is bad. I'm in deep with this woman. We only met a week ago, and I feel more obsessed about her than can possibly be healthy.

Thankfully, we don't have cameras in the secure hall, or I'd be deleting footage faster than Olivia Pope on an episode of *Scandal*. I realize belatedly that there is footage of us kissing in the security room, but that space isn't live monitored, at least.

But seriously, I need to get my head on straight.

I need rules.

Off site only. At least while we're secret.

And think about the damn cameras. They're everywhere in the halls and elevators. The front desk is triple covered.

In fact, that raincheck I asked for on our first night was a dumb one. I know damn well that every hotel has a security camera in the elevators. It's standard.

Even if we sneak into an unused room, there will be a log of my key opening the door, camera footage of us entering.

I never thought of these things before.

Because I never did anything illicit before.

I mean, this isn't theft or murder, but it is secret. And it does put Mila in a bad position.

I shouldn't do that.

But we're doing it anyway.

There's a knock on my door. I quickly slide my mouse around to wake up my computer and say, "Come in."

Anna, the head of housekeeping, steps inside, closing the door behind her. That's not a good sign. Most people who pop in are quick and don't bother shutting the door.

I turn my chair to face her. "Everything okay?"

"That boy of yours, Maverick, is trouble."

I keep a straight face, but inside, I'm thinking that he made it five days before someone other than Raya got upset. Not bad, really.

"What's going on?"

"He's got all the girls in the laundry room fighting. I understand he's sleeping with more than one of them already. And less than an hour ago, he was all over that girl from room service right here in the back hall!"

And I was all over an intern in the haunted wing. Pot, meet kettle.

"I'll speak with him."

"You better. The last time we had one of these lotharios about, I lost three good workers over it."

I remember that. A maintenance worker. Trey fired him for disappearing during work hours. He couldn't technically do it because of the women, but he could for the time.

I'm about to have to do the same if Maverick doesn't shape up.

"Thank you for bringing this to my attention, Anna. I'll call him in."

She gives me a sharp nod and leaves the office.

Maybe there's something in the water. Maverick, all over this new cache of available women. Me, all over this intern I met before I knew who she was.

I rest my chin on my hands, but then there is that smell of her again.

God. I can't escape it.

I should get up. Wash my damn hands. Get some control. I'm thirty-damn-two. I shouldn't be acting sixteen.

And I have an ugly confrontation with Maverick ahead.

That cools my jets.

As I head to the bathroom, I consider the speech I'll give him.

And how I can possibly apply the same rules to myself.

When I pop into the meeting room slightly ahead of five, only Raya is inside. No interns. No Mila.

She looks up from where she's collecting papers from the long table at the front of the rows of chairs. "I sent the interns off early. There's only so much reviewing the risks of salmonella you can do."

"How do you feel now that you've had a week with them?"

She shoves her reading glasses up on her head. "Ilsa has the best work ethic. She's responsible and competent."

"But?"

"Nobody likes her. She's too cutthroat. She wants the position too much."

I perch on the end of the table. "The event manager has to be personable."

"I know. Your Maverick is probably a little too personable. I can't stand him, but he's won over everyone in the kitchen. They already requested him for next week, like I don't have a schedule already."

"He never went to HR?"

"No, he did dish room Monday and Tuesday, then Cristal in laundry snagged him the rest of the week. I let it go."

I consider telling her that Anna complained about how he's seducing the young women there, but think better of it. I'll handle him.

I'm itching to know what she thinks of Mila, but I wait it out.

"Owen is the friendliest, but he gets flustered easily. He's like a golden retriever who gets distracted by every squirrel."

"So not organized."

"Not in the least. Both Brooklyn and Mila were away from me the most, so I don't have a good read on them. They were with you at the front desk. What's your assessment?"

I didn't expect this turn. "They were both excellent. They quickly learned how to handle the most common problems. They interfaced with guests both at the desk and in rooms. They learned how to program the alarm clocks, reset the TVs, adjust the thermostats. They can check guests in and out. They have a pretty good lay of the guest-facing areas of the hotel."

"Good. I think the front desk is where we'll see their strengths."

"Who is on it next week?"

"Just Owen. I'm trying to mix them up. Brooklyn and Maverick were supposed to be on room service, but with Maverick in the kitchen, maybe I'll put Brooklyn there, too. My schedule will need to be reconfigured."

"You can say no."

She frowns at me. "I know that. I'm assistant manager." She huffs, like she might like to say more, as if I've disrespected her.

I'm used to it.

I don't say anything. It's best to let her work it out. More talking generally makes it worse.

Finally, she says, "Maverick is easier to control in the more rigid environments like the dish room and kitchen.

I think I'll leave him there. I don't want to manage him."

I'm itching to know where Mila will be, but I know better than to ask.

"Sounds good."

"How did Mila do on that sensitive matter you had?" Raya asks.

I carefully control my expression. "She did well. The guest asked for a female employee, so I sent her in. Everything resolved."

"Good. I have her in HR next week."

So that's where she'll be. HR isn't on my usual path unless someone there needs me, so the temptation will be significantly less.

"The interns have the weekend off?"

"I'm going to keep them Monday to Friday for the first month, then the cycle spreads out."

"Sounds like a plan." I hop up from the corner.

As I head down the hall, I pull up my contacts. I keyed in all the interns' phone numbers mid-week, when Raya had the day off and I was in charge of them.

I text Mila.

It's the weekend. Dinner?

I'm back at my office before she replies.

Mila: Can we do tomorrow? Have a thing here.

A thing. I wonder what the thing is.

Me: Absolutely. Text me tomorrow. I have an easy day.

I'd prefer to nail down when I get to see her, but she's made friends here. That's good. I'm glad.

Mila: I will! Sorry. I'm kinda needed. I didn't expect it.

That's some fast bonding.

Me: Not a problem.

I shut down my computer and lock my office. I already checked on Sasha, who runs the night shift at the front desk on the weekends. There's nothing else for me to do. Having extra hands this week, plus it being the start of the offseason, has made for light work.

Plenty of time to obsess about a dark-haired intern.

21

MILA

Brooklyn and I walk the aisles of King Soopers, a grocery chain I've never heard of. It's bright and well stocked, and while maybe not as great as H-E-B back in Texas, has everything we're looking for.

Except maybe a cure for rage.

Because Brooklyn's hit the angry stage over Maverick. As we push our buggies up and down the rows, she continues a circular rant that began in the car on the way here.

"And what the hell was he trying to do, showing off his next lay? What did he expect me to do? Tear her off him and declare my undying love?"

"I don't think Maverick's looking for love."

"So I got too clingy, and this is how he gets rid of me?" Brooklyn's cart skids into a display of tortilla chips at the end of the row. I leap forward to straighten the stacked boxes before the whole pyramid tumbles.

"I wasn't even clingy! I'm not a clinger! He came, he conquered, he went to his room!" She taps my shoulder so I'll stop examining the chip display for structural integrity. "Is this a clingy face?"

I turn and she has this dreamy look, like maybe this moment is the best thing ever happened to her.

"Is that the look you gave him?"

"It's my standard post-sex look to make sure they know I want them to come back!"

"Do you give it to everyone?" This whole concept is new to me.

"Heck, no. Only the ones I want to come back."

"Do it again."

She shifts from anger back to the content expression so quickly that I wonder if she missed her calling on the big screen. "It looks a little on the love-sick side."

"What!" She shoves so hard on her cart that it rams the tortilla display again. Several loose chip bags tumble from the top, and I lunge to catch them.

When I have them back in place, I slide her cart away from the stacks. "I mean, maybe not?"

"No, no, no. Go with your first impression." She pulls out her phone and switches to selfie mode. She makes the face. "Oh, God. I look like I'm in love with him. Do you think he thought I was in love with him?"

"Maybe?" Brooklyn is still new as a friend, so I'm not clear about the best way ahead, not like I would have been with Camille.

"Damn it!" She shoves hard on the cart, and that's it. It rams the chip boxes, and the bottom row shifts, then the upper section tumbles.

Chip bags fall from the top, banging their way down

like rocks careening off a cliff. Crunch, rattle, crash. Boxes and packages pile onto the floor.

A store employee heads our way.

"We gotta go!" I tell her.

She snaps out of it, and we race with our buggies up the aisle, speeding past mothers with toddlers in the seats, shoppers contemplating brands of peanut butter, and a stocker or two filling shelves.

When we're at the other end of the store in produce, we hide behind the display of apples, which has a tall cardboard sign describing the different varieties.

Then we laugh. It starts as a giggle, but moves on to a full belly-quaking takeover. We sit on the floor between our carts, holding our stomachs, tears in our eyes.

"All this for a dumb boy," Brooklyn says.

"Maverick is the poster child of dumb boy."

She closes her eyes. "He sure is good in bed, though."

This makes me think of Sebastian. I have nothing to compare him to, but does that matter if I love what he does?

Brooklyn smacks my leg. "You're thinking about boning. Somebody good. Who was it?"

I stammer a moment, my brain not able to come up with any name but Sebastian. "Just a guy."

"Did you leave some poor broken-hearted cowboy back home?"

"No. Definitely not."

"Someone recent?" Now she's sitting up, as if she's about to get at something.

I shouldn't have been so emphatic that it wasn't from home. I could have embellished some old boyfriend.

Except there aren't any.

"It's Sebastian, isn't it?" She lowers her voice. "Everyone thinks you two are doing it. Did you do it in the haunted wing when he came and got you? Everybody thinks you two were doing it."

Oh my God. How? "They do?"

A woman passes with her cart, staring down at us like maybe she wants to call the manager.

Brooklyn grabs the base of her cart and pulls it in front of us so we're less noticeable. "You can tell me. Did you know Sebastian before?"

I weight the inequity of our confessions. I know all about her and Maverick. But she knows nothing about me. And if one day Sebastian and I become open with our relationship, this one new friend I've made at my job might feel betrayed by my secret.

And yet, this secret could get me fired, or at the very least, on the bad side of Raya and probably HR, and maybe Havannah wouldn't be as understanding as Sebastian thinks.

But Brooklyn's already judged my hesitation. "You did! Did he get you hired on? Are you guys a couple on the sly?"

"No," I say quickly. "I only met him a week ago, the night before we moved in."

Brooklyn's face lights up. "Where? How?"

"At a bar."

"Did you have sex with him? Are you a thing?" She's excited.

"Please don't tell anyone. He didn't know I was an intern. I had just gotten into town."

"So you *did* have sex with him?"

I don't know if I should straight-up admit it. "Our contract says we can't date anyone who is more than one rung higher in the chain of command."

"That's like *everyone* for us."

"Exactly."

Brooklyn sighs. "I guess we can date the kitchen and housekeeping staff."

"And the other interns." I shouldn't have said that, because Brooklyn's face immediately collapses into upset.

"I'm sorry," I add. "I don't know what Maverick is thinking."

Brooklyn tugs at her hair. "He'll probably get fired anyway. Raya is not going to put up with him."

"That's true."

We sit for a minute, peering through the silver bars of our carts to watch people walk by.

Then the ridiculousness of where we are hits us both, and we start laughing again.

"Are we hiding behind carts at a grocery store over men?" Brooklyn asks.

I can barely get the words out over my giggles. "We are."

She unfolds her long legs to stand and reaches a hand down to me. "Well, it's time we get up and face the world."

"Even a manager who might be upset about his tortilla chip tower?"

"Nobody saw it. Can't prove anything."

I laugh at that. "If you're Bart Simpson, who does that make me?"

We push our carts as Brooklyn thinks it over. "In the *Simpsons* world, I think you're the sexed-up teacher who seduces the principal."

If only she knew I had no power to seduce anyone. But I like that she thinks I could. It's exactly what I was going for when I started this whole wretched business of ditching the cherry. To seem experienced. "I can live with that."

"Let's get some revenge. Do they have itching powder in grocery stores?"

"Unlikely. But you could always smear petroleum jelly on his door handle. And if you ever get in his apartment, put plastic wrap over the toilet."

She laughs again. "Mila, you look so sweet and innocent, but behind that pretty face is one malevolent bitch. And I mean that in the best way possible."

We head to the checkout, and I fairly glow with happiness. A new bestie, and an amazing man on the sly.

This job is working out so much better than I could have possibly hoped.

22

SEBASTIAN

I don't hear from Mila until the next morning.

Despite what happened the night we met, and in the haunted wing, I don't feel we're close enough for me to ask her what she did last night. I play it light when she texts.

Mila: Brooklyn, Owen, and I are walking the castle today. Any highlights we should hit?

Me: Go out to the barn and meet Jed. He's from Avalonia, where those laughing miniature donkeys originate. He has lots of great stories.

Mila: Are these the donkeys about to give birth?

Me: Yep. You all will be helping.

Mila: It sounds fun. And possibly gross.

Me: The miracle of life is often gross.

I wait after that to see if she will offer up a block for time for us, but no more texts come.

I sip coffee on the back porch, looking at the mountains. It's warmed up again, Colorado being its normal indecisive self.

Arya slides the door open and drops into the chair next to me, bundled in a blanket. "Oh, it's not cold anymore." She lets the blanket fall to her lap.

"It'll be a nice weekend."

"You spending it with this new girl?"

I haven't told Arya about our torrid scene in the haunted wing, nor do I plan to. "She texted me this morning, but we haven't made any plans."

"Hmmm." She holds her mug with both hands, her black hair a snarl of a messy bun. I wonder why she never dates. I haven't seen her with a boyfriend, or even trying to acquire one, since she moved in with me the first time.

I have a sense something went sideways with a guy while she was in college and I was working in Denver.

When I decided I hated banking and came back to Boulder, everything changed on us. Mom moved to India.

I bought this house and moved Arya in with me.

Then we had the Haley situation.

Maybe Arya has never felt security, particularly with Dad leaving when she was so little. I probably did my part when I was blindsided by a woman.

Am I doing it again? Is this why Arya seems so quiet since learning the one-nighter is staying around?

"You okay?" I ask her.

"Mmm hmm." She sips her coffee, her eyes on the mountains.

I turn my attention to the view. "Remember what Mom used to always say?"

"Devi, the earth, is a goddess to be protected and

admired." She smiles against her cup. "Do you still touch the ground when you wake up to apologize for stepping on Devi?"

Now it's my time to smile. "I do. It's a habit. Sometimes I touch a window, if I'm not on the ground floor."

"Really? That's a good idea. I always thought it was silly to touch the rug, especially on the second floor."

We both get a good laugh at that.

"I should call her," I say.

"I did yesterday. She's good. All the aunties keep her busy. They want to find her a proper man."

"She should get divorced." This was one of the situations with my father that stuck in my craw when I learned about it. Since they never had a legal agreement for separation, he never paid child support.

I don't have any use for the man.

Arya romanticizes him, only knowing him from the pictures where he's tossing her in the air or tucking wildflowers behind her ear. Even now, at twenty-six, I'm not sure she understood all the ways in which our father screwed Mom over, meeting her in New Delhi, getting her pregnant, which I totally blame him for, and dragging her to America.

Then, just leaving.

Of course, Mom was educated and smart. She had been studying to be a doctor when she was whisked here. She shifted to training as a physical therapist since she could finish quickly and support us. We ended up fine.

He hadn't helped at all.

My phone buzzes.

It's a photo of Mila with the donkeys. My heart feels pierced as I look at her, laughing with one of the miniature animals nibbling her ear.

Arya leans over to look. "Is that her? She's pretty. And young. Younger than me." Arya leans away again. I sense her unease.

"Nothing's going to come between us. I won't do that again."

"It's fine. You have a life. I should get one of my own." She presses the mug to her cheek. "I can't mooch off of you forever."

"But you love your art class."

"It doesn't work for paying the bills. I know that. I just…I don't know. I feel lost."

"How can I help?"

"You already do. A place to live. Food. I've noticed how you keep taking my car to fill it with gas."

"I don't mind."

"I know I don't really contribute."

"Hey. It's fine. You figure things out. There's no deadline."

But she glances at my phone and Mila's picture.

And maybe she thinks there is one.

I text Mila back.

Me: Love it.

Mila: We're heading into town later, but tonight should be free. Anything else you want to teach me?

That sets me on fire. I shift uncomfortably in the deck chair. Maybe I need to take this one inside, away from Arya.

I quickly tap out a line.

So many things.

Time to flee. I hurry inside, feeling the buzz of another message.

I leave my cup in the sink and race up the stairs like a teen boy trying to get away from prying eyes.

Mila: I'm starting to understand the whole hot for teacher business.

I lie across my rumpled bed. I can picture her tangled in the sheets.

Me: Should I procure glasses and a tie?

Mila: As long as there's nothing else.

She's killing me.

Me: And you in a tiny plaid skirt, thin white shirt, no bra?

Mila: This is hot.

Me: You're hot.

Dots appear, then disappear.

I can sense her hesitation. She's unsure of herself. How many times has she said she's never anyone's choice?

Me: I will choose you every time. In jeans. In a Castle Hotel-issue vest. In a sexy nun costume.

That gets her. The text comes quickly.

Mila. A NUN????

Me: Wrong kink?

Mila: Kink is fun. Except when you're handcuffed to a wall and hotel staff has to rescue you.

Me: Welcome to the industry.

Mila: I want to hear all the stories.

She must be away from the others for such a long text conversation.

Me: I'll tell you more tonight. Show you a few.

Mila: Handcuffs?

Me: That can be arranged.

Mila: Not sure I'm ready for that. But I do have a skirt that is woefully short.

Me: You're killing me.

Mila: Done. Dinner, then?

Me: Absolutely. How about I cook for you?

Mila: You cook?

Me: Totally.

Mila: And safer. Can't run into other staff. You probably know everyone.

She's not wrong.

Me: It's only for now.

Mila: Ok. I've been spotted hiding in the hay room. Later!

I set the phone down and roll over onto my back. How is it that I feel sixteen again with her? Because she's so young? It's rubbing off on me?

The age difference doesn't seem to be an issue.

Just the job.

Bringing her here for dinner is a good idea from a privacy standpoint.

But Arya will be here.

And that worries me. Is Mila ready to meet my family? Will Arya feel pushed out again?

And how soundproof is my room, actually?

I guess we'll all have to figure it out.

23

———

MILA

As I drive to the address Sebastian sent me, I wish I had told Brooklyn more. She could have advised me on underwear. Front hook versus back hook bra? And how serious was Sebastian about the short skirt? I had offered it up, but was that just banter or was I expected to follow through?

I know nothing.

Camille was little help over Facetime. Ever practical, though, she suggested I carry an oversized purse that was clearly a purse and not any sort of overnight bag. Pack the short skirt. Then I was covered.

So I did.

At every red light, I fuss with my hair and clothes. I settled on a normal-length skirt with red flowers, and a red silk shirt that buttons down the front.

I'm terrified I've chosen poorly, although I'm not sure why. It's dinner at his house. Should I have been casual? Jeans?

This is worse than the nights I dressed thinking I

would have my one-night stand. I never planned to see those people again.

This is looking to be a long-term thing.

Medium term?

I have no idea.

My longest relationship was three months, as a freshman in high school. My curves were in all the right places then, and the boys were trying for anyone they could get.

We did stuff, all the kissing and touching things. But Brock had the fear of God put into him about getting a girl pregnant, and he had some weird concern about condoms having holes.

Anyway, we hadn't lasted long enough to get that far. And the freshmen quickly settled into their cliques. I was a band geek, and that served me well with friendships and things to do. There was always a game or a pep rally or a fundraiser to be involved with.

But nobody in our friend group dated. Not one-on-one.

I didn't go to prom, not even with the group. I looked for a dress, but the style at the time was sparkly and very, very short, and I couldn't pull it off. Mom tried to put me in more traditional things, but I looked like a toddler trying on old lady costumes.

So, I didn't go.

It was fine.

I bet Sebastian went to prom. I bet he looked incredible in his tux, and he had the most beautiful girl on his arm.

Self-consciousness bites me again. I mostly do fine, but in moments like this, the old fears rear up.

I smack my hand on the steering wheel as I rev through an intersection. "You are bold. You are beautiful. You are what you're meant to be." This rolls into the lyrics of "This is Me" and I start singing that until my phone lets me know that I have only a quarter mile until my turn.

Then the nerves come rushing back.

As I pull up to the gorgeous two-story house Sebastian directed me to, I feel struck by everything I am not.

I am not successful. Not yet. I am not in my thirties or have things figured out. I might never figure things out.

I have never been in a house like this, much less dated someone who owned one.

Inferiority washes over me, and it's all I can do not to turn around.

The exterior of the house is made of stones carefully fitted together in a beautiful tapestry of earth tones. Behind it, the mountains loom large and majestic.

Above the oak entrance is a balcony with two glass double doors. The driveway is long and curves in front of the porch. I roll slowly up to the front.

Of course Sebastian has a nice house. He's bound to be very well paid as the GM of the hotel. He's got experience behind him, years of working and saving.

I have student loans, a free studio apartment, and feel excited when I can buy a new outfit.

We are a mismatch in every way.

He is casual and experienced with sex. I know nothing.

He's managed a million real-world situations. I freak out over calls about my car's extended warranty.

I stop in front of the door, but I don't put the car in park. The brake feels liquid beneath my foot, like maybe I should hit the gas and take off.

But then it's too late. Sebastian comes outside with a wave.

He looks like the night I met him, no longer in the suit and jacket. With the warm weather, he's switched to a short-sleeved button-down in pale yellow, and jeans.

He's not wearing shoes.

How can this be real? This man? His house? This situation?

When I don't move, he tilts his head. "You okay?" I can't hear him, sealed up in the car, but I get what he's said.

I have to calm down. I put the car in park and kill the engine.

You're here, Mila. He's the same guy you've been working with all week. Remember the first night! Remember the haunted wing!

This gets me out of the car.

I sling the big purse over my shoulder. I stand inside the open door and look at him over the top of my car. "Hey."

"You made it!" He walks around, taking my hand to pull me away from my hiding spot. "I hope you like curry. I didn't make it too spicy."

I've never had curry. Mom said it singed her mouth

off the one time she tried it, and Dad would rather go to a steakhouse any day.

"I'm sure I will like yours," I say. But a whole new set of fears crop up. What if I don't like what he cooks? What if it makes me sick?

What if we're in bed, and suddenly I have to like, *go* go?

Oh, God.

He leads me to the house. "My curry is a crowd pleaser. Do you eat Indian food much?" He opens his front door and gestures for me to go inside.

"Pretty much never, but I'm game."

"I don't always cook it. I'm decent on the grill, too."

I enter the foyer, which opens up to a living room with soaring ceilings. A staircase to the right leads upstairs.

"You can leave your purse anywhere. My sister Arya is normally here, but she's gone off with a friend tonight. She took our pup dog Alfalfa with her, so you won't have to worry about her slobbering all over you on the first visit."

I set my bag on a table next to the sofa. "You live with your sister?"

"I do. Our mother moved back to New Delhi about six years ago, and I helped Arya finish college."

"So she's younger than you?"

"Six years, yes."

And four years older than me. I follow him into the kitchen, which is separated from the living room by a long bar lined with stools. "Do you visit your mother much?"

"Once or twice a year. She hasn't returned to America since leaving. But we enjoy our time in India. We didn't see our mother's family much growing up."

"Are both of your parents from India?"

I don't miss the shadow that briefly crosses his face. "No, Dad was Colorado born and raised."

"Is he still here?"

"I don't know where he is currently. Last time I talked to him, he was in California."

Oh.

I sit on one of the stools. "My parents were born Texans and are still a little miffed I've left."

Sebastian lifts the lid of a pot to stir something spicy and aromatic. "Ah, yes. The Texas migration to Colorado is something of a pipeline."

"I've heard stories. I was advised to get my car plates changed to Colorado as soon as possible."

"Not a bad idea."

He closes the lid. "How hungry are you? I'm about to sear some chicken. Do you eat meat? I can do tofu if you are vegetarian."

"You forget all the prime rib sliders I put away."

"That's right. Good."

"Aren't a lot of Indians vegetarian?"

He shrugs. "I was born here. I am way more American than Indian. My father was not, I guess you'd say, a big fan of my mother's traditions."

I feel lucky with how I grew up. "Is Arya your only sister?"

He nods, swiftly cutting chicken breasts into strips. "She is. We are close."

"Does she work?"

"She teaches art to small children. She has a degree in fine arts."

I turn to the living room, taking a longer look at three tall paintings on the side wall. "Are those hers?"

"They are. Most of the art in the house is Arya's."

"Has she sold any?"

He shakes his head, sliding all the chicken into a bowl. "She tried to get into galleries early on, but the rejection was hard on her."

"It would be for anyone."

He nods, swiftly throwing spices into the bowl without measuring. This is something he's comfortable cooking.

"Did your mother teach you how to make curry?"

"Absolutely. After my father left, we were able to make more of it than before."

"How old were you?"

"Eight."

So Arya was only two. That's hard.

"I need to let that sit for a while," he says. "You want something to drink? We can do wine, or I found that cider we had at the bar."

"Really?"

He grins. "Really." He heads to the fridge.

Camille is going to die. He got the thing we first drank together.

He extracts two cans. "You want a glass? Never mind. Of course you do. We're not heathens."

I laugh as he pours the cider into tall, clear glasses. He has everything. A whole life.

I feel like mine has barely started.

He passes me a glass, and we tap them together.

"To our one-week anniversary," he says.

He's right. It's come around again.

The cider is cold and crisp. Sebastian sits on the stool next to me. "You did great this week. You and Brooklyn both."

"You think so?"

"Completely. Raya asked how you handled the haunted wing incident."

My cheeks burn, not for what we saw, but what we did after. "What did you tell her?"

He leans in close. "That I made you orgasm in the hallway."

"Sebastian!"

He laughs. "I said you were commendable and discreet."

But he doesn't move away.

Our gazes meet. He takes my glass from me and sets them both on the bar.

"I'm afraid I might kiss you a lot tonight."

"You will?"

He slides his fingers through my hair to hold the back of my head. "One for every time I wanted to during the week but couldn't."

When his mouth meets mine, every worry I had leading up to coming here falls away. He takes his time, his lips gentle, then gradually adding pressure.

We open to each other, him tasting tangy, like he was checking his curry before I arrived. It's good, and he's delicious, and I want to melt into him.

He pulls me from my stool to his, my legs straddling him. His hands hold my back, keeping me tightly against his body. I can feel him responding, hard beneath my thighs.

Our tongues mingle, and I figure out how to settle in, not holding my breath but relaxing into him.

His hands roam, one shifting to my ribs, his thumb sliding against the bottom of my bra. The other grasps my butt, fitting me more firmly against the hard length of him.

I ache to do more things, new things, all the things.

My breathing speeds up again. My skirt has slid up my thighs, and his hand on my shirt makes its way down, past my waist, until it finds the bared skin of my leg.

"I like skirts on you," he murmurs against my mouth.

His fingers tap dance along my skin as he pushes the skirt higher, until he's reached the lace edge of my panties.

I suck in a breath, anticipation flooding me. I feel high, like I'm breathing pure oxygen.

His thumb flirts with the satin in his way, running along the border of my skin and the underwear.

I can barely breathe, almost vibrating with energy, wanting to move forward, to explore.

Much of our first night was lost to fear and worry, although I distinctly remember his mouth down below. I've never felt anything so intense, so good.

His kiss slows down, and his lips move near my ear. "I'm going to do so many things to you."

My heart hammers painfully. I can feel it in my throat. I don't answer, just try to breathe as he hooks a finger on my panties, and tugs.

Of course, I'm straddling him, so he doesn't get very far.

"Hmmm," he says, letting them go to put both hands on my waist. He lifts me easily onto the bar.

Now he reaches beneath the skirt with both hands, yanking the underwear down and tossing it behind him. For a moment, the tile surface of the bar is cold on my skin, but swiftly warms up.

I'm high up on this counter, and with Sebastian sitting on the stool, my knees are at his chest level.

"I like this," he says. His gaze holds mine as he reaches for my shoes, slipping them off and letting them fall to the floor.

His fingers circle my ankles, then begin their journey up, sliding along my shins and cupping my knees. These he spreads wider, then continues, moving my skirt up as he goes.

I brace myself on my hands, watching him look at me. His mouth goes to the skin of my inner thigh, and I suck in a breath as he nips lightly.

His path is achingly slow, and he reaches up to unbutton my shirt as he makes his way.

He's nimble and quick, and my shirt gapes open.

His eyes shift to look up at me, and he pulls away from my thigh for a moment. "Front hook. I love those." With a quick snap, it's open.

The tension of the band pulls the bra cups aside.

"Mmm," he says. "I love this view." He pulls me to

the edge of the counter so he can push the shirt and bra off my shoulders.

Then his mouth has closed over one breast, his hand on the other.

My head falls back. I look up at the beautiful tiled ceiling, reveling in his touch and attention.

It's hot, so hot, to be half-naked in his kitchen, sitting on the counter.

Camille told me years ago about her fumbling sex with high school boys.

This is nothing like that. If her experience was back-yard karaoke, Sebastian is an opera, lush and flawless.

I'm glad I waited.

"Mila?"

I glance down.

"I'm going to taste you now."

I nod, my breath hitching in anticipation.

He spreads my knees again, pushing the errant skirt out of his way. His hands go beneath me to slide me forward, then he's there, his mouth hot on me.

My arms buckle for a second, but I straighten them to hold me up. All the blood in my body rushes to where he works me. Forget oxygen. I must be breathing in stars, because I feel alight from within.

He takes it deeper, reaching up to spread me wider and allow him more access.

I lose my head for a moment, so dizzy that I'm not sure which way is up or down. Then the lightning bolts of pleasure flash out from where he works me, like Zeus has brought down his scepter in that very spot.

"Oh my God, Sebastian!" I grip his hair with one hand, holding on.

He sucks on something that makes me nearly rise from the counter. I can't bear it, the pleasure is too intense, too crazy. I will break.

Then I do, fragmenting as every part of my body flashes hot.

It pulses, like I've fractured into waves. I don't think I breathe. I can only focus on the ecstasy of it, the overwhelming emotion.

"Sebastian, Sebastian." It's the only word in the universe. My legs quiver, my arm gives out, and I almost crash to my elbow. Sebastian catches me, holding my back, his mouth on my inner thigh, kissing his way to my knee, like it's time to come back home.

I shiver, slowly coming off the high.

"How do you do that?" I ask, lifting his face from me so I can look at him. "How do you know what to do?"

I almost regret asking. He could say, "Practice." Or, "From all the girls I've loved before."

But he grins, his fingers tracing lazy circles around my nipples. "You are easy. You make me feel like I know everything."

My throat tightens. I wrap my arms around his neck. He allows me to pull him in, his cheek resting on my chest. Who is this man? How did I find him in some backwater bar?

I realize I've been the recipient of all the attention. And I want to explore, too. I want to play. I run my finger along his ear. "Hey."

He looks up. "Yeah?"

"There are some things I'd like to try. Will you be my guinea pig? I might not be very good at it."

"Absolutely." He stands up and holds out his arms. "I'm all yours."

I draw in a deep breath.

I'm going to be brave. It's time to practice those things that women do to men.

24

SEBASTIAN

L ooking at Mila on my counter, topless, her knees spread, her colorful skirt pushed high, is about to be my undoing.

I want to plunge into her, but she's new to all this. If she wants to practice on me, I'm going to be patient.

She sits there a moment, contemplating me like she might have to work up her nerve.

Then she glances at the door. Is she thinking about running?

I drop my arms. "No pressure. We can go back to dinner."

She shakes her head. "No, I was thinking, when is your sister due back?"

Good point.

"She'll probably make herself scarce, but I see your point." I bend down to retrieve Mila's clothes. "We can take this upstairs."

She nods. I sling her things over my shoulder and wrap my arms around her to lift her down from the counter. For a moment, I consider carrying her upstairs, but again, she taps on my chest to let me know she wants down.

Just like the first night.

"You sure? I've always imagined carrying someone up my stairs."

She tilts her head. "You never have?"

"Nope."

"Okay, then."

I laugh, whirling her around in a circle. Then we're heading up, so fast that she hangs on for dear life, her hair bobbing, along with her soft breasts. I vow not to be distracted, although doing things *on* the stairs with her has just hit my bucket list.

My bedroom door is open. I turn us to edge inside. I've made my bed today, not normal, but I knew she might be here. I hoped, anyway. I had this house built with double master suites, one downstairs, and one up. I wanted both views of the mountains, the foothills and the peaks.

Plus, the entire back wall of this bedroom is glass, and I rarely lower the electronic shades because there is nothing behind it but mountain range, trees, and near the top, a hint of snow.

"Oh," Mila breathes as she catches sight of it. Dusk is falling, so the colors are brilliant. "It's breathtaking."

"The deck up here is amazing." I use my elbow to press a button near the wall and two glass panels slide open to allow us out on it.

The cool air billows in, making Mila's nipples

pucker, but the warm front that blew through last night means that it's not uncomfortably cold.

This time when Mila taps me to be let down, I set her bare feet on the smooth polished wood deck. Her hair is wild, her skin golden in the fading light. She can't stop looking at the view.

I can't stop looking at her.

She turns, the outline of one breast against the backdrop of the mountains, and for the first time in my life, I wish I was the one with Arya's gift of painting. I want to burn this image into my brain.

I step forward to tug at the waistband of her skirt.

She holds it a minute, almost shy, but I lean in. "You are a goddess and I'm going to worship every inch of you."

She lets go, and I slide it over her hips, kissing skin as it's revealed.

The wind rushes through the trees, making leaves dance in its wake, some of them fluttering across the deck.

"I feel reckless," Mila says. "I don't think I've ever been naked outside."

I remain kneeling in front of her, the skirt puddling as she steps out of it.

"You're about to do a lot more than be naked out here."

She lifts her eyes to mine. "Can I practice some things first?"

"I am all yours."

She taps my shoulders to get me to stand up, then tentatively works on my shirt buttons.

I wait her out, looking at everything. Her hair curls over her shoulders, brushing the tops of her round, delectable breasts. I can't help but touch them again, running a thumb across the tight nipples.

She smiles at that, but moves my arm as she pushes the shirt down my back.

She reaches for my belt, sliding it through and unlatching the hook. Then she unsnaps my jeans, and the zipper eases down with a gentle hiss.

Mila bends close as she pushes the jeans down. I step out of them as she kneels to bring them over my feet.

Then, they are gone, and Mila is still on the ground, looking up at me with those big, brown eyes. Her hair blows everywhere, and those tight nipples are rosy with the light of sunset. I could not be any more erect, and my gray boxers damn near block my view with how they tent out.

She reaches up, taking a deep breath and letting it out slowly. She touches me outside of the boxers first, running a shy hand along the length. Everything in me twitches, from my fingers to the tip of my cock.

When she reaches the top, she grasps the elastic band and tugs it down.

Of course, the elastic catches on me, and she has to reach in to pull it out of the way.

Her hand on my throbbing skin sends precum sliding out. She touches it with her fingertips, spreading it on the head.

I groan. She's killing me.

"You like that?" she asks.

"I like everything."

"I don't want to mess up." She holds the boxers open with one hand while reaching in with the other, wrapping her fingers around me.

"You can't mess up. It's all—" Whatever I was going to say next ends in something even I can't decipher.

She's gaining confidence. I can see it in her smile and how she pulls the boxers down.

She sits on her knees, holding my cock, contemplating it. "It's purple. I didn't think it would be so colorful."

I grip the rail, trying to hold onto control.

She goes on. "And a bit comes out. You could probably get pregnant from that."

Shit. Right. Condoms. They are inside.

"I can go in and get—"

"No, not yet. And I've been on contraceptive forever. How long did you say it was before me?"

"Almost two years. Work has been a lot."

She nods. "Good enough for me. I guess I'm obviously okay."

I let out a long rush of air. She's picking up a rhythm with her strokes, and it's getting hard to think. "Yes."

"So, we're good? I want to feel your skin in me this time."

God, I'm going to explode all over her if she keeps talking this way. "Okay."

She pays close attention as her hand moves along my length, her gaze moving between her hands and my face, as if gauging my reactions.

I close my eyes. The mountain air is brisk and smells

of pine and earth. This gorgeous woman is naked at my feet. I feel high.

She shifts closer until her hair tickles my belly. God. I look down.

Her lips open and she slides me inside her mouth.

It's warm and soft and I grip the deck like I'm hanging from the edge.

She sits higher so she can get a better angle. She takes me in until I can feel myself bump the back of her throat. Her breasts brush my thighs.

Fuck. I'm going to lose it. She's too beautiful. This is too incredible.

But I hang on. She's curious. Experimenting. She sucks on the end, and that's it.

I release the rail and snatch her up. "I'm going to fuck you below the sky," I growl into her ear and drop her onto the oversized chaise lounge near the door.

She lies back on the cushions, her hair falling off the edge. "Please do."

I put one knee on the lounger, glad I chose something so solid and sturdy. I'm about to test its limits.

Then I spread her legs, dragging her close to me. I lift her hips, giving me a perfect view down the soft plane of her belly to her breasts and face and hair.

I would paint this, too, if I had the skill.

I run my thumb over the edges of the glistening pink in front of me.

Mila sucks in a breath, then reaches up to grasp both sides of the chaise where it rises in the back.

I make slow lazy circles over the nub, until she's writhing on the cushions, her body flushed with color.

When she starts breathing fast, I plunge into her, and God, it's like homecoming. I haven't had sex without a condom in a decade, probably, and it's slick and warm and tight inside her.

I keep working her body, reaching up to thumb her nipple.

She's crying out already, and I can feel the spasm of her around me. I keep everything steady and even for her as she comes, her body thrusting against mine.

Her strangled words disturb a few birds who haven't thought to migrate yet. Then she grabs my arms. "Come inside me, Sebastian. I want to know what that feels like."

Fuck. I hold onto both of her hips and crash into her like I've never let myself go before. The world is a wash of orange sky and mountains, and her skin, her hair, her glorious body.

I unleash into her, warm and wet and with a release so complete I feel like I've poured my soul into her. I collapse over her, propping myself up on my arms.

But she draws me down to her. "Lie on me. I'm sturdy."

I wrap my arms around her neck to cradle her head. I drop my face to her shoulder. Her skin is soft and smooth and a comfort. She wraps her legs around the backs of my knees and locks us together.

I don't know how long we stay there like that, but the sun sets completely and the air cools. And even as a chill ripples over my back with the arrival of night, I do not want this moment to ever end.

25

MILA

The weight of Sebastian feels good. I need to be grounded after so much intensity. I haven't quite lost the sensation of drifting into the sky.

It's full dark, and the only light comes from the hallway outside of Sebastian's bedroom.

I've heard people say, "This is a moment I want to freeze in time." But I'd never had one of those experiences until now.

I don't want to move on with the evening. The night. Even life.

I want to feel exactly this way, protected by his body. Warmed by his skin despite the cooling air.

Desired even though I've never believed I could be.

I'm afraid of breaking the magic. That Sebastian will sit up and think, "Oh, it's just her." And find some polite way to get me out of here.

Then, it's too late. The insecurities have invaded, and the moment has passed after all.

I couldn't hang onto it.

I shift beneath him, and he rises away from me. "It's getting chilly," he says.

"And your curry is going to burn."

He chuckles. "It could cook all day. But it will get too spicy." He takes my hand to lift me from the chaise, and now that we're beyond the act, I feel exposed and self-conscious. It takes everything in me not to snatch up a cushion to hide my belly, the wide hips, the thick thighs.

I hate these voices in my head. Stop it, I tell them. I am worth this.

It quiets the noise.

Sebastian picks up my skirt and his boxers. We dress as we walk, gathering the rest of the clothes from where he left them in his room.

I think we will simply walk down the stairs, but Sebastian swings me into his arms again. "What goes up should go down the same way."

I laugh, hanging on tight as he rushes down the stairs like I'm nothing to carry. He doesn't set me down until we're back at the stools.

"Let me check the curry." He takes a fresh spoon from a drawer, dipping it in the pot. He tastes the red-orange sauce.

"Verdict?" I ask.

"Dreamy. I think I'm making it as well as my mother. You want to try?"

I nod.

He walks around the island and brings me the same spoon. "I don't think it's spicy, but I'm fairly tolerant."

The spoon is warm, and when the sauce hits my tongue, my first instinct is to brace myself.

And there is spice, but it's smooth and aromatic.

Sebastian tilts his head. "And?"

"Perfect," I say.

"Excellent!" He sets the spoon in the sink. "Let me stir fry the chicken."

He takes out a large wok and sets it on a burner. I take in the kitchen again, and the living room, picking out more details than before.

There are ceramics and sculptures and stacks of books everywhere. I hop off the stool and sort through several novels piled on a table beside the sofa.

I lift one up. "*What My Mother Doesn't Know?*" I call out to Sebastian.

He laughs. "It's Arya's favorite. She's read it a dozen times."

"Not you?"

"Oh, I have, too. She made sure of it. I thought it was good. First love and all that."

Huh. I sit on the end of the sofa and open to the first page.

And I'm completely sucked in. It's adorable and sweet and told in verse.

Soon, Sebastian taps on my shoulder. "It's ready."

I look up. Fifteen minutes have passed. "Oh! The book got me."

"It does. Arya might kill me if I loan it to you, but I'll get you a copy."

"Oh, I can do that."

He presses his lips to my hair. "I'd like to."

I set the book down. "Okay."

He leads me by the hand to the stools. Two wide bowls are filled with rice, chicken, and the thick orange sauce. "What's this called?" I ask.

"Murgh makhani, or butter chicken. It's tomato-based, with garlic and butter and spice."

"It smells heavenly."

"Do you want wine? More cider?"

"More cider is good. And maybe water, just in case."

He grins. "Absolutely."

I wait until he's brought the glasses back, then I fork a bite of the chicken.

I almost swoon at my first full-fledged bite.

"It's so good, Sebastian. Where has this been all my life?"

"I'll take you to some Indian places in town. There are good ones."

"When you can cook so well at home?"

His face relaxes, and I realize, he was nervous too. Worried I wouldn't like his mother's dishes. That I might not be able to eat it.

I take his hand. "Thank you."

He squeezes my fingers.

I wonder if I will stay the night, and if I do, what I'll do if I get caught sneaking back into our hall. I should have brought casual clothes, not something that too obviously looks like I went out.

But nobody saw me leave. No one would really know.

Sebastian touches the crease between my eyes. "What's worrying you?"

"Just thinking about the hotel crew."

"About them finding out about us?

Is there an *us*? I suppose there must be. It's been a week. And we've been all over each other.

"Is this how it always is?" I ask him.

"What do you mean?"

"It's been exactly one week, and we've had sex twice, made out in a security office, and did pretty serious stuff in a hallway."

He laughs at that. "No, it's not always like this."

"What does it mean, do you think?"

"That we're on the intense side?"

"Are we?" I have nothing to compare it to.

He turns to me, running his hand along my leg. "I think it's means we're a good match."

"Even with all the complications?"

"Even so."

I eat a few more bites before more questions erupt. "I know we're going to try to be discreet, but what if we are found out? What happens then?"

"I'll go to straight to Havannah and explain. Then we'll probably meet with HR. You'll probably be asked to come in separately."

I can barely swallow my bite. "Separately?"

"They'll want to be sure I'm not coercing you, or using my authority in any way. I would expect them to be sure."

"Okay. What do I say?"

He squeezes my leg. "It will be okay, Mila. It's a relationship, not a crime. I know I'm the head honcho or whatever, but in reality, it's Raya who is your sole supervisor, and it's Havannah who decides if you are promoted."

"What if we break up?"

"That might happen. I guess we'll do our best to be kind to each other. Maybe skirt each other at the hotel when we can, at least until the pain lessens."

He would be in pain over breaking up? He already knows this?

"I've never broken up with anybody," I say. "I mean, I dated a boy freshman year of high school, but technically, we never broke up. We just sort of stopped hanging out. There was no drama."

"That's the only relationship you've had? At age fourteen?"

I frown. "I ended up with good female friends. None of us dated much in high school."

"And in college?"

I can't look him in the eye. "You may not have noticed, but I don't exactly have hot girl summers."

He spins my stool so I face him. "Don't say that about yourself. Don't even think it."

"It's hard not to. Do you know how hard I tried to go home with somebody in college? And all summer?"

He holds up a hand. "I can't help that most boys are dumb." He takes my fingers and brushes a kiss on the back of my hand. "I think you are incredible. And I hope that if we ever get to the place where we're not together anymore, you still believe it when I'm no longer allowed to show you."

So this is what it's like to date someone who's fully

formed into adulthood. Who knows what he likes. Who isn't afraid to say it.

Tears smart my eyes. If going through eight years of rejection and loneliness were what it took to get me here, on this stool with this man, then I know one thing is absolutely true.

It was worth it.

26

SEBASTIAN

Mila decides she would rather sneak in late at night, so not too long after dinner, she heads back to the hotel.

I definitely understand. She's less likely to run into anyone at one in the morning, when she leaves, than midmorning, when any number of the interns or other staff members might notice her arrival. We both recognize the necessity of being discreet.

When I come downstairs Sunday morning, Arya is in her usual position on the sofa, Alfalfa on her lap.

"I left you some coffee," she says.

"Thanks."

"Which one of you touched my book?"

I smile inwardly. "I didn't let Mila take it. I knew you would have a cow."

"Exactly. She can get her own copy."

I pour myself a cup of coffee and sit in the chair opposite of her. "Thanks for giving me space. It won't always be necessary. Mila is nothing like Haley."

Arya shrugs. "I'm sure. Haley was a real piece of work."

Mom always said I was blind to women's faults. Then she would laugh and say thank goodness. It certainly is useful for her and my sister.

But Mila isn't like that. I'm sure of it.

Right?

Would I be able to see it?

Arya pets Alfie's black head. "Besides, there is only so much that noise canceling headphones can really cancel."

"What kind do you have?" I ask.

"I don't know. Whatever came with my phone."

"I'll get you a new pair."

"I hear those pricey Apple AirPods are great."

"Done."

She sits up. "I like this. What else can I shake you down for?"

I reach out to nudge her with my foot. "You don't have to shake me down for anything. I am more than happy to attend to your every need. You don't ask for much."

Her eyes light up. "A one-hundred-dollar gift card to the children's art supply website I like."

"Done."

"Wait. I meant to say two hundred."

I laugh. "Done."

She shakes her head. "You shouldn't spoil me. It makes you an enabler."

"I think it makes me a good big brother. I was in a hurry to be all adult and independent. Let me tell you from this side, it is not all it's cracked up to be."

"I shall take that advice, big brother." She takes a long sip of coffee and sighs happily. "You didn't say how it went."

I settle back in my chair. "Really, really well. I like her a lot."

She clasps her mug with both hands. "You're a lot less grumpy in the mornings when you've gotten laid."

I reach out to nudge her again, but she swings her legs to the other side, disturbing Alfalfa. He lifts his head with a yawn.

"When do I get to meet this mystery woman?"

"Soon, probably. Home is the safest place for us to be if we're going to stay quiet about our relationship."

Arya strokes Alfie's ears. "True. You could run into anybody if you go out."

"Especially as more and more of the staff meet her."

"Will it be this way forever?" Arya asks.

"It will get out eventually. She's just so new. I want to delay the inevitable."

"You guys are hitting it pretty hot and fast. Sounds like another relationship I remember."

Did I dive in like this with Haley?

But between Arya's current concerns and my mother's old one, I start to wonder. Are we headed to certain disaster? Can something like this ever work?

She'd been so vulnerable last night. She's so young. And her experience is even less than I thought. Only a boy early in high school? And nothing after?

High school feels like eons away for me.

When I was graduating high school…Mila was in second grade.

I rub my forehead. What am I doing? I should let her find someone her own age.

Then I remember the feel of her in my hands. The way we fit together. How she trusted me.

I'm not letting her go. No way.

In fact, I pick up my phone to text her.

Me: Good morning, my mountain goddess.

Mila: Hey.

Me: Feeling okay this morning?

Mila: Amazing. Maybe a little worried. Is this fast? Sometimes it feels fast.

So she's thinking it, too.

Me: You want to slow things down?

Mila: No. I was already thinking about coming over this afternoon for more.

I force my dick not to jump. I have an audience.

Me: I'm down.

Mila: But will you be down there?

Me: You bet I will.

Mila: Three?

Me: Definitely. Here?

Mila: If that's okay.

I look up to my sister. "I think Mila's coming back this afternoon."

Arya's eyebrows lift. "Is your dick made of gold?"

"Maybe."

She shrugs. "Cammie and I were going to go see

Casablanca this afternoon anyway. They're having a live band play the music."

"What time?"

"Two-thirty, I think."

"Perfect."

She scrunches her face. "You guys won't be naked somewhere downstairs when I get back, will you?"

I press my hand to my heart. "I vow not to be naked with Mila in any open area of the house after four-thirty."

"Deal."

I tap a message back to Mila. *Sounds great.*

I told Mila not to listen to any negative voices in her head.

Time for me to do the same.

27

MILA

The Monday morning meeting is tense.

I spotted Sebastian on my way to the staff room, and I'm trying not to think terribly dirty thoughts about him as Raya introduces the proctor who will administer our certification tests.

We all sit at different tables. Brooklyn is near the door. I'm by the wall. Ilsa is behind me. Owen is behind Brooklyn.

And Maverick? He's nowhere to be seen.

Raya's lips pinch tightly together as she taps messages on her phone. Brooklyn's face is a neutral mask. I probably should have spent more time with her over the weekend after the Maverick incident.

But all I wanted was to be in Sebastian's bed. And I was. Sunday afternoon was languid and easy. But I'm sore today after all our activities, and I squirm in my seat. Who knew so much sex in a two-day period could be this hard on your body?

I vow to hang out with her today as much as possible, and definitely suggest dinner. I assume we'll be together again this week as we rotate.

When five minutes pass and still no Maverick, Raya says, "Let's go over the assignments for the week. When you are done with your exam, you'll go straight to your position." She taps on her iPad. "Maverick, never mind, he's not here. Brooklyn, you will be in the kitchen today. Ilsa, you will be at the host stand in the main restaurant. Owen, you move to front desk. Mila, you will be in human resources."

I almost wish for laundry or kitchen work to keep my hands busy and my mind free, but HR is good. I'll meet more staff.

Be far from Sebastian.

And all the empty rooms.

The hallways with no security footage.

I glance in the corners. There are no cameras in this room. Sebastian and I discussed this last night. All the halls other than the secure ones have them. So do the elevators, lobby, and restaurants. Anywhere money changes hands is watched. So are all exterior doors.

But most of the employees-only areas are camera-free. And of course all the guest rooms. It's getting in and out of them that gets recorded, plus the system logs all employee scans through locked doors.

Sebastian and I are not breaking laws here. Just a little fraternization clause. But I suppose if something did go wrong, it wouldn't take much to find out all the places we went together.

Not that it would come to that.

A few more minutes pass. The balding proctor sips his coffee, shaking his wrist to reveal his watch from beneath the cuff of his white shirt.

Raya's face is bright red. "Okay, go ahead and start. We can give Maverick his late."

The proctor lifts a stack of exams. "Mark your answers clearly and plainly. I will grade them as you turn them in. We'll fill in your digital certificates upon completion, and the printed ones will be mailed to you."

He walks between the tables, dropping the booklets on the desk. "If you fail to pass the exam, you can opt to review the correct answers, and take it again immediately. I'm here until noon. Otherwise, you'll need to schedule a test on your own time at one of our exam locations."

I write my name on the front page of the booklet and wait. I've taken this exam twice already in Texas, once when I worked at a resort in high school, then again as part of our college coursework. I'm not worried. Eighty percent of it is common sense. The rest is about food temperatures and safety.

The proctor returns to the front of the room. "This test is untimed. When you are finished, bring it to me. You may begin."

I flip to the first page of questions.

The door opens with a whoosh and Maverick comes in, followed by Sebastian. Both are scowling.

My stomach turns. Did Raya make Sebastian go find him? I haven't asked Sebastian about his relationship to Maverick, but everyone says he's related, and that's why Maverick isn't taking his internship seriously.

I glance at Brooklyn to see how she's faring with his appearance, but she stays focused on her test booklet, rapidly circling answers.

Sebastian waits for Maverick to sit down like he's a kid skipping class, then for the proctor to pass him a test.

Raya realizes Maverick doesn't have anything to write with and heaves a huge sigh as she fetches a hotel pen from a container near the front of the room.

Her pointed look at Sebastian could have withered a tree.

His eyes briefly meet mine before he turns and heads out again.

I look behind me at Owen and Ilsa.

Owen spots me and makes a grimace. Ilsa pretends to focus on her test, but she keeps glancing over at Maverick.

Maverick kicks a leg out, spinning the pen in his hand. He clearly does not want to be here.

Maybe it would be better if he was gone. Brooklyn would be relieved, I think. Hopefully she didn't relapse with him over the weekend.

Raya clears her throat, and I spot her looking at me.

Right, the test.

I focus on the questions and start plowing through them.

Handwashing. Food temps. Food-borne illnesses. Perishable items. Cleaning solvents.

The room quiets, only broken by the occasional scratch of pen on paper or a muffled cough.

Ilsa finishes first, walking confidently to the front like a star pupil showing off. The proctor compares her pages to his answer sheet.

"Perfect score," he says. He takes a moment to type in her information from the front cover. "You're all set."

Raya walks her to the hall. "Hunter will meet you in the restaurant. Go in through the back."

I check my booklet. One more page.

Brooklyn finishes, passes, and is sent to the kitchen. Then I'm done.

I only miss one question, the safe time of transport of frozen foods. Even so, I'm annoyed to have checked the wrong answer.

Raya points to the door of HR. "Have you been back there yet?"

"No."

"Suze will be at her desk near the door. She'll tell you what to do."

"Thanks."

Owen stands up as I'm leaving. Maverick doesn't appear to have turned a single page. Yikes.

I walk down the hall, but when Raya is out of sight, I pause to text Sebastian.

What's the deal with Maverick?

He doesn't respond right away. He might be with a guest.

This will have to wait.

I open the door to HR. It's a big room with three women at desks, plus a larger, closed office near the back.

A woman in a flowing maxi-dress printed with

daisies stands up. She's grinning a mile a minute. "You must be our intern! I'm Suze, the administrative assistant. I'm the one who handled all the applications."

I remember her name now. I extend a hand for a shake. "So glad to put a face with the emails."

"We're so excited you're here. Everyone's all abuzz at who might be the event manager. We're so glad Havannah decided to hire more help. She's going to have her hands full with that baby!" She gestures for me to follow her. "This here's Georgia and Emily. Our head of HR is Jessie, but she's not here at the moment. You'll meet her later. Everyone, say hi to our intern Mila!"

The other women wave from their computers.

For a moment, I wonder which one of them would call me in if someone ratted out me and Sebastian.

Suze leads me to a spot on the side wall with a small table and chair near a wall of filing cabinets. "We keep hard copies of quite a few documents. Jessie thought it might be useful for you to get an idea of what we do here if you learned the system and put some things away. Mostly applications, vacation requests, timesheets, and things like that. Stuff that was taken to meetings, or needs physical signatures, you know. Nothing too sensitive."

"Okay."

"Familiarize yourself with all the labels, then here are a few stacks of things. We put newest in front."

"Got it."

"Let me know if you need anything! There are a few hitches in the organization that might need explaining."

I turn to the drawers. Most of the labels are what

Suze said. Applications. Timesheets with date ranges. Toward the back are more interesting ones. Exit interviews. Investigations. Contracts. Violations. These are locked.

I try not to imagine printed screenshots of me and Sebastian in one of those cabinets and open the first folder stacked on top of the cabinets. "Intern finalists." Huh. These were clearly passed around, as there are multiple handwritten notes on them.

I don't look too closely as I head to the cabinet for applications. There are sections for Housekeeping, Kitchen, Security, Maintenance, Guest Relations, and Professional.

I check Guest Relations, but that's room service, front desk and bellboys.

I head into the section for Professional. This is for management, accounting, operations, tech, and internships. I find a folder marked "Interns." It's thick with all the people who didn't make the final cut.

My phone buzzes in my pocket. I'm not sure how the others feel about me using a cell on the clock.

At the front desk, nobody dared to pull one out unless they were on break. Other than Aisha. She would flaunt hers when the lobby was empty and announce whatever was happening. "Just got a text from Ray! He wants to get pizza. What you all think? Cosmo's or Nick-N-Willy's?"

I face away from the other HR staff, folder in hand and a drawer pulled to look busy at a glance. Then I take a peek.

It's Sebastian.

He's a mess.

That's all he'll say, I bet. And I get it. We're in that place where personal and professional cross.

I've only gotten halfway through alphabetizing the finalists when there's a commotion in the hall. A male voice is yelling.

Suze looks at the others. "What in the world?"

She circles her desk to peer out the door, then turns back. "It's that good-looking intern."

Emily hurries forward. She's young, mid-twenties, and wearing a form-fitting sweater dress I could never pull off. "Maverick?"

Suze nods.

The two of them peer out the door.

I'm painfully curious, although Georgia remains at her seat, so probably I should as well.

Suze turns to us. "He's yelling at Raya!"

And then we don't need a play-by-play, because Maverick's voice is loud and clear. "I'm not taking that stupid test again. You can shove it up your ass!"

Suze steps back as he passes, a mere blur in the gap.

"Oh my!" Suze says.

Then, she rushes back to her seat, and so does Emily, who scurries to her desk.

Moments later, Raya bursts into the room. "Where is Jessie?"

Suze looks up as if nothing has happened. "She's at an appointment this morning. We expect her back around eleven."

"Tell her to call me the minute she returns."

I focus on my folder until she's gone.

The women all abuzz with excitement.

"Maverick's going to get his butt fired," Georgia says, shaking a head full of braids. "He's done screwed the pooch with Raya."

"By screwing half the laundry crew," Emily says. "Everybody knows it. I heard Anna already went to Sebastian about it."

Anna. Anna. Was that the head of housekeeping? I keep my eyes trained on the folder in my hand.

Then I realize, I'm down to our applications. Mine, Brooklyn's, Owen's, Ilsa's. I've hit the ones who were accepted.

I shouldn't have these.

But I do.

I glance quickly at the others, but they are still talking animatedly.

"We want the details," Suze says. "Is it Cristal? Zara? They always go for the hot guys."

"Them and more," Georgia says. "There's the redhead in room service."

"Kennedy," Emily says.

But I already know all this. I want to find Maverick's application.

I lift Ilsa's, expecting to see his.

But it's not there. I reach the back of the folder.

I turn it to the front. "Intern finalists."

It holds the four of us who won. And about fifteen who almost made the cut that I already filed.

I nonchalantly stand and finger through the alphabetized drawer of everyone who was passed over.

No Maverick.

He never even applied.
There were a thousand entries.
That's some powerful nepotism.
No wonder Raya's mad.

28

SEBASTIAN

That boy is going to be the death of me.

He walked out of the exam without taking it and shouted at Raya.

And that's *after* I hauled him out of his apartment, that *we* pay for, half an hour late.

I should fire him.

Instead, I head to my office and call Uncle Roger.

He picks up on the first ring. "What's he done already?"

He knows.

"Just looking for some tips before he gets axed. He's pulling some real shit."

Uncle Roger sighs. "I was hoping getting through college would give him some perspective."

I swivel in my chair. "He bucks all authority. How did he even graduate?"

"It took some doing." He sighs again. "We got him a campus advocate. She had the most to do with it."

"Really? What did she do for him?"

And more importantly, could I hire her?

"I don't know exactly. She did some paperwork. Got what she called 'accommodations' for him. He doesn't talk to me, and since he's an adult, she couldn't get me his grades or anything. But he walked the stage. And he got a diploma, I know that. It came to the house."

"Do you have her name?" Maybe she can shed some light on how to make him straighten up.

"Sure. I'll track it down and send it to you."

"Thanks."

Uncle Roger sighs. "I appreciate it, Sebastian. I know it's a burden. I didn't know what to do. He wasn't going to get anywhere if I didn't intervene."

"He didn't have it easy. Neither did you, picking up where your sister left off."

He's quiet. Both of us imagine all the scenes from the past, and those only Maverick witnessed.

His mother Maura, Roger's only daughter, is in jail for life. She did every drug imaginable, broke every law in the land other than murder, and very nearly did that too, with how she treated her only son.

I was twelve when a five-year-old Maverick appeared at Uncle Roger's, where we spent every Sunday afternoon to give Mom a bit of time to herself.

But I remember. He was scrawny, mean, and half-feral. Bruised from eye to knee.

There were social workers all the time, even on Sunday. Therapists. Someone helped him with his speech.

He didn't go to kindergarten that year. And when he did, he got held back. This made him bigger and tougher than the other kids, and he used that to always be on top.

We called him cousin, even though Uncle Roger was a family friend. But our lives were tightly intertwined growing up.

He seemed to be straightening out when I left for undergrad. I only heard the stories as told by Arya.

Maverick dated a lot, showed off his girlfriends, broke their hearts. This was a different track from the one where he sucker punched anyone who crossed him.

Now I wonder if he's ever recovered. It's like he wants to hurt the world for the hurt he got when he was little.

But apparently somebody in college found a way to make him productive. Someone who was helping him as recently as last year.

I'll be calling her the first chance I get.

I've played it straight at this job for five years, but I'm really in it now. Forcing an intern into the program. Having an affair with a subordinate.

I rub my forehead. I would fire me, if I knew. At least call me in.

But I'm the one in charge. Havannah has already moved into a hands-off approach for everything she can pass to others. She only does the event management, her favorite. She's been hiring an outside team to implement her visions, but that's something she hopes to give to the intern she thinks can handle it.

In our meetings about the interns before they were hired, she liked all of the choices. Ilsa had shown true leadership, getting glowing reports from her professors and hotel references alike. She had a double major in business and hospitality and got things done.

Brooklyn had charmed everyone, and sometimes was given a difficult bride or mother-of-the-bride at the hotel where she did her undergrad internship. She excelled at handling hard customers.

Owen was a teddy bear of a choice, able to work with anyone, loyal, and thoroughly reliable.

And Mila. I only vaguely remember those discussions, before I knew their names, and overlay that early impression with what I know of her now. Hardworking. Diversity of experience. Minored in interior design.

I had forgotten about that. Havannah had been particularly interested in this combination of skills, since her ballroom decor was one of her most treasured elements of her parties.

There's a rap at my door.

"Come in."

Jessie from HR appears, her white-blonde hair more freshly dyed than yesterday. She smells of a salon.

"Hey." She sits in the chair opposite my desk.

I have a feeling I know what this is about.

"I like the hair."

She touches it. "You always notice." She twists her wedding ring, and I figure her husband probably doesn't.

"What's up?"

"What are we going to do about Maverick? I've got a written report from Anna, which states she already spoke to you and got no action. Raya is ready to throw him off the interstate, I think. I have two reports of him yelling in the back halls earlier today. And one girl from laundry left an email citing an 'unbearable work environment' as the reason she didn't come in over the weekend." She sits back in her chair. "We have to intervene."

I'm glad I talked to Uncle Roger. "I have a lead on someone who can rein him in."

Jessie looks skeptical. "You think that'll help? He's wreaking havoc."

"I'd like to try it before we chuck him. It's only been a week."

She lets out a sharp laugh. "I'm not sure we've had anyone cause this much friction in only a week. And he lives on site! Raya is on the warpath."

"Give me one more week. If we don't get him in line, I'll let him know he's out."

"Okay, boss." She stands up. "Please don't add a legal mess to the already problematic personnel one. He's not going to do something irrevocable, right? Havannah doesn't need this."

"I'm on it."

"Okay."

When she's gone, I lean back. This is a lot.

I reach for the phone. Normally on a really bad day, I'd text my sister.

But today, I pull up Mila's thread and add a message.

This has been a doozy of a day.

She's in HR, so she might not be able to text back for a while. I set my phone on the desk and turn to my computer. Havannah has sent the fifteenth draft of who should handle her various tasks when she goes on maternity leave.

But then my phone buzzes.

Mila: I'm heading to lunch. Know somewhere safe to meet?

My body instantly stirs.

Me: I do.

Mila: Tell me where and we'll turn this day around.

I shouldn't.

But my fingers don't get the message. They text out what they want.

Me: Meet me in the princess tower.

29

MILA

I stop by the sandwich cart for two ham and cheese on my way to the tower. I don't know if Sebastian likes them, but I want to do something for him. I'm guessing he got an earful from Raya about Maverick.

I met the HR director, Jessie, but only for a minute before she hurried out. She was gone for almost an hour, and when she returned, she closed herself up in her office.

I bet that was about Maverick, too.

He's making a real mess of things.

Sebastian has to be feeling pressure for bringing him on. I'm powerfully curious, but I don't want to ask inappropriate questions. I'm guessing part of the fraternization clause that isn't explicitly stated is that underlings can get access to information they shouldn't have.

When I reach the base of the tower, Sebastian isn't there. Just in case, I scan my ID card and press the up arrow on the elevator. Nothing happens. Right. Sebastian told us on our princess tour last week that our IDs weren't coded to work here.

I can access the stairs, and they have cute windows to look out, but all the doors that lead into the circular lobbies of each floor are secure from curious guests or random visitors. I'd get nowhere.

My phone buzzes.

Sebastian: I recoded your ID for the elevator. Go to 11.

Really? I scan my badge. This time when I press the up arrow, it glows yellow.

I hear the carriage coming down with a gentle rumble. After a bright ding, the doors slide open.

It's empty.

I step inside, remembering the bright mirrored interior, and press the button for 11.

Nothing happens.

The happy voice reminds me, "Please scan your room card."

Right. I forgot.

I scan my ID. The voice says, "Welcome, staff member. Please choose a floor."

I press 11.

The elevator glides upward with no dance party, since I'm staff. "You have arrived on eleven," the voice says.

I step out. There are three doors. One is marked as the "Cinderella Suite." One is the stairwell. And the third, a janitorial closet.

A well fortified one. Unlike the doors I've seen in other parts of the hotel, this one is solid metal, not painted white with a metal kickboard on the bottom.

And the locking mechanism looks incredibly sturdy, not a simple deadbolt.

I hold my key card up to it, but nothing happens. That's odd. I thought I had access to broom closets.

I wander the small space, waiting. The stairwell door opens, and Sebastian pops through. My heart leaps, like it does every time I see him.

This one is somehow mine.

I simply take in the dark waves of his hair, the suit jacket on broad shoulders. And those hands.

Oh, those hands.

"Hey," he says. "You ready for an adventure?"

"With you? Absolutely."

"That's what I like to hear." His grin is infectious, and we stand there a moment just smiling at each other.

I point at the blue door. "Are we headed to the Cinderella suite?"

"Better. Come on. You can never breathe a word of this to anyone."

I lift the hand not holding our sandwiches. "Scout's honor."

He presses a quick kiss to my mouth, and that's how I know there's no camera here. "You were never a Scout."

I laugh. "Were you?"

"Troop 69, Greater Boulder." He clicks his heels.

"You were not 69."

"Oh, yes, we were. Google it. It was a great joke, even though half of us had no idea exactly what it meant."

I'm twenty-two, and I have only a vague idea of how

it works, two people locked together in opposite directions.

I bet Sebastian knows everything.

He presses his key card to the janitor's closet lock.

The first lock engages, then there's a slow turning of another one. Finally, the door pops free.

"Fancy," I say.

"Oh yes," he says. "We upgraded and slightly rerouted this path last year when someone leaked photos."

Ohhhh. "Is this the secret suite?"

He holds a finger to his lips. "Come on."

When we enter, there's a set of shelves filled with cleaning supplies. But something's wrong. They aren't labeled correctly. I try to pick one up, but it's glued to the shelf.

"False front," Sebastian says. He reaches down to pull on a yellow bucket.

Something clicks.

The entire shelf swings away from us, revealing a narrow set of stairs that definitely aren't the usual ones with the windows overlooking the front of the property. They only go down, even though there is a floor above us.

"This is positively banger," I say.

"Banger. I guess that means cool?" He's grinning, like I'm talking "young people" slang. As if thirty-two is old.

Although Camille thinks so.

"Totes," I say, even though that's not a thing we've said since high school.

He laughs again.

Lights pop on as we descend the skinny stairs. The walls are painted in a pastel rainbow, and each wall sconce is a metal cloud.

We arrive at the bottom to another door requiring a card. Sebastian uses his.

"Who all can come here?"

"It's locked down pretty tightly nowadays. Most of maintenance can get in, usually once you've worked here about six months. But only two members of housekeeping have access. And any room service is handled by the manager on shift. All front desk calls are routed to the manager. We deliver towels or food or anything they need in person."

"Wow."

"It's an important secret. Part of the castle's mystique."

We step out of the stairwell, and everything is sky. The white carpeting is lush and thick. The walls are perfectly blue, brighter on top than at the bottom.

Clouds are suspended from the ceiling by invisible wire, some high, some low. It feels like you're walking among them. I reach out to touch one. It's softer than cotton but just as fluffy and white.

"This is incredible," I say.

There's a door ahead. It's marked "Secret Suite." Below it is a plaque that reads, "All who enter here agree to keep the secret."

He turns to me. "Do you?"

"Of course. So no one is staying here?"

"They checked out last night. The next person arrives tomorrow. It's a rare empty day."

The first room is an extension of the clouds in the foyer, but colored like a sunset in pale pink and orange. It's filled with pastel furniture, and soft white curtains frame grand windows that look out on the mountains.

"This is magical," I say.

"It's only the beginning," Sebastian says. He turns a dial by the door.

The sunset fades into night, and I realize the walls are actually screens. Soon, the room is filled with the chirping of insects.

He moves it again, and dawn shifts the colors from black to dark blue to the pale rising of the sun.

"That's amazing."

"And that is only the setting for time of day. There are themes."

I spot something shifting in another room. "Does it affect the entire suite?"

"Yes, you can sync every room, or do them independently. The bathroom isn't automatically included so that no one is surprised in the shower if someone moves to the pirate ship."

"Pirate ship?"

"It's a cool one, but I think that one is best in the bedroom."

The bedroom.

My body tingles, forgetting that it was sore a few hours ago. Funny how that works.

Every day is a revelation.

I follow Sebastian through an archway into the next

room. A huge round bed matches the circularity of the room itself. Everything inside mirrors this shape — the cushioned chairs, all the tables, a desk with a round mirror.

He turns a knob by the door and this room cycles through the day, breaking its connection with the living room. Then the room darkens into night, and a constellation of stars appears overhead. The walls become the hull of a ship and a lone lantern sways on its post.

Waves crash all around us, and I startle.

Then come the rush of smells. Seawater. Wet wood. Salty air.

"This is amazing," I tell him.

"Come over here." He takes my hand and draws me to the bed.

Only when I sit down do I realize it is part of the experience, gently rocking with the movements of the lamp, and the glint of moonlight on the water beyond the ship.

"This is an immersive experience," I say.

"State of the art."

But, my ever practical mind is already whirring. "Does it break a lot? Who does the programming?"

He chuckles and draws me close. "We hire an outside company to maintain the tech in this room. We haven't had too many problems."

I look around, our bag of sandwiches on my lap. "It's amazing."

"You brought lunch?" He picks up the bag and opens the top.

"I did. Ham and cheese." But I'm still in awe of the

room, the shifting of the bed. "Can I try the other settings?"

He pulls out a sandwich. "Absolutely."

While he eats, I fiddle with the knob.

The pirate ship dissolves into a green twilight. Trees surround us, thick with leaves and vines. The wind rushes through the room, and my hair blows gently away from my face. In the distance, I hear the quiet chatter of monkeys and the call of an elephant.

"A jungle?"

"Mmm hmm." Sebastian has a mouth full of bread.

I sit beside him and take the other sandwich. "I love this one. What does the bed do?"

He gestures to the wall behind us. It's the deck of a tree house, like in Tarzan. The bed rests partially inside the bamboo walls, and partially outside, beneath the canopy of trees on the ceiling. Occasionally, the leaves will part in the breeze to reveal a piece of sky, the bed will creak, and shift ever so slightly.

"It's like we're in another world," I say and take a bite.

We sit in the scene while we finish our lunch, then I hop up to move to the next option on the dial.

We're surrounded by sand, the ocean stretching into the black night. Waves crash in a lulling rhythm, and the tangy smell of the sea fills the room, brighter and cleaner than the version on the pirate ship.

"Turn the inner ring that controls time of day," Sebastian says.

I shift my fingers and twist, and the colors of dawn spread across the walls.

He drops his empty sandwich wrapper in the bag. "You can sync it with the actual time of day, but most people choose their favorite."

When the pinks and oranges radiating from the ball of yellow on the water begin brightening into dawn, I stop twisting. Seagulls call, and the waves lap on the edge of the sand.

Behind the bed is a hut, open on one side so the occupants of the bed can see the ocean. I sit next to Sebastian to admire the view. Birds wing out over the water. In the distance, a dolphin leaps into the air and splashes back down.

"There will be a whale, too." Sebastian slips an arm around my waist and draws me close.

"This is lovely. Why does Havannah want to keep it secret?"

"She likes the idea of a secret club of people who have slept here."

"I guess it must be very expensive."

"Actually, Havannah doesn't charge for this room."

"Really? She could charge hundreds a night. A thousand!"

"She doesn't want an experience like this to only be for those with money."

"How is it booked?"

"Her special guests, mainly. She sometimes will accept a request. Her assistant Sarah goes through them. We've hosted a few very tiny weddings."

"Like celebrities?"

"More like hospice cases."

"Oh. With those stairs?"

"There's a back way on the tenth floor. A secret passageway from the other suite on this floor, through a bookcase. Someone has that suite at the moment or I would have shown you."

I close up our sandwich bag and set it on the floor. "It's amazing. She's amazing."

"She's great. She had some struggles. It gave her perspective."

I snuggle up against his shoulder. The waves continue to crash, and low on the wall, near the bathroom door, a turtle makes his way along a piece of driftwood and holds his tiny head up to the sun.

Magical.

I wonder if we've already used up too much of whatever ill-defined lunch break we have, when Sebastian's hand lifts to my chin and turns my face to his.

When his lips land on mine, I think, yes. This is what we're here for.

30

SEBASTIAN

I'm glad we got plenty of leisurely time over the weekend, because this brief break isn't going to last.

I kiss her easy and light for a moment, testing the waters. We are, technically, at work.

But when she presses closer, that's it.

The sun rises on the walls and the waves crash all around us as I unfasten her vest and drop it to the floor. I've certainly never removed a hotel uniform off anyone, and the thrill of it makes me move faster.

I unbutton the shirt beneath, feeling more frenzied as I go. Then the bra.

Her breasts are heavy and warm in my hands, and I groan against her mouth.

She breaks away, her breathing heavy. "Teach me what a quickie is, Sebastian. I hear about it."

She doesn't have to ask me twice. I stand her up and walk her to the bathroom, clicking the sync button as we pass by so that the ocean laps against the edges of the garden tub. I take her to the long counter topped by an expansive mirror.

The sun has risen, tipping her naked breasts with gold light. I spin her around so that she can see herself, palm trees behind us as if we're undressing on a deserted island. She braces herself on the counter, her eyes cast down to the sink.

I lift her chin. "I want you to see how gorgeous you are when you come."

I unfasten the hotel-issue pants. In one swift yank, I've jerked them to her ankles, her cute pink panties with them.

My hands snake around to her breasts. "See how I fill my hands with you?"

Her gaze is on my fingers, cupping the fullness.

"This is perfection right here." Our eyes meet in the mirror, and I bite her bare shoulder.

She sucks in a breath.

I let go with one hand to unbuckle my belt and unsnap my dress pants. "A quickie happens anywhere you can get away with. No fuss." I incline my head toward the perfectly made bed. "No muss."

She nods.

I pull myself out of my boxers and glide along her skin. Then I use my foot to push her legs slightly farther apart, as far as the pants around her ankles will allow.

My fingers slide inside her. "You're so wet," I say, my breath feathering across her back.

"Mmmn hmm." She closes her eyes as I work her.

When her legs tremble, I thrust into her in one swift move.

Her eyelids fly open.

"Watch yourself," I tell her. "Watch how your body flushes pink."

I move inside her, taking my time, reaching around to finger her.

Her chest moves in and out with her labored breaths, then slowly gets more rosy.

I run my free hand across the swell of her breasts. "Like the sunrise."

Then I grasp her hip, moving faster. She holds onto the sink, her hair swinging. I work the sweet nub, watching her in the mirror.

Her breasts sway, her body undulating as we move together. Her breath catches, and a long, low moan escapes.

I can feel the shuddering of her muscles and wrap my arm across her belly to hold her steady.

More of her blossoms red.

"Look at that glorious body," I whisper.

She cries out, her body lurching against mine.

I hold her tightly, locking us together, crashing into her.

A stuttering groan emerges as I relinquish control. It's intense and overwhelming, a full-body cascade of tension and release.

I let her go, and she collapses forward, her hair spilling across the gleaming ivory counter.

My body moves gently behind her, taking a last few long, easy strokes. I bend over her back, leaving a trail of kisses across her shoulder blades.

She laughs. "That was crazy."

This makes me chuckle. "Everybody loves a nooner."

Her body shakes as she keeps giggling. "I can't believe we did that."

"On the clock." I bend down to whisper into her hair. "You are a naughty, naughty intern. I'll have to punish you by doing it again tomorrow."

She laughs and stands up. "I get why people like role playing. It's fun."

"We all want to escape who we are every once in a while." I pull away from her, quickly cleaning up and fastening my pants. "You might have a bonus reminder of this in a few minutes."

Her head pops up. "I know! I got a big surprise when I got out of the car at the hotel Saturday night and this gush came out! It was you! Your stuff!" She turns to push on my shoulder. "You had a lot of stuff!"

Now, my laugh is full-on. "Sorry. We can go back to condoms."

She unspools a handful of toilet paper. "No, it's kind of fun. A little reminder of what we did."

"I think you can do Kegels to make it come out faster."

"Kegel? What's that?" Then just as quickly, "Never mind. I'll Google it."

I head into the bedroom to collect her other things. When I return, she's looking in the mirror in pants and nothing else. It's hot.

"I might make this your unofficial uniform when we're alone during work hours," I say, bending down to give one nipple a long lick.

"Hey!" She swats my head. "Give me those." She takes her bra, shirt, and vest.

I lean against the doorway as she dresses.

"I could watch this all day," I tell her.

She shakes her head. "Is this how we'll spend every lunch break?"

"Don't tempt me." In truth, I've ignored several phone buzzes. They'll have to assume I'm in a meeting.

When she's presentable, clothed, and her fingers run through her hair, we head to the bedroom and shut down the beach.

"I do love it in here," she says.

"It's a dream suite."

We hold hands as we leave through the door and enter the small private cloud room. The secret stairs are too narrow to walk side-by-side, and when we arrive in the janitor's closet, I pull her close for one more long, slow kiss.

"You go out first. I'll give you a head start."

She nods. "See you later."

I wait as she slips out of the closet and closes the door. I turn to examine the fake boxes of Kleenex, cleaners, and the trick bucket.

Probably I shouldn't indulge myself like this while I'm working.

But Mila is irresistible.

And on a day like today, when everyone is skulking around about Maverick like I don't know what they're saying, I needed the break.

Now I have to go out there and face my day job.

31

MILA

When I return to HR, Jessie, Suze, and Emily are talking near Jessie's office. They pay no attention to me, so I sit before the filing cabinets and resume sorting a mess of punched time cards from the kitchen and housekeeping staffs that need to be organized and filed.

I make two stacks, my brain checking out as I make the piles based on which machine was punched.

Then something Jessie says draws my attention to their conversation.

"The fraternization clause is there to make sure there is no disruption to work tasks."

Suze clucks her tongue. "I'd say banging three different girls in laundry and room service is a disruption."

Jessie sighs. "I'm sure they were on break, not that we have a solid timeline, but the fact that Cristal and Zara got in a physical altercation over it is enough."

Emily frowns. "But are we going to bring in Cristal

and Zara over what Maverick is doing? He's clearly baiting them."

Suze speaks up. "I agree. He's the one who's the problem."

Jessie fiddles with her hair. "He didn't make Zara punch Cristal."

I glance over there as often as I dare. Jessie is clearly annoyed by the situation. Suze looks to be there for the gossip. Emily wants to protect the women.

They don't seem to know about Maverick and Brooklyn.

That boy gets around.

But I circle back to the first thing Jessie said. It can't cause a disruption in work tasks.

Would a quickie in an empty room count? I'm pretty sure I took too long for lunch, even though nobody said anything when I came in.

And while I know there are no cameras in the secure hall or that secret staircase, I'm clearly in the elevator and security might ping that a lowly intern suddenly has access to an area where I'm not supposed to go.

At the same time, Maverick is drawing all the attention. A few glances between me and Sebastian, or an occasional disappearing act, aren't going to get noticed with all this other drama.

Jessie seems to realize I'm back, because she breaks up the conversation. "I'll call him in. And the women. This is going to be a thing."

Suze heads to her desk. Emily lingers for a moment at the back of the room as if she has more to say, then sits in her chair.

I keep my head down for the better part of an hour, sorting time cards.

Suze eventually wanders over. "You're moving fast. I'm sorry there is such a backlog. We rarely find time to do it."

"No, it's great. I learned a lot at the front desk about handling guests, and here, I'm learning a lot about the shifts people work, and how many employees there are."

"These are just the hourly workers, of course. There are no time cards for the salaried ones like you and me. Have you worked in the kitchen or laundry yet?"

"No, but it's coming. My friend Brooklyn has the kitchen today. And there were others in the dish room last week." I decide not to use Maverick's name.

"Raya won't leave you long on those shifts, but it's good to get a feel for the different parts of the hotel. The laundry crew is tight, normally. They do happy hours and see each other after hours. Housekeeping doesn't get to interact much, as they are in teams of two. The kitchen is full of cliques, and the deli is a party all the time. They like to do conga lines, and it's become a tradition for them to pause at the top of every odd-numbered hour to do one with the guests."

"That's fun."

"They gelled from the beginning. Duke is the primary manager, although the original manager Calypso still takes shifts."

"I haven't met any of those crews."

"It's a big place."

"How many employees?"

"Around four hundred."

"Whoa."

Suze gestures to the time cards. "You're looking at them. The vast majority are hourly."

"Why are these physical cards? Isn't it all electronic now?"

"We were all electronic in the beginning, but then a data crash caused a huge disaster. Havannah switched us to the punch/electronic combo, and everyone liked it because you could walk by the punch card wall and spot who is on shift."

"I haven't seen it."

"There are two. One is on the back wall of laundry, where the housekeeping and janitorial staffs punch in. The other is on the back wall of the kitchen, where all food service and prep people check in."

Suze checks her watch. "Jessie and I will be leading a new employee orientation at two. We have six new hourly staff plus a new security guard coming on board this week. You're welcome to sit in if you want to see how those go."

"That sounds fun."

Suze smiles. "And a break from the filing cabinets."

That too. My lower back is starting to complain.

Or is it from the bathroom incident?

Either way, I'm thrilled to follow Jessie and Suze out of the office a half-hour later to set up the staff room.

The proctor from the tests is long gone, and the tables have been shifted back to their usual configuration against the walls.

One young man in jeans and a T-shirt sits in the front row of chairs.

"We have an early bird!" Suze says. "We'll have coffee and water in a minute."

The man nods politely.

Suze turns to me. "Mila, why don't you check in with the kitchen staff to make sure they're bringing drinks to the meeting room?"

"Anyone I should ask for?"

"Not Monique, or she'll growl at you. She'll have the tallest chef hat. Filo will be good. He's the food manager. He's a big guy, also dressed in chef whites. Most of the regular workers will have short caps."

"Got it. Just water and coffee?"

"I think I ordered some cookies, too."

"I'll ask."

"Thank you." Suze heads over to where Jessie is spreading paperwork out on a side table.

I haven't had time to explore the kitchens, so when I turn down the tiny hall that cuts from the big service hall to the food prep area, I'm not prepared for the heat and the noise.

"Desserts up for Banquet 2!" A tall woman with a shock of black hair firmly encased in two tight balls below her high chef hat waves her arms at a half-dozen servers carrying trays of chocolate cake on white plates. "We do *not* have extras. Do *not* have any mishaps in the halls!"

The line of servers files past me for the service corridor. Another one pushes a cart carrying three additional shelves of cake plates. It must be a big gathering. The main ballroom was shut tight when I passed it earlier, so they must be at the smaller one on the western side of the castle.

The tall woman looks at me. "Who are you, and why are you in my kitchen?"

I have a bad feeling this is Monique, the very person Suze told me to avoid. "Suze wanted me to check on the water and coffee for the orientation?"

"I am a chef, not a delivery service." She walks off.

Ooookay.

I stand there a moment, trying to spot the man Suze mentioned. Large. Also, a tall hat.

Everyone is moving swiftly, mostly people in white caps rushing around with bins of vegetables or stock pots.

Monique leans over a pair of women stirring huge vats on a long stove. "That smells too much like fennel. Fix it!"

I slip quietly along the wall with the staff offices, hoping to spot Filo.

Kennedy, the red-haired woman from room service we spotted kissing Maverick in the hall, glances up. She sits in front of a phone console with two screens.

Does she remember me from last week? Does she know I'm friends with Brooklyn?

I can't worry about it.

"Do you know where Filo is?" I ask.

"Three doors down. If he's not in his office, check the bakery. They messed up the dessert numbers, and he's probably trying to figure out whose fault it is."

Great. I've come during a crisis. That might be why orientation doesn't have drinks.

"Thanks."

I pass the open door to a huge pantry filled with dry goods. Then several yards of stainless steel that is cold to the touch. Must be the freezer or fridge space.

Finally, I reach a double office with two facing desks, separated by a tall bookshelf. One is neat as a pin with a computer, inbox, and pencil case.

The other is a wild mess, papers scattered, half-opened boxes, and… Is that a rutabaga on the chair?

I don't want to be stereotypical, but I can't imagine Monique in the messy space, so I assume it belongs to Filo. He's not there, though, so I keep going, past the rows of stainless-steel chopping tables, to the corner near the delivery bay.

To the left is clearly the bakery part of the kitchen that leads to the corridor where I came in on the first day. Several workers in short white caps stand around tables covered in flour and chocolate, their plastic-gloved hands clasped in front of their uniforms.

A large man with wild black hair paces in front of them.

"And who did the ratios and prepped the supplies?" he asks.

One diminutive woman raises her hand. "I did, Chef Filo."

"And did you think you were Jesus?"

She glances left and right. "Um, no, Chef."

"Did you think you could use two loaves of bread and five fish to feed two hundred executives chocolate cake?"

I've found Chef Filo, but I can't interrupt. I hold very still, not sure if maybe I should back away.

"No, Chef."

"Did you have anyone double check your figures?"

"No, Chef."

"And why is that an important step, particularly for banquets?"

"Because I might get it wrong, Chef."

"And did you get it wrong?"

"Yes, Chef."

He huffs out a slow breath. "There's no fixing it. We can't miraculously generate more cake. Hopefully not everyone will want dessert."

"Chef?" Another woman near the back raises her hand.

"Yes?"

"We have some frozen cake in the freezer. It's not the same recipe, but it is chocolate. We could frost it the same."

"Now, this is what I like. Someone solving a problem, and not causing it." Filo raises both hands. "Get to it. Now! It will thaw by the time you have it frosted."

The crew scatters.

I wait by the wall, wishing I had not been sent on this mission.

He turns and sees me.

"Yes, madame? Clearly you are not a kitchen worker with your hair everywhere."

I touch it self-consciously. "Suze asked about the refreshments for the orientation."

"Right. Yes. Of course. We have had a mishap, and

it slipped my mind. I will get it sent down right away. Coffee and water?"

"And cookies."

"Of course."

"Thank you, sir. I mean, Chef."

He laughs. "Do not look so frightened. You didn't short a banquet by six cakes!"

"Couldn't they cut the pieces smaller?"

He laughs. "We could have, if someone had counted the cakes before we started cutting. But I like your thinking. Tell Suze we are on our way."

"Thanks." He strides for the noisy kitchen and Monique.

Nope, not getting near her again.

I decide not to cut through that way, but to escape to the main corridor, when I hear Brooklyn.

That's right. She got the kitchen this morning.

I turn around to see if I can spot her.

Her voice is shrill. "Don't even look at me, buster!"

Who is she talking to?

I move closer to the delivery door so that my wild hair and I aren't too close to anybody cooking. When I pass the first row of work tables, I see her, an apron over her black vest, a white cap covering her blonde hair.

I inch closer as she says, "Find your own work station!"

Then I see the culprit.

Maverick. He must have been given kitchen duty, too. Or else he's still on dish room duty. The far corner hosts a line of sinks and commercial dishwashers, as well as three workers madly loading stacks of plates, probably from the banquet. Brooklyn and Maverick stand between the sinks and the last row of work tables.

"Don't be like that," Maverick says. "You know we were a good time."

Two of the dish washers glance at each other with a smirk.

Brooklyn lets out another indignant squeal. I think she's about to smack him with a ladle when Monique arrives.

"Interns, knock it off. Maverick, you're wanted in Sebastian's office immediately. Brooklyn, I assume you will be able to complete your soup without the distraction."

"Yes, Chef," she says.

I step to my right so Monique won't see me again. I'm trapped, but I want to check on Brooklyn.

When the head chef has moved on, I approach Brooklyn's stove. She stirs a pot of something lemony yellow.

"Hey."

She looks up. "Oh, thank God for a friendly face. This has been the worst day."

"Has Maverick been here the whole time?"

"No, he just showed up. There's a banquet, so everyone has been insanely busy. I don't think my soup is edible." She dips the ladle in it and lifts it, letting the thick, chunky yellow liquid fall back into the pot. "It's the only task I've been given."

"I'm in HR. It's been wild. Maverick is the talk of the hotel."

"Don't say his name." She smacks the ladle against

the surface of the soup as if it's Maverick's head.

"I have to get back. We'll talk later? We can do dinner in my room."

She nods. "That'll be good. If I get fired for killing that son of a bitch, it's been nice knowing you."

I laugh. "Good luck."

I hurry along the back wall through the bakery kitchen where they are already slicing the newly frosted cakes. They're fast.

My body only relaxes once I get to the corridor. The kitchen has been the most stressful part of the hotel so far.

I hurry to the orientation room. Six people sit in chairs, and Jessie points a remote at the projector attached to the ceiling.

I move close to Suze. "Filo says the drinks and cookies are on the way. They have a banquet today, so things are intense in there."

"Oh, right. The banking people. Thanks."

"Should I sit down?"

"Absolutely. Just hang out. When the drinks get here, maybe help with that. Or collecting paperwork."

"Sure."

I move a few rows back near the table where we always had our breakfast and lunches served during our first week. I assume that's where they will set up.

The castle seems like a well-oiled machine from the guests' point of view, which is what I could see the first week from the front desk. But there are definitely behind-the-scenes complications.

And many of them revolve around Maverick.

32

SEBASTIAN

Maverick stalks into my office like a middle school troublemaker angry he's gotten caught.

I lean back in my chair, as casually as I can make myself do it. "Close the door."

He whirls around.

"Don't slam it."

His hand makes a fist, but I understand him better than I did before I talked to Carly Sutton, the campus advocate who somehow got this ball of fury to graduate from U of B.

He closes the door hard enough to make a point, but not enough to qualify as a slam.

"Take a seat."

He falls onto the chair, sprawling with legs out, hands clasped behind his head. "You must love this," he says.

This catches me off guard. "Love what? Taking two to three meetings a day, all about you?"

"Your superiority. Sebastian, the big boss. Head honcho. Is it time for me to pack my bags?"

Carly told me he'd come at me with what looks like an offensive, but is really a defensive maneuver. He was the king of trying to be the one to control a situation, even if it meant sabotaging it.

I've had a crash course on Maverick, as much as she could tell me without breaking confidentiality. I read between the lines that all the strategies and coping mechanisms she was about to mention would be helpful.

She also suggested he call her. She was happy to follow up.

"I am kind of a big deal around here," I say. "Which is why you're still sitting in this building. I've bought you another week, but we should come up with a game plan to get you in good graces."

"I don't give a shit what anybody thinks about me."

"A good plan, honestly, but there are some minimum requirements to get a paycheck."

"Banging the hotties isn't against the law. I can't help it if they get territorial."

I hold up a hand. "I hear you on that. You could use some discretion, but I'm in agreement that you can't be held accountable for their reactions."

"And Henry and Beto in the dish room got along with me fine. And the kitchen staff *requested* me. How about that?"

"I did see all those good marks for your first week. That's something to build on. Do you want to stay in the dish room and kitchen? I can make that happen. You don't have to be in the running for event manager.

You could be a liaison with events from food management."

"I sure as hell wouldn't have left fifty executives without dessert."

I heard about the banquet snafu. "They fixed it."

"Is this the kind of outfit you run?"

Back to an offensive. "I never said I was a *good* head honcho."

"Are we done?"

"Not hardly. Why didn't you take the exam this morning?"

"I already have my Colorado certification. It was stupid to take it again."

"Are you curious why Raya wanted it done in-house?"

"Not really."

I draw upon the well of patience I use with belligerent guests, like the mother who wanted the Grumpy dwarf ejected. "Raya wants everyone's expirations to be in sync so she can track them. It's for your long-term employment."

"Sounds like I'm not very long term if you're going to chuck me in a week."

"We're here to avoid that." I try a new tactic. "Do you want to be chucked? Are you trying to get fired so you can leave?"

He frowns at that. "No."

"Do you like it here?"

"Some."

"What have been the parts you like?"

"The apartment is dope. The chicks are banger. The

food is good." He sits up. "Did you know there's a kickass tower on the hiking trail? Killer place to hook up. The view is sweet with their tits swaying over a gorge."

"I'm glad you've found some things to enjoy." I clear my throat, the vision of my encounter with Mila briefly passing through my thoughts. I may be more like Maverick than I expected. "But this exam isn't optional. Now you have to take it off site."

"I won't."

I sigh. "Why is this the sticking point?"

"It's dumb. I already took it."

"When?"

"Sophomore year."

"Then it's about to expire. You have to take it again. That's why we sync it here so we can offer the test to employees when they need it. If you're in the system, you go on the list. You do it here at the hotel, on the clock. You get paid to take it!"

Maverick's hand starts rapidly tapping his leg. Carly mentioned that, too, that people who struggle with frustration might use body movements to calm their nervous system. It's both a tell and a coping strategy.

"Are you worried about passing the test?"

"Of course not." Maverick's face screws up like I said the dumbest thing ever. "A third grader could pass it."

But his hand moves even faster. This is exactly what he's afraid of.

Carly mentioned that some people — not necessarily Maverick, of course, as his diagnosis was confidential —

but some people did better when written instructions were read aloud.

So if there are parts of his job requiring complex comprehension of written material, I should find a way to offer an oral version.

"It's hard for some. We have an employee with dyslexia and another with ADHD who are coming due for their re-certification. So we'll be doing another test for them, this one read aloud. If you think you can handle the read-aloud option, I can put you on the list to take it then. Will that work?"

"Who the fuck needs it read aloud?"

His voice is full of disdain, but his hand has stopped tapping.

We're getting somewhere.

"Lots of people. We have a couple of low-vision employees as well, but they aren't due yet."

"Fine. If Raya's going to have a damn fit about it, I'll take it then."

Another element of Maverick's struggle unlocks. Reading is a challenge. He gets angry if he has to do something that should be easy, but for him, is hard.

I wonder if this is why he was so awful in school. Why wasn't he tested? He probably hid it well. Charmed the teachers, maybe.

"I'll let Raya know to put you on the list for the oral exam."

"If I'm still here, of course."

There's that. "I think if you keep doing good work on your rotations, it will be fine. You shouldn't be around Raya that much."

"Good. She's a piece of work."

I don't disagree with him there. "You're in the kitchen today?"

"Yeah, Monique likes my chopping technique. I told her I'm good with my hands."

"She said that?" Chef Monique is one of the toughest nuts in the hotel. Even I give her a wide berth when I can. She's single, though. It would be wild for our forty-something chef to get entangled with an intern.

"I'm not going to fuck her," Maverick says. "Even I know better than to strike that high."

I almost agree that it's unwise to break the hotel policies like that, but decide it would be better not to bring up the very fraternization clause that I'm quite decidedly breaking myself.

"Wise words." I stand up. "Good luck in the kitchen. You there all week?"

He stands, too. "If Brooklyn doesn't get me kicked out."

"You're not getting along with her? She seemed very likeable on the front desk."

"If you mean lickable, yes, that."

"Oh, I see." She's one of the scorned. "It's a big kitchen. Maybe avoid her."

"Where's the fun in that?"

Before I can chide him further, he's out the door.

That kid is going to be the death of us all.

But he's right. My situation with Mila is a problem.

There's just no way I'm going to give her up.

33

MILA

The week is easy.

I move from filing in HR to learning the software that runs the complex scheduling. It determines how many rooms are booked, and from there, provides an algorithm of how many workers we need in housekeeping, the kitchens, and in the restaurants.

Anna allocates the hours for her employees, and Filo schedules out the kitchen, room service, and bakery. The restaurant has a manager, as well as the deli. They all log in to figure out their weekly shifts.

I've worked with it for a couple of days when I realize there are some missing pieces.

"Suze?" I ask from the extra desk they've set up for me in the corner.

Suze looks up from her cell phone, where she spends way more time than I would have expected. "Yeah?" We're alone in the office at the moment.

"The secret restaurant isn't on here. How do you know how many workers to schedule for that?"

"Oh, it's closed for the season. It'll come back near the holidays when things pick up."

"Have you been there?"

"I've seen it. But I can't afford to eat there, not even with the discount."

"Really?"

"Really. It only takes five reservations a night, and each meal is personally prepared by Chef Monique. She has two assistant chefs and there is one server and one sommelier available each night. It's only open at dinner Thursday through Sunday when it's in operation."

"And it's profitable?"

"At those prices? Yeah."

"Like, what kind of prices?"

Suze uses her phone as a mirror to press her hand against her wild mass of hair. I try not to think of Marge Simpson's sisters, but that's the exact look. "I don't think you'll leave for less than four figures."

"A thousand dollars?"

"Per person."

"Whoa." I wonder if Sebastian's ever eaten there. I'll have to ask.

Speaking of eating. It's almost lunch. Sebastian and I sneaked into an unused staff apartment yesterday, one far from the intern wing.

No cameras. Nobody looking at those door key cards. He coded my ID to get in.

I've decided nooners are my thing.

I'm keen to get back there and meet him, but Suze says, "Jessie wants to take you to lunch in town, show you around. I asked Brooklyn and Ilsa, too. Girl's trip, you know."

Oh. Dang.

"Okay. Sounds fun."

Although not as fun as getting naked with Sebastian.

I text him a quick note that I have to spend lunch with HR.

Sebastian: They aren't nearly as fun as I am.

Me: Don't I know it.

Sebastian: Tonight? Arya is taking an art class.

Me: Yes. Definitely.

I feel better. I know I'm on a roller coaster with a tunnel that keeps me from seeing the end, but I sure as heck am enjoying the ride.

Suze drives us all to a place called Blackbelly. As she parks in front of the brick building, she says, "Now, this isn't hazing. Nobody's going to make you do anything. But we are going to order a plate of crispy pig ears, and we hope you all try them."

She glances over at Jessie in the passenger seat and they dissolve into laughter.

Ilsa, Brooklyn, and I are squeezed in the back seat and glance at each other in alarm.

"Pig ears?" Brooklyn asks. "I thought I'd tried everything."

Suze opens her door. "This is a very trendy restaurant and market. Don't worry. It's good."

We scoot out and cross the parking lot to enter the

bright open space. There's a butcher and meat counter, and countless tables. Everything is rectangular, from the bricks to the wood tables and square stools.

Suze gets us a table and we look through the menu.

Ilsa sets hers down. "I'm vegetarian."

Brooklyn laughs. "Nice try. We saw you eating those steak skewers the first day."

Ilsa glares at her.

"They have a lovely lunch menu," Suze says. "Tomato soup. Grilled cheese. There's no need to eat meat."

Jessie leans forward. "Other than the pig ears."

We place our orders and Suze asks for the pig ears to come out first. When they arrive, it's different from what I expected. I'm not sure what I was picturing, maybe a pile of pink triangles.

But they come out as a stack of crispy fried strips, thin like the tortilla strips you find in migas or tortilla soup. The mound is topped with a fried egg.

We're each given a small plate.

"Dig in!" Suze says.

Ilsa's eyes narrow. "You first."

Jessie laughs. "It's not poison!" She scoops a hefty chunk of the stack onto a plate, making a great show of stabbing a bite and popping it in her mouth.

It was a big bite. They can't be all that bad.

We watch as she chews and swallows. "I won't say it's my favorite thing in the world," Jessie says. "But it's unique and interesting."

Suze follows suit, taking a solid spoonful for herself and eating a bite.

"I think you've done this before," I say.

Suze and Jessie exchange a smile. "Normally only with new HR hires. But it's great fun to have interns."

I take my turn, placing a daring bit of egg and pig ear on my plate. I wait for Brooklyn and Ilsa to do it as well. The two are completely opposite in every way. Brooklyn is bright and happy with her shining gold braids touching her shoulders. Ilsa is brooding and suspicious, her inky hair piled on her head.

"On the count of three," Brooklyn suggests, her fork buried in her modest pile.

Ilsa and I nod.

"One, two, *three.*"

Brooklyn shoves hers in her mouth and I take in mine. Ilsa hesitates, then follows suit.

At first, I can't taste much of anything. It's all texture, crunch and egg.

Then I bite into the strips of ear. It's crispy on the outside, but chewier inside. I get why it comes with the egg. It prepares you for the variation in texture.

The taste isn't much of anything. It's not bacon. Or even pork. It's spices and egg.

I swallow. "That isn't so bad."

"See?" Jessie says.

Brooklyn takes another bite. "Rattlesnake is chewier."

I nod. "For sure."

Jessie and Suze both set their forks down.

Suze speaks first. "You both have had rattlesnake?"

I shrug. "It's not that hard to find in Texas."

Brooklyn takes more. "Florida either. Alligator meat is common, too."

Ilsa is quiet. After a moment, she brings her napkin to her mouth, and I'm fairly sure she spits the pig ear out.

"These interns have more experience than any of us," Suze says. "And here we were, trying to shock you."

Brooklyn stabs more egg. "Unless you've scraped a beaver off the side of the road and had it for supper, you aren't going to one up me."

"You didn't," Suze says.

"My Uncle Barton said no meat should go to waste."

"Aren't you from Florida? Didn't you go to college?" Jessie asks.

Brooklyn grins. "You two sure are gullible."

Jessie sits back with a laugh. "You got us."

"Serves us right for making them eat pig ears," Suze says.

This is fun. Brooklyn waggles her eyebrows at all of us, and everyone laughs, other than Ilsa, who looks like she'd rather be doing anything else.

The regular food comes. We talk about the hotel events, how long Jessie and Suze have worked there.

Everyone is getting along great, other than Ilsa, who hasn't said a word. She watches the rest of us like we're the ones acting weird.

But she's obviously stewing, because in the next lull in the conversation, she drops a bombshell of a topic.

"So, Brooklyn, how is it working in the kitchen with your ex? Or is he actually your ex? How is it that nobody wants him to be their ex? They just keep hitting it?"

Brooklyn tenses beside me.

Suze clears her throat. "Maverick might not be the best subject for any of us." She exchanges a worried glance with Jessie.

But Brooklyn wants to know what Ilsa knows. I can feel her trying to hold back, but she can't. "Who else doesn't want him to be their ex?"

"Cristal. Zara. Kennedy."

Jessie and Suze go still, but they don't say anything.

"Not possible," Brooklyn says.

"So you are sleeping with him even now," Ilsa says.

"I didn't say that."

Ilsa shrugs. "Then you don't care about the rest of them. He disappeared with Kennedy into the supply room of the restaurant for a full fifteen minutes."

Brooklyn scoffs. "Why would he do that when he has an apartment?"

"Why does he do anything?" Ilsa stabs a piece of lettuce. "Except to show off."

Brooklyn's face and neck have gone pink, like on that day in the staff room after we saw Maverick in the hall with Kennedy.

I want to ask her if this is true. Is she still sleeping with Maverick? She hasn't said anything to me since hiding behind the carts at King Sooper's.

But her eyes glisten. And that's answer enough for me.

"I have to pee," I tell the table. "Brooklyn, come with me?"

She doesn't resist as I drag her to the back of the restaurant and into the women's restroom.

"You okay?" I pull a paper towel from the dispenser and pass it to her.

She looks in the mirror and dabs at her eyes. "I know I'm stupid."

"Is he acting like you're the only one?"

"Not really. We're mostly in 'don't ask, don't tell' mode."

"And you're okay with this?"

She tosses the paper towel in the trash. "I'm not. Of course I'm not. But I can't seem to stop. When you're with him, it's like you're the most important, most beautiful woman in the world. He's so good. So convincing."

I know how that feels. I try to imagine what I'd do if I found out Sebastian had other girls on the side. It would kill me, but so would letting him go.

"I'm sorry he's such a gorgeous, sexy asshole."

She lets out a strangled laugh. "They often come in that precise package."

"You've been here before?"

"It's a type. And it's apparently *my* type."

"He's going to get himself fired over all this."

She washes her hands and presses cool water under her eyes. "I don't think so. Did you know he and Sebastian grew up together? That's how he got the job. He thinks nobody can touch him."

That explains things. "They could go over Sebastian to Havannah."

"Mav doesn't think so. Not with her so close to having a baby."

I lean against the counter. "Are you going to keep seeing him?"

She shrugs. "I don't want to. But then he knocks on my door, and I let him in."

I get that, too. I doubt I'd be able to say no to Sebastian.

We're about to head back to the table when I hold out a hand to stop her. "What do you think Ilsa's game is, bringing this up in front of Suze and Jessie?"

"She wants to win. The more we look bad, the more likely she'll get chosen for event manager. They'll never pick Mav, and he doesn't even want it. If I'm a hopeless whore, then it's just you and Owen she has to beat. Owen doesn't have a competitive bone in his body."

"So then it's just me."

"She'll come after you next, I bet." She hesitates. "Are you still seeing Sebastian, or was that a fling?"

I consider saying we're done, or even saying we only see each other off site. But it's all a lie.

"Never mind," she says. "It's clear you are. Don't let Ilsa find out. Because once she knows, everybody knows."

She opens the door and holds it for me.

I walk out in a daze.

Sebastian and I have to be more careful.

34

SEBASTIAN

Mila suggests we hold off until the weekend to see each other after her lunch with HR. She feels like they're watching her.

I regularly check on Maverick in the kitchen, but he's getting along with everyone, including Chef Monique.

Unless you count Brooklyn, who stays as far from him as possible. I don't blame her. He's screwing everything that moves, and both Zara and Cristal threatened to quit when they found out that he's also hooked up with another woman from laundry.

He's got to be doing a new one every day. Sometimes I try to sit down and do the Maverick math, and it doesn't add up.

Maybe he's the one with a dick made of gold.

By the time Saturday rolls around, I'm more than ready for time with Mila. I tell Arya we'll stay in the downstairs master suite, so she has the upstairs without worrying about bumping into us.

Mila is shy and adorable, walking in with her overnight bag. Alfalfa bounds up to her like a Labrador puppy and not an overfed eight-year-old, but Mila kneels down to give her plenty of attention.

Watching the two of them together does funny things to my heart. Despite everything Mila told me about her HR lunch, and her fear that Ilsa would discover us and ruin her chance at the event manager spot, I feel confident everything will work out.

Mila walks toward me, Alfalfa devotedly trotting alongside. "I've missed you," she says.

I take her bag and lead her to the downstairs bedroom. "You don't know how many times I wracked my brains for excuses to go into HR to get a glimpse of you."

"Maybe next week I'll be more accessible, and not closed up with four gossipy women."

Except then we might take bigger risks.

Footsteps bound down the stairs. I drop Mila's bag inside the door of the bedroom.

Arya appears. "She's here!" She turns to Mila. "You're here!"

I squeeze Mila's hand. "Mila, this is my sister Arya."

"I love all your art," Mila says. "Every time I come here, I discover another beautiful piece."

"Really?"

Mila nods, absently petting Alfalfa. "The triptych in the living room? I see something new every time I look at it."

"Ooooh, tell me."

The two of them take off for the next room. Mila

tells Arya what she sees, and Arya talks excitedly about what she planned.

Mila goes on about the layout of the room and how the art is perfectly situated, asking if Arya has done any interior design.

My sister is eating it up.

I smile to myself as I watch them. This never happened with Haley, not once. Their instant friendship gives me peace of mind that I won't have a situation where Arya will ever feel pushed out.

"You want to see my studio?" Arya asks.

"Heck yes, I do," Mila says.

The two of them disappear upstairs.

And, she's been stolen.

This is good. Very good.

I open the fridge and survey the contents. I bought several options for meals this week. I rummage around and set various packages of meat on the counter to consider.

I've started crushing garlic when they finally come back downstairs.

Arya hops on the kitchen island. "I like her. I loaned her one of my books."

"You don't even loan *me* any of your books!"

Arya reaches down to snatch a slice of cheese I set out. "You got crumbs in them!"

"Once! When I was twelve!"

"How can I trust you after that?" Arya steals a cracker from the tray.

I catch Mila smiling at the two of us. My heart swells. This is the best. The absolute best.

"I was thinking about grilling ribs for dinner. You staying?"

Arya hops down. "And watch my brother make out like a lovesick goon? No thanks. But you can leave out some leftovers. I'm heading to Vicky's this afternoon, anyway."

"I'll make extra."

"I'll be around in the morning if you want to make French toast," Arya says. And then to Mila, "He can really cook. Be very bad at it and you'll be all set."

"Noted," Mila says.

"Hey!" I swat at Arya's head.

She ducks and laughs and bounds up the stairs. Alfalfa barks and runs after her.

"And we got rid of them both," I say. "I need to let this meat marinate for a while."

She wanders around the island as I scrape the crushed garlic into the container with the meat. "Whatever will we do while we wait?"

I seal the lid over the meat. "Play Parcheesi?"

She squeezes my waist. "Sure."

I slide the meat into the fridge. "Or to the bedroom?"

Mila grins up at me. "I thought you'd never ask."

We lie on the big bed that faces a wall of plate glass with a different view of the mountains than upstairs. The deck beyond the door connects to the one outside the kitchen and living room, and a small hiking trail is a winding scar through the trees and underbrush.

Mila rests her head on my shoulder. "Do you like to hike?"

"I used to do it a lot. Work often gets in the way."

"Does Arya hike?"

I laugh. "Almost never."

"Did your mother?"

"Almost never."

"Dad, then, or were you too young?"

I trace lazy circles on the leg of her jeans. "We did it some. But it's not something I think about doing with him. It was Uncle Roger who took me most."

"The Uncle Roger who raised Maverick?"

"You know about that?"

"Brooklyn is still seeing him. He told her."

"I see. Yes, except most of the hiking was before Maverick came along. When Dad left, Uncle Roger was pretty angry at him. He tried to make up for it by being a father figure to me."

"Did it work?"

"I had a hard time the first year. Uncle Roger helped."

"Do you think you'll ever have a relationship with your dad?"

"At this point? Unlikely."

She wraps an arm around my waist. "I feel lucky to have parents who put us kids first. Even if they were a super big pain."

"It is lucky." I hesitate. "Do they know you're seeing someone?"

"Not yet. My best friend Camille does. She keeps insisting I slip her a picture. She's having to go by your hotel headshot."

"You want to take something to send her?"

She hesitates, and I pull her close.

"No?" I ask.

She bites her lip. "I've been reluctant to have…evidence."

Ah. I get it. "It's not a bad thought. There are no pictures of us together." Well, other than camera footage of us in the halls, perhaps. And I never scrubbed the security camera kiss from the first week, not that anyone will go looking. It's long buried in miles of files, all shoved onto a backup drive who knows where.

"I keep imagining I'll scroll through my phone looking for something and someone will spot the picture."

"Makes sense. We'll make up for it one day by taking a million."

She nods.

I lift her onto my lap and slip my fingers beneath the bottom of her sweater to find her skin. It's warm and smooth. I want to sink into her.

"So, you have some new positions to show me?" She wraps her arms around my neck.

"Oh, do I."

35

MILA

The next week, Sebastian and I get better at being sneaky. I'm in housekeeping, so I scan in and out of rooms all over the place with the other workers. During lunch, Sebastian figures out which rooms are empty in the halls I've already scanned into, and we meet in one.

Afterward, I replace the sheets myself, and drop the others in the laundry. It's the perfect cover.

Ilsa is also in housekeeping with me, but thankfully, she gets sent to a completely different wing. If she was even on the same hall, I would never have risked seeing Sebastian during my break.

We're like little kids, dashing in doors and around corners. I've never had so much fun in my life.

While Ilsa and I vacuum carpet, Brooklyn gets to do an event with Havannah, a fiftieth anniversary gala for a local politician. It's extravagant and beautiful, and I often pause with my housekeeping cart when we pass the back doors to admire the decorations and set up.

Brooklyn is in her element, practically glowing as she directs workers and runs errands for Havannah.

Lucky duck.

Except if I were doing that job, I would have no chances to see Sebastian.

For my fourth week, I get the maintenance rotation with Trey.

We spend Monday morning working on the security camera that covers the corridor between the western banquet hall and the wedding suite wing. It's feeding nothing but static to the security monitors.

Trey determines it can't be fixed and puts in a requisition to order a new one.

"How long will that take?" I ask him.

"A good week, probably," he tells me. We move on to look at a running toilet in the princess wing.

But I think to myself — the wedding hall is *unmonitored*.

On Tuesday, Trey and I scan into the bridal suite because the couple who checked out that morning reported the hot tub jets weren't working very well.

We determine it's only buildup in the sprayer, easily handled.

I look around the fluffy white room with a heart-shaped bed and en suite hot tub. I want to be here with Sebastian.

The bridal suite is rarely occupied during the week. Most couples stay the night of their wedding, then leave for their honeymoon. The companies that hire out the hall for meetings aren't interested in the themed room.

When it's time for lunch, I message Sebastian.

I scanned into the bridal suite earlier today, and it's unoccupied.

He writes me back.

Be there in five.

I wander the suite as I wait for him to arrive. It's pure white everywhere, with sheers on the walls, birch hardwood floors with fluffy rugs, and a satiny white bedspread on the bed.

There's a gentle tap, tap on the door. I toy with the idea of quickly stripping out of my clothes and opening the door naked, but I chicken out. If it's maintenance or housekeeping, who always knock before entering even if the room is empty, I'll never recover from the embarrassment.

I pop the door open only a crack.

Sebastian grins at me. "Your groom has arrived."

The very idea of us being married brings heat to my whole body.

"I guess that makes me the bride."

He steps inside and closes the door behind him. "And it's time for us to break new ground on our sexcapades." He gestures to the hot tub. "Under water."

"Really?"

He heads over and turns both levers. "It takes a while to fill, so I'm going to leisurely strip you naked while we wait. Any objections?"

"None."

When he's satisfied with the temperature of the water coming out, he sets the plug and turns to me. "Where should I start?"

Something impulsive takes over, and I say, "You'll have to catch me first!"

I dash behind the circular dining table.

"I like this," he says. "Every time I catch you, I'm taking something off."

"Good luck."

As he rounds the table, I stay ahead, always on the opposite side. We continue this for a moment, then he lunges across the top, snagging my vest. He pulls me by the edge over to him. "So this has to go." He unfastens it.

I squirm away as he pulls it from my arms, kicking off my shoes so I can run across the huge bed. He does the same, leaping to catch me before I'm over the far end.

"No pants for you," he says in my ear as he unfastens them and tugs them over my hips.

I fight my way out of his arms, losing my pants in the process.

He shucks his jacket and ID. That's a good idea, and I pull mine over my head and drop it to the floor.

I head into the bathroom proper, then realize this was a terrible mistake, as now I'm trapped.

He runs in behind me, and I let out a squeal as my hotel shirt is pulled over my head.

Even so, I duck out of his grasp and return to the main room. There's a small kitchenette and bar, so I dash to it.

But I'm trapped again, not that I care all that much.

He stalks me in there, dropping clothes as he goes. He's down to boxers.

"I've got you cornered." He presses me against the wall and in seconds, my bra is unsnapped and flying over the bar.

"One of my favorite things in life." He bends down to take a nipple in his mouth.

I melt against the cool luminous wallpaper. I live for this. I want it all the time. Every day, whenever I can get him.

Sebastian makes his way down my body, dragging my panties away. He lifts one of my legs onto his shoulder, and then his face is there, his mouth exploring me.

I'm lost. I reach out to hold onto the counter as he works his way deeper.

My breathing is ragged. This will never, ever get old.

He ever so gently slides his finger along my thigh, then presses against another part of me, one he's never touched.

At first I tense, then realize, this is good. Really good. I relax as he doesn't seem intent on going in, but massaging where he is.

The two parts of me getting attention at the same time wind me more tightly than I've ever been before. I flatten against the wall, my one leg barely holding me.

I'm not sure how to handle what I'm feeling with two points of pleasure. The intensity of him working both places makes me gasp for air.

Sebastian works faster, his hair tickling my belly. He sucks hard, and that's it, everything lets go. I cry out, my head rolling back and forth against the wall. It's bright and wild and even the sun couldn't compete with the shine in me as the orgasm flashes through my body.

He holds onto me as I come down, keeping me steady. Then he swoops me into his arms. "Water's ready."

He carries me to the tub, which is two-thirds full. He sets me down on the side, letting my feet dangle into the water. It's warm and feels so good.

I'm about to slip down when he says, "Let me get your hair."

Right. Wet hair might be a giveaway when I go back to Trey and the crew.

He takes the clip that is holding back the front of my hair, then gathers all of it in his hands. He twists it until I feel it tightening against my head. Then the clip goes back in.

He lets go, and I expect it all to fall down, but it stays.

I lift my hands to my head. "How did you learn to do that?"

"Baby sister. Mom with a heavy workload."

"You're full of surprises."

He leans close to my ear. "Wait until I fuck you underwater."

My heart hammers. How can anything be this amazing, this hot?

How is this happening to me?

He slides into the hot tub and shuts off the water. It reaches his thighs when he's standing, but he drops down, his bottom half becoming a wavering blur.

Above the water he's all muscle, biceps and chest, a tattoo on his left arm. All places I've come to know and love about him.

"Come here," he says, grasping my hips and sliding me down into the water with a light splash.

Sebastian kisses me, his hands all over my body as he leads me across the heart-shaped hot tub to the point, where there is a bench.

He turns us around and he sits on it, bringing me down to his lap. He kisses me again, his hands caressing my breasts, my waist, and sliding my thighs apart.

Then he lifts me, buoyed by the water, and when I come down again, he slides into me.

The water sloshes as I move into position, then rocks gently against our bodies as he works me up and down.

It's soothing and relaxing, a wholly different experience than any of our other encounters.

Sebastian can be fierce and fast, or slow and easy. But this is comforting and rhythmic. I drape my wet arms on his shoulders, closing my eyes and letting the water do the work.

For a while, I float over him, feeling him enter and glide. Then he begins to speed up, his arms flexing.

This sets off something in me, because that need for him gathers, tightening and tensing.

He reaches between us to touch me and this makes everything move so much faster. I clutch at him, pressing his face into my chest. He nips at my breasts and I lean in. "Bite harder."

He does, and the force of it goes straight to the core of me. I cry out, everything bursting. The water splashes wildly, and Sebastian groans against my skin.

We cling to each other, not moving, riding out the

storm. Between us, muscles clench and release, clench and release.

The water goes still. It feels cool against my back.

We hold on a while longer, our chests heaving.

He kisses everything he can reach. "Mila…"

I hold the back of his head where damp hair has curled against his neck. "We got wet."

"We did."

From somewhere in the room, a phone buzzes. Duty calling.

"We have to go," I say.

"Damn it, we do."

He opens the plug and the water gurgles down. Thankfully, there's a rack of towels right beside us.

We climb out and dry off with minimal mess to the room.

"I'll drop these off," Sebastian says, picking the towels up.

I nod. "I'm probably missed in maintenance."

"I'll cover for you if Trey has any questions."

I shake my head. "No. I'll take whatever he dishes out about my tardiness. It's better that way."

Sebastian nods. "We should stick to quickies."

"I'm willing to get in trouble over this one."

Sebastian picks up his phone. "The buzzing wasn't mine."

I find my cell in my pants pocket and pull it out.

Brooklyn: I hate it here and I'm going to leave.

Uh oh.

I race to get my pants on, scrolling through messages.

"Everything okay?" Sebastian asks.

I was worried this might happen. She's been in laundry all week, which was a big letdown after doing events last week. Plus, she has to deal with all the drama of the other three girls there who were having sex with Maverick. He's apparently dumped them all.

This made her happy at first, but then Maverick stopped coming to see her, too.

I read all her messages quickly.

Brooklyn: I found out why Mav's too busy for anybody.

Brooklyn: He's fucking Chef Monique!

Brooklyn: A kitchen staffer walked in on them in the deep freeze!

I let out a strangled cry of disbelief. The deep freeze?

Brooklyn: I can't do this anymore!

The last message was only a minute ago.

I quickly tap out, *Where are you?*

Sebastian comes up behind me. "Everything okay?"

"Apparently, Chef Monique and Maverick got caught having sex in the deep freeze."

Now he's the shocked one. "The deep freeze?"

"We got the better location."

Sebastian runs his hands through his hair. "Jesus. Can't anybody in this hotel keep their pants on?"

"We are just as guilty."

"I know. I know."

Brooklyn: My room. I left my shift. I don't care. I'm packing.

"Brooklyn's going to quit. I have to go."

"Definitely. I'll tell Trey there's an issue you have to handle."

"No. I'll do it. He doesn't need to know you are keeping tabs on me. This is one of those moments where it's important to be apart."

He nods. "You're right."

I stand on tiptoe and kiss his cheek. "See you later?"

"Okay. Keep me posted."

I'm almost out the door when he calls out, "Mila?"

I turn around.

He holds out my ID badge. "Don't leave this."

God. That would have been hard to explain. "Thank you."

I snatch it and take off down the hall, feeling the damp base of my head. I release the hair clip to hide the wet parts.

This is a hot mess of a situation all around.

There must be an aphrodisiac in the water of Boulder, Colorado.

36

SEBASTIAN

I make it back to my office to find three people already there.

"And where the hell have you been?" Raya demands. "While half the staff is at each other's throats?"

"Dealing with the broken security camera in the bridal wing," I say easily.

Raya's stance is angry, and she glares at Chef Monique, who hovers in the corner like a kid in trouble. This is wild, as Chef is normally hell on wheels.

The other person is Maverick, looking pleased with himself. Of course he does.

I sit in my chair. I have to pretend I don't know what this is about. "What's going on?"

"We have a fraternization issue between a superior and a subordinate," Raya says. "And inappropriate sexual conduct on the hotel grounds."

Neither Chef Monique nor Maverick reacts to this.

"Is Jessie coming?" I ask. "This is an HR matter."

"She's on her way," Raya says.

"Okay. Everybody, find a seat. We'll figure this out." I have a small conference table opposite my desk, and the three of them find chairs. There's one for Jessie. I stay where I am, worried I might smell of the hot tub or sex or Mila or all three. My stomach rumbles and I realize I used up my lunch hour without eating lunch.

Still worth it.

Chef Monique steals a glance at Maverick like a smitten schoolgirl, but Maverick taps the surface of the table and avoids her gaze.

Raya looks back and forth at both of them like a principal ready to send them to detention.

We've definitely had inappropriate liaisons on the clock among staff members before, but never a wild card like Maverick, and never between someone so low on the hierarchy and our head chef.

Still, it's not lost on me that I better handle this well, knowing that at some point, this meeting will be looked upon in a new light once my relationship with Mila is revealed, hopefully by us, on our own timeline.

Jessie rushes in. "I'm here." She sits in the empty chair at the table, then hops up again to close the door. "Should we call in Havannah?"

"Let's not trouble her with this," I say. "Besides, she's off site at a doctor's appointment today." She texts me each morning with her schedule, particularly if she'll be out. "Jessie, what is the procedure here?"

She flips her blonde hair behind her shoulder and opens a notebook. "HR will conduct an investigation as to whether there has been preferential treatment or inconsistent distribution of duties."

Maverick scoffs. "I'm an intern. I've been washing dishes and stirring pots. I'm not even allowed to cook anything."

Raya leans forward. "You have been repeatedly taken off the intern schedule I set and placed in locations that are near Chef Monique."

"You're the one who sent me to the dish room on day one!" Maverick kicks back in this chair, arms crossed. "Everyone else got sweet gigs in HR or the front desk or fancy parties, and I've been carrying trays and scrubbing pans."

Raya is undeterred. "You say this as if that was my plan. Kitchen requested you." She looks pointedly at Chef Monique. "Then you were in the restaurant, where you tended to work the kitchen, anyway. Then Monique wanted you in catering because of the meeting banquets they had to serve early this week. If anything, I tried to get you away from the kitchens."

Jessie scribbles notes on her clipboard. "Raya, you approved all these schedule changes for Maverick?"

"I did. The requests seemed reasonable."

And it got Maverick out of her hair. She'd told me so. But I'm not getting any more involved in this than I have to.

"Monique, when did you first request Maverick for the kitchen?"

"After I saw his work ethic and camaraderie with the dish room staff. He was a good addition, and the men all got along." She folds her hands together.

"And at what stage was your relationship at that point?"

"Nothing. I barely knew him, other than everyone was buzzing about him."

"Buzzing?"

"Saying he was an enjoyable coworker."

Jessie bites her lip at that, and I'm trying not to react, either. I bet he was enjoyable.

Jessie turns to Maverick. "How would you characterize your relationship with Chef Monique right now?"

He chuckles. "She's hot enough to melt the permafrost on the shelves inside the freezer."

That quiets the room.

Monique's face goes pink, but I don't think she's upset by what he said. If Maverick can win that one over, he's got real skills.

Jessie makes more notes. "I'll want to talk to each of you separately. But while you are together, are you two planning on reporting your relationship to HR officially? I can email you both the form so it's done while we sort this out."

Monique and Maverick answer simultaneously.

Monique: "Yes."

Maverick: "Hell, no."

Monique turns to him. Now she's upset. "Why not?"

"I'd have to file for half of laundry too." He stands up. "Now, if you'll excuse me, I need to check on my blonde hottie."

Does he mean Brooklyn? Geez.

I stand up with him. "Actually, Maverick, you stay

right here. Everyone else can work out the schedule of interviews with Jessie for her report."

Both Raya and Jessie throw me looks that tell me they are not thrilled that I appear to be taking Maverick's side, but they file out.

Maverick sits back down. "Now what?"

I move to the table. "What the hell are you doing, Mav? Do you have to shove your cock in everything with a vagina?"

"I'm not hitting on your chick."

This stops me cold. "Who is my chick?"

He props his feet on the table like he's perfectly at home. "The one with tits for days. Mila. I left her for you."

My anger floods me so fast, I don't think. I just yell. "Pack your shit, Maverick. You're out. Fired. Gone. Empty your apartment."

He drops his feet to the floor. "Fuck. I figured that would be the thing to get you. Don't worry. I'm not going to narc on you. I'm not like that." He stands up to leave. "But seems to me, you and me are in the same damn situation."

He's right. "Sit down," I tell him.

He drops into the chair.

"I assume Jessie won't find any preferential treatment for her report?"

He shrugs. "Can't. I've been doing grunt work."

"So the biggest thing we can get you two on is inappropriate behavior."

"If you get us on that, you'll have to take out half of

laundry, plus room service, plus one of the other interns."

Now it makes sense. Spread your misdeeds out and it becomes impossible to fire everybody.

"Do you even like Monique?"

"She's a hard-ass bitch. I dig it. But I'm not having chef babies with her or anything. She's a freak in the sheets, though. I'll give her that. The freezer was all about ice on her—"

"I'm good." I don't want any more details. "There's nothing to cater today. What is your assignment?"

"Nothing. That's how we freed up time for the freezer," Maverick says. "I'm just hanging out."

"You're moving to HR today, then. Suze will give you work."

"Cool." He heads for the door. "That Emily chick in HR is hot."

Damn it. I should have sent him to maintenance.

But Mila's with them this week. I don't want him near her.

I want to tell him not to do anything stupid in HR, but he's already gone.

I feel like I'm reeling. The wildness in the bridal suite, then abruptly being dumped into this meeting. I run my hand through my hair. It's curled up from being wet.

Yeah, Chef Monique's situation will be mine, eventually.

I text Mila. *How's Brooklyn?*

It's a minute before I hear.

Mila: She wants to know if he's fired.

I shouldn't answer that. It's out of protocol. But I do.

Me: Not yet. Convince her to stay.

It's a while before another one comes.

Mila: She's calming down. Can she have the day off? Can you make that happen?

Another breach of protocol. Technically, this is Raya's call, since she's over the interns. But I do it anyway.

Me: Why don't you and her go check on the pregnant donkeys when you feel up for it? I'll tell Raya you two were needed out there and I pulled you from today's rounds.

Mila: I like that. Thank you.

I sink back in my chair. One problem handled.

Now for the other.

Maverick has figured out about me and Mila. That's a powerful secret.

I wonder who else knows.

37

MILA

Sebastian and I cool it for a few days, but when everything settles down after the Chef Monique situation, we're back at it.

As the weeks pass, we feel invincible. We're like addicts, sneaking together whenever we can. It's part of the thrill.

It's half-dark in the unused staff apartment, which I sometimes like to think of as ours. We discovered it three weeks ago and it became our go-to location.

But it's our last day to use it, as Havannah hired a new social media coordinator. He'll be arriving over the weekend to take it over until he can find an apartment.

I'll miss having this space, which is easier to sneak into than empty guest rooms. No hall cameras. Nobody monitoring the door lock scans.

We have such a long way to go until Havannah chooses her event manager and we can go to HR with our relationship. Four months at least.

Sebastian's hair tickles my skin as he leisurely makes

his way down my body.

Neck, chest, belly, thighs.

He lifts a knee and dives in.

I clutch the bedspread and arch my back. He knows exactly what gets to me. He always did, but after almost two months of paying attention, he's a master.

I'm getting better, too. There's this place I can touch that makes him crazy. I looked it up after I discovered it. It's called the perineum.

He likes it.

I suck in a breath. He's got me, the world starting to spin. I live for this. I can't believe I was twenty-two and graduated before I got to do it. Next month I will be twenty-three. Sebastian will turn thirty-three one week later. We're both Scorpios.

His finger shifts, and that's it, I'm there. My breathing is wild, and that familiar pulse begins to throb.

Then I freeze at a strange sound.

Voices.

Close.

The front door pops open.

"Make sure it's all ready," Raya says, then stops cold. She's seen us.

She stares at me, as there's a direct sightline from the main door into the bedroom. God, I'm naked, with Sebastian's face down below.

Sebastian notices a heartbeat later than me. He throws the bedspread over us, but it's way too late.

Raya steps back into the hall. "You know, let's come back after lunch," she tells someone we can't see. "Out we go."

The door clicks.

My entire body flashes so hot, I feel like I'm incinerating.

She saw us. Saw me. Naked. Having sex.

I can't deal with it.

I roll away from Sebastian and race to the bathroom. I don't have time to get the toilet lid up, so I throw up into the sink. I've skipped lunch, so there's nothing but sticky fluid that I have to spit to get out of my mouth.

He comes up behind me, but I wave him away. As if Raya seeing me wasn't mortifying enough, now he's watching me puke.

I rinse out my mouth a half dozen times, although it doesn't take the acid taste away. I catch sight of myself in the mirror and grimace. My hair is everywhere. My mascara has smudged.

My boobs are saggy despite my age. My belly has a fold in it when I bend over that gives me a terrible pouch. I'm blotchy and gross, and I can't bear any of this one minute longer.

I let out a sob, and Sebastian's there. He wraps his arms around me. "Hey. This was always a possibility."

I can't stop crying. I'm so humiliated, like all my secrets were just announced at a school assembly. I want to run away and hide.

I know exactly why Brooklyn wanted to leave after the Chef Monique fiasco. It's too horrible to think of facing people who know about your mistakes, your misdeeds.

But she stayed.

And Maverick got put permanently in the barn to keep him away from the offices. He's been building a whelping pen for the pregnant donkeys to give birth in.

Things had calmed down.

We got complacent.

And now this.

"What do we do?" I ask.

"I'll call a meeting with Havannah and Raya and Jessie. I'll officially report our relationship. You'll be called in and asked about it, too."

"What do I say?"

"The truth. The truth is the best. We met before you started. We intended to avoid seeing each other again, but we are in love."

I suck in a breath and look at him. "We are?"

He smooths my hair across the top of my head. "I've been feeling it for a while. I know being a couple is new to you. I didn't want to say anything to rush you."

He…loves me?

He kisses my hair. "We're going to be okay, Mila. We will. Let's imagine the worst-case scenario for a moment. The absolute worst."

"Okay?"

"We're both fired. You move out of the castle. You stay with me. I look for a new job. You look for a new job. We work somewhere else. Maybe it's not the castle, but we're happy together."

I like this. It's not the castle, but it's still pretty great. "Okay."

"We've got this, Mila. We're going to be okay."

We walk out to the bedroom and slowly dress.

My fingers tremble as I pull my ID over my head.

He takes my hands in his. "I don't like leaving you, but I'm going to have to call this meeting."

I nod. "I know."

"Why don't you check if Brooklyn can do lunch? You're in security, and Hank won't notice how long you're gone."

"Okay."

"Take a minute." He kisses my head again.

He's about to leave when I grab his hand. "Can you say it?"

He tilts his head quizzically, then he realizes what I'm asking.

His smile is big and broad. "I love you, Mila Simmons, my raven-haired beauty, watcher of stars, keeper of secrets. *I love you.*"

Despite everything that's happened in the last ten minutes, my heart absolutely soars. "Thank you."

He kisses my hand, then slips out the door.

I sit on the end of the bed. He loves me.

Sebastian Young loves me.

I press my hands to my cheeks. I want to write it on all my notebooks, surrounded by hearts. I want to wear his letter jacket. Sit on the bumper of his car in the student parking lot. I want to dance with him at prom and tuck our picture in my mirror.

It happened late. But it's happened.

Somebody loves me.

And not anybody.

Sebastian Young.

Now we just have to get through this terrible part.

38

SEBASTIAN

When I arrive in Raya's office, she's sitting with her hands clasped on her desk like she's been waiting for me.

I take a chair across from her. I'm the superior. I should handle the hard parts of this conversation.

"Would you like me to call in Jessie and Havannah?" I ask.

Her face is solemn. "Yes. I should not have to bear the brunt of this betrayal alone."

Betrayal. Raya is ready to blow this up.

"I'll call them." We've seen less of Havannah lately as she hits full term, but as far as I know, she's in the castle. She has a suite she uses for her family when things get busy. Its location is almost as secret as the hidden one I showed Mila.

I step out of Raya's office and into the hall to make the calls. There's no reason to do it in front of her. She's angry, as if she can barely hold it in.

I call Havannah first. She picks up on one ring.

"What's wrong?"

I usually text, so she knows something is up. "Hey, we have a serious staffing matter to manage."

"Can it wait?" Her voice sounds strained.

"I don't think so."

"Really? Is Maverick seducing more upper management?"

If only. "No, this one is about me."

"Oh."

"Raya's upset with me. You might be, too. I'm going to ask Jessie to sit in as well."

"Can you and I talk about it first?"

"We can, but Raya's waiting in her office. She wants action right away."

She lets out a long slow breath. "I see. I'm not sure I'm in a condition to even waddle over there."

"We can come to you."

"Can you do that right away?"

"I'll assemble everyone."

"I'll be in my front room." She ends the call.

At least she realizes the gravity of this.

Now for Jessie. Since I'm so close, I decide to walk into HR. It's still the lunch hour, so only Emily is inside the big room. I wonder if she hooked up with Maverick like he planned. Not my business. They are close enough on the hierarchy that it doesn't matter.

Thankfully, Jessie's having lunch at her desk, holding a sandwich from the cart in the lobby as she clicks around on her mouse.

I lean inside her office. "Can I borrow you for a bit?"

She looks up. "I'm deep in payroll approvals."

"Havannah is waiting for us."

"Oh." She wraps her sandwich up and sticks it in a tiny fridge in the corner. "Who is it this time?"

"Me."

"Oh."

Emily watches us as we cross the office to the hall. I pop my head into Raya's room. "Havannah is meeting us in her suite. You ready?"

Raya rises from the desk, picking up her ever-present iPad. I don't carry one, preferring to keep tech out of my interactions. I take my notes afterward. Raya uses hers like a shield.

Havannah's suite is tucked in the same tower as the private restaurant. I scan my card, and we are silent as we ride to the tenth floor, which can only be accessed with four IDs in the entire staff. Me. Trey, head of maintenance. Anna, head of housekeeping. And Hank, head of security. We have to escort anyone else who goes there, or Havannah does.

But that's how much trust she's put in me. I hope I haven't wrecked it.

We step into a small foyer outside the elevator. There are two doors. One to the stairwell, which is similarly secure, and Havannah's door.

I knock on it.

Havannah's husband Donovan answers. "Hey, everyone." He nods at us. "Come on in. Please make it quick."

"Nonsense," Havannah calls from inside.

We all enter the soothing cream and lavender interior. Havannah is propped on pillows on a chaise. She wears a loose pink dress that reaches her ankles.

"You feeling okay?" Jessie asks.

Havannah waves away her concern. "Bored out of my mind. Someone isn't letting me so much as log onto a tablet." She shoots a look at her husband.

Donovan pinches his lips. "Havannah is hardheaded when it comes to doing what she wants. I'm insisting she takes six weeks to recover after the baby comes."

"Two," she says.

"Four," he volleys back.

"We have it handled," I say. "You take all the time you need."

It's then that I notice a tightness in her expression. She grips one of the pillows so hard that her fingers are white.

Donovan scowls.

They are more upset about this meeting than they are letting on.

"Everybody sit down," Havannah says, gesturing to the sofa and scattered chairs. "Sebastian sounded all doom and gloom, which isn't like him. Let's get to it."

Jessie and Raya sit on the sofa, and I take a wide armchair. I consider how I will start this without being too shocking.

But Raya does it for me. "Earlier today, I discovered our general manager fraternizing with one of the interns in an empty apartment on the staff wing."

Jessie turns to her in shock. "What do you mean, fraternizing?"

"I think we get what she means," Havannah says.

"Okay, so we have another situation like Monique and Maverick, only with a more direct line of command?"

Jessie fumbles for words. "Sebastian? Really? You're everyone's boss. This is highly inappropriate."

Despite all the times I pictured this moment, I hadn't quite prepared myself for their judgment.

"Should we take a moment for me to explain the circumstances?" I ask.

Raya fairly sputters. "The circumstances? How about the circumstances where you are naked, our intern is naked, it's business hours for both of you, and you are on hotel property?"

Ouch.

Donovan's mouth twitches, like he's trying not to show any reaction. Havannah is grimacing, her usual control of her expression faltering as well. She's got the pillow in a death grip. This has to be my fault. She's put her trust in me, and I've failed.

"I'd like to hear it," Jessie says. "I'll be the one filing the report."

Havannah lets out a long, slow breath. "Can you give us the short version?"

The strangled sound of her voice alarms me, like she is going to react far more fiercely than I expected.

I need to calm everyone down. "I met Mila before she began working here. I wasn't involved in her hiring, so I had no idea—"

Donovan interrupts. "Havannah?" He straightens her dress, where a dark spot of pink expands.

"Damn it," Havannah says. "I was trying to hold that in."

"I told you this one was for real." Donovan lunges for the wall and mashes a button. "Sarah, bring the hospital bag. It's time!"

Raya leaps to her feet. "Sebastian! You sent Havannah into labor!"

"No, no," Havannah says. "I've been having contractions for two hours. I went too early last time with Rebel and embarrassed myself. I was trying to be sure, then Sebastian called. Uh oh—" Her words dissolve into a keening cry.

Oh, geez.

Everyone stands to help Havannah up.

"I'm fine. It's just a baby." Water pools at her bare feet. "Donovan, can I get some shoes?"

"Which ones still fit?"

She smacks his shoulders. "Hush. Get the Crocs."

Sarah, Havannah's primary assistant, barrels into the room with a black suitcase. "All ready. I'm ready."

Donovan returns with pink Crocs and bends down to place them on Havannah's feet. "You're really wet," he says. "I think you'll slip."

"I'll get a towel." Sarah rushes off again.

"Do I have time to change dresses?" Havannah asks.

"You nearly had the last baby in the limo!" Donovan says.

"No, no," Havannah says. "You're forgetting. We thought I was going to have the baby in the limo, but then it took another twenty hours."

"Oh, right."

Havannah looks at all of us. "It was our first date. It was a lot."

None of us know this story, and Jessie, Raya, and I exchange glances. We knew Rebel had a different father, but not that Havannah gave birth to him on her first date with Donovan.

"I insist on a new dress," Havannah says again. "And dry underwear."

"Well, come on," Donovan says. "Let's get you changed." He gives us all an apologetic smile. "We'll have to table this for now."

Havannah holds onto the back of the chaise as she takes small, mincing steps toward the hall. "Handle it as close to what we did with Maverick as possible," she says. But then she bends over, letting out a long moan. "Ohhh, here we go again."

Sarah returns with the towel. "You all are still here? Handle this situation yourselves." She passes the towel to Donovan and herds us out like cattle. "She'll let you know when she's ready to talk business again."

Then we're out in the foyer by the elevator.

"This is so exciting," Jessie says. "The baby is coming."

"No, it's ridiculous," Raya says. "Sebastian has committed a fireable offense."

Jessie scans her ID, realizes it doesn't work, then looks at me. "We didn't fire Monique."

"We got them separated, though," Raya says.

I don't interrupt, but step between them to call the elevator.

"This is different." Jessie twists her hair into a long rope. "Maverick was causing problems beyond his relationship with Monique."

"So, we should send Mila out to the barn, too?" Raya asks.

Jessie searches my face. "I think this one is probably a more long-term relationship, am I right?"

I nod.

"I should handle it," Jessie says. "Raya, you seem very angry, and as a direct subordinate, you should not be involved."

"But I am Mila's direct supervisor."

The elevator doors glide open and we step inside.

"Don't fire her," I say. "If anyone should take responsibility, it should be me."

Jessie holds up a palm. "It's out of your hands, Sebastian. You say you met her before, but you kept seeing her after you learned she was an intern."

"I did." There's no sugar coating that.

"And this is a consensual relationship?"

"Yes."

"He's going to plot with that girl to make her say what he wants," Raya says. "We need to call her in right away."

"I'll call her in," Jessie says. "Sebastian, do I have your word that you won't contact her until I let you know we've concluded our interview with her?"

I nod.

"All right then."

We step out into the lobby.

Jessie turns to me. "Sebastian, I'm going to ask you to take the rest of the day off. We'll call Mila in today."

I shove my hands in my pockets. "All right."

"I'll be in touch."

She and Raya head down the hall toward the lobby.

I turn the opposite direction to walk outside to the employee lot.

When I get in my car, I check my phone.

Mila has sent several messages.

Everything feels too normal. How are the meetings going?

I'm guessing this will take a while.

Are you okay?

Even though I have told Jessie I won't contact her, I do. Mila is more important than my job. More important than anything.

I send one quick message.

Meeting done. Jessie will talk to you. It's going to be just fine. I love you.

Then I toss my phone onto my seat and head home.

39

MILA

My legs tremble as I head to HR. Raya texted me, saying to drop everything to meet with Jessie.

I hope Raya isn't there. I'm not ready to face the person who witnessed me naked with my boss. Even the thought of it makes my face burn.

Walking through HR feels very different from the week I worked there.

Suze is settling into her desk, probably in from her lunch break. She tilts her head as if to ask why I'm here, but she doesn't.

Georgia's chair is empty.

Emily watches me walk by like maybe she knows something.

Jessie stands as I approach. "Come on in. Sit down." Her voice is falsely bright, making my nerves jangle.

She shuts the door with a click. Jessie only closed her door twice the week I was here.

I'm shaking so hard my teeth almost chatter. I'm a

rule follower. A good girl. I never get in trouble. I never visited the principal's office.

This is the worst.

Jessie sits down and leans forward, her elbows on her desk. "You're not in trouble, Mila. I'm involved only to make sure that all parties in this relationship were there of their free will. When we have a gap in the chain of command, there is always the possibility that there was a power dynamic at play, even if it was only implied."

I try to find my voice, but it won't come. So I sit there.

"Did you at any point feel like your job was contingent on your relationship with Sebastian?"

I shake my head no. "We met before I started."

"And when you realized he was the manager, what did you do?"

"We agreed not to see each other."

Her forehead crumples, as if she didn't expect that answer. God, did Sebastian tell her something else? He said to tell the truth.

"Did he later convince you to start seeing him?"

"No, it just happened."

"He didn't pressure you in any way?"

With his kisses? His attention? Why had I changed my mind?

"No. I liked him."

"Because he had such a high position here?"

Was that an accusation? "No! That was the problem, actually. Why we decided not to date."

"But you did."

"It just happened." My body shakes again, and I feel tears forming.

Jessie gives me a small smile, like I'm a kid who needs a warm hug. "You're all right, Mila. I'm making sure that you never felt like you had to date him or else face consequences at work."

"I didn't. Raya is my boss. Sebastian was clear that he wasn't in charge of the interns."

"Good."

So, I got one answer right.

"Did you ever feel he was giving you extra attention over the other interns?"

That's a hard one. I always felt it. "He didn't move me anywhere or have me do anything special."

She nods. "Did you take steps to keep your relationship with Sebastian secret?"

"We didn't tell anyone." Only after I say it do I realize it's a lie. I did tell Brooklyn. But I don't fix it. I don't want to get her in trouble.

"Why did you think it should be a secret?"

"There's a clause in the policy we signed."

"Did Sebastian tell you about the clause?"

I fidget in my chair. "I read it when I signed it."

She nods. "Good. But you did it anyway."

"Not at first," I say again. "But then it just happened." I'm repeating myself.

She asks about any special privileges I got. I say none, even though seeing the secret suite probably counts, and having additional access on my ID card.

She looks out the window of her office. "Mila, you live on site, so it's natural you would do…the things you do in a relationship on the premises. But I need to ask you not to do them while you are on the clock, or anyplace inappropriate."

God, this is mortifying. "I understand."

She fiddles with some papers on her desk. "You can return to your duties. Sebastian isn't on site today, but you can resume your conversations with him while Raya and I decide what to do."

Not Havannah? Sebastian was counting on her stepping in. But I simply say, "Thank you," and escape the room as quickly as possible.

I race down the employee hall and duck into the empty staff room. I text Sebastian.

Me: Just got out of HR. They haven't decided what to do about us. Jessie said she and Raya would decide. What about Havannah?

Sebastian: She went into labor during our meeting. She's out of the picture for now.

Me: Oh, no. That's bad, isn't it?

Sebastian: It will be okay.

But it's not okay.

Me: Jessie said you're not here.

Sebastian: I got sent home to avoid Raya's wrath.

Me: Can I see you later?

Sebastian: Absolutely.

I sink into a chair. I'm not sure where to go or what to do. I feel like there's an axe hanging over my head, and any minute it will fall.

Although these meetings ought to be confidential, I don't know who was with Raya or what they saw. Emily might blab.

If I've learned anything from Maverick's situation, news of this is going to hit any minute, and everyone will be looking at me.

I'm supposed to be with security, but Hank is off today and I've been stuck with Wendell, who I dislike.

Sebastian was a break from dealing with him. It feels mean that I have to go back to Wendell. I don't want to sit in the locked-up room while he makes commentary on all the video screens. It's been the worst rotation so far.

"Mila?"

I jump in my chair.

Raya enters the staff room. "Come along. I'll be taking you to your new assignment."

New assignment?

She holds out her hand. "You won't need your uniform. You can wear the white shirt and black pants for now, but hand over your vest."

Where am I going that I don't need a uniform? Even the laundry and kitchen workers wear the black pants and white shirt.

I unfasten the vest, my face flaming because it feels weird, like I'm undressing for her. I pass it over.

"Your ID card will be reconfigured. It will unlock the exterior door that opens at the end of your apartment hall and, of course, your apartment door. And that's all. You will no longer have access to any elevators or employee corridors."

"How will I get around?"

She smiles, but it's forced. "You won't need to. Like Maverick, you won't be working inside the castle."

Maverick got pushed to the barn after he was caught with Chef Monique. The only time I ever see him is if we happen to pass each other in the staff apartment hall.

"Will I be in the barn, too?"

She heads out of the staff room, and I rush to catch up.

"No. You will be working at Havannah's other business."

Other business? Does she have a satellite hotel? I haven't heard about it.

We walk through the lobby to the front door.

Bertie tips his hat at me, then tilts his head as he realizes I'm in partial uniform. His eyes move to the vest in Raya's arms.

Outside in the front circle, the castle shuttle bus is waiting, its sides emblazoned with a gorgeous summer-time view of the hotel and the mountains. The driver opens the door.

Raya leans in. "Take Mila to the Tasty Mango. Please arrange to pick her up at five."

The Tasty Mango? What is that?

"I have a car," I say.

Raya steps back. "You will take the shuttle for the rest of this week. Next week, you can drive yourself, one we've established Sebastian's situation."

His situation? What does that mean?

I take the steps up onto the bus. "Is he going to get fired?" I ask.

"That's not for me to decide," she says brightly, as if everything is working according to plan.

I sit in the first seat.

Raya stands by the hotel entrance, arms crossed in front of her, my vest dangling from her fingers, as the driver closes the door and takes off around the circle.

When we're headed for the highway, I ask the driver, "What's the Tasty Mango?"

He grins. "That's the Boudreaux sisters' deli. One of the finest sandwich places in all of Boulder. Havannah and Magnolia opened it years ago, before Donovan built the castle for Havannah. Magnolia still runs it with her husband, Anthony Pickle."

"Pickle?"

"You know, the Pickle family. They have delis from California to New York. Anthony owns the Boulder Pickle. The Pickles are tight with the Boudreaux, although it wasn't always so. It's quite a tale how the Pickles and the Boudreaux married betwixt themselves to avoid both their delis falling apart. You should look it up."

So I do, finding the Tasty Pepper, the original Boudreaux family deli, the opening of the Boulder Pickle, and the whole crazy business between Magnolia and Anthony when they were on a cooking show circuit.

We pull up in front of the bright orange building.

"Here we are," the driver says. "I'll be back for you at five or thereabouts, depending on where I am with guests."

I nod. "Thank you."

I step down in front of the big glass windows. Above them, a pink and orange awning flaps in the wind. There are quite a few people seated inside, and a couple more in line at a long glass counter where employees make sandwiches to order.

The bus drives away.

So this is what happens to people who break the rules.

There's nothing left to do but open the door and introduce myself.

40

SEBASTIAN

I don't hear from Mila for hours. I assume she's at the hotel and surrounded by people. Knowing her, she feels she's broken enough rules and won't take out her phone for anything until she's off work.

At five, when she should be done, I text her again. *Let's have a nice relaxing evening.*

Nothing.

My stomach clenches. Has something gone wrong?

I'm not waiting around. I don't care if I'm not supposed to be up there.

Arya looks up as I stomp past the sofa. I told her Mila and I had been outed today, although not the circumstances. "You all right?"

"Mila's not responding."

She leaps up and manages to beat me to the door. "Stop. Use your head. What was the last thing you two said to each other?"

"She asked to come over. I said absolutely."

"When was that?"

"Around one."

Arya frowns. "That's hours ago."

"I assumed she was working, but now she shouldn't be."

"I'm coming with you."

"Why?"

"So you don't do anything dumb!"

I lift her and set her aside. "I don't do dumb things."

"You do dumb things when women are involved!"

I don't have time for this. I wrench the door open, but when I get my car unlocked, Arya is already in the passenger seat.

"Did you lock the front door?" I ask her.

"No."

"You going to go do it?"

"No. You'll drive off without me."

She's right.

"Sebastian, use your head. What if she's upset? What if she needs a minute? What if she's on her way here?"

I drop my head against the back of the seat. "What if Raya's giving her hell and she needs someone on her side?"

"Should that be you?"

"Absolutely."

"Well, go lock the door," she says.

I look down at her bare feet. "Go get some shoes and lock the door. I won't leave without you."

She stares at me a moment. "I'm not sure I believe you."

"I swear on my grave."

"Swear on Alfalfa's grave."

Gah. She's got me. "I swear on our puppy dog's grave."

She opens the door and gets out.

I consider gunning it, but I don't. She's probably right to come as a buffer. She and Mila have totally hit it off. She's been showing Mila how to paint while Mila teaches her interior design principles. They're always up to something when I'm cooking.

I grip the steering wheel. Am I prepared to jettison this job over her?

Totally. Absolutely.

Arya launches back into the car, a pair of yellow Converse in her arms. "Let's go."

I race to the hotel, cursing myself for accepting Jessie and Raya's insistence that I leave for the day. I should have been there. Mila is bound to be upset.

When we get to the hotel, I get my first shock of the evening when my ID won't open the back door.

What the ever-loving hell?

It's five-twenty, and most of the professional staff will have left already. Housekeeping and the kitchen staff will be there, though.

"Should we drive around front?" Arya asks.

We might have to.

I stand there, knowing that only Raya currently has the level of access to cut me out with Havannah gone. The only other person is Hank in security, but he was off today.

Why would she do this? They can't make a decision as big as firing me without Havannah's involvement.

Unless they are planning to put me on a leave of absence until she returns.

"All right," I say. "Let's go around." It won't help much, as I'll only be able to go into the lobby without my own ID badge working. Sasha will be there, though, and her clearance is pretty high.

We only take about three steps when the door pops open. I turn around.

It's Maverick of all people, holding a bin of what appears to be chopped hay.

I grab the door before it can close. "What do you have there?" I ask, mainly to stop him so I can judge if he knows anything.

"Jed had the kitchens mix some greens into the hay for the pregnant donkeys." He heads on, but manages to toss back, "I heard you finally got busted." He laughs. "We're all black sheep."

I exchange a glance with Arya.

"He didn't even say hello to me," she says.

"Well, we learned two things," I say. "People know about Mila, but not that I'm pushed out."

We walk inside the hall to the competing smells of laundry detergent and cooking, which is like home to me.

"I haven't been up here in a while," Arya says.

I text Mila again. *I'm at the hotel.*

Still nothing.

An additional concern hits me. What if they told her she couldn't talk to me anymore? How did they threaten her, exactly?

My anger surges. Now I'm pissed.

"Who do you think leaked the information?" Arya asks. "It should only have been a very small group who knew."

"Raya came in with someone. They might have seen."

Anna's office is locked up and dark.

"Or else Raya leaked it for her advantage."

"Could be."

Raya's door is open. She's still here.

I'm ready to go in, guns blazing, but Arya must know because she grabs my arm. "No, no. Not her first. Let's see if Jessie is around."

It takes everything I have not to charge in there, anyway.

But she's right. Ordinarily, Jessie would have to sign off on my access getting cut. If she didn't, Raya did it on her own.

"Let's go around," I tell Arya, and pull her toward the kitchen.

We cut through the bakery, walking alongside the wall with Monique and Filo's office, the pantry, and the walk-in freezer.

The scene of Maverick's crime.

A few cooks notice us, but nobody looks at me with surprise, like they know something. It's not common knowledge, not yet.

How did Maverick find out?

We cut down a narrow passage between the kitchen and the main hall, beyond Raya's office. It leads straight to the staff meeting room, which is also dark. Then HR.

I check the door. Unlocked.

I pop it open. The three desks in the main room are empty, but Jessie's office is lit up.

"Wait here," I tell Arya. I hand her my phone. "If Mila texts, tell her I'm with Jessie."

She sits in Suze's chair, touching my screen to keep the phone unlocked.

I stride quickly to the back.

Jessie looks up in surprise. "Sebastian? I thought we asked you to stay home."

I throw my ID on the desk. "So you all could cut off my access to the hotel?"

She picks it up. "What are you talking about?"

"Did you or Raya tell Mila she couldn't contact me?"

She pushes back away from the desk. "We did not. Or, I didn't. Is something wrong with Mila?"

"She's not responding to my messages."

Jessie's expression flickers. "She was shook up after her meeting with me. She might need some time to herself."

"She would write me back. I know it. Unless someone told her something bad would happen if she did."

She picks up my ID again. "Let me check this."

She scans it on the machine we use to program the IDs. A message flashes on her screen. "No records."

"What?" She scans it again.

"No records."

She takes her own ID and scans it.

The screen fills with information. Jessie Styles.

Human resources. There's a long list of security and lock access notes.

"I'm not authorized to change your high-level ID," Jessie says. "Who is?"

"Hank, Havannah, and Raya."

Her mouth goes in a tight line.

"I saw Maverick, and he knew about Mila. Who all knows?"

She shakes her head. "This is bad. And Havannah is out." She sighs. "Couldn't you have gotten caught on a day the owner *isn't* in labor?"

"My priority is Mila. Did you tell her to take today off, too?"

"No. We were trying to figure out what to do with her, given Havannah's last request was literally to make it like Maverick."

"Did she go to the barn?" Maybe reception is bad out there.

"No." Jessie bites her lip.

"Spit it out."

"Raya came in with the idea so fast that I think she might have already known what she wanted to do."

I lean forward, both arms on Jessie's desk. "Where is Mila?"

"She's been stripped of access to the hotel, other than her room. She's been sent to work at the Tasty Mango."

"The deli? She has a degree in hospitality!"

"I know, I know. I figured it would be fine for a couple of days, until Raya calmed down."

I back away. "Is she still there?"

"I don't really know. Raya went to tell her."

"And probably told her not to talk to me. And also cut my access. Is this her way of gunning for my job?"

"I don't know."

"What else could she do?" I pace the small office.

"Do you have other secrets?"

"No."

"Then you have nothing to worry about." Jessie comes around the desk. "Go home, Sebastian. Take the rest of the week. Let Mila work at the deli. It won't kill her, and if anything, it will endear her to Havannah. I'll deal with Raya. Let us handle it."

That's the last thing I want to do.

Arya comes to the door. "She texted."

"Mila?" I lunge for the phone.

Mila: Worked at Havannah's deli today. Up to my elbows in pickle juice. Shuttle still hasn't come for me. Can you pick me up?

A thousand rivers of relief course through me. I don't care about the hotel as long as Mila is all right.

Me: Absolutely. Be right there.

I turn to Jessie. "I'll stay away. But Raya has broken protocol herself now. Watch her."

Jessie nods. "I will."

41

MILA

Well, this has been a day.

I started at the hotel, watching security footage with Wendell.

Got caught banging my boss in an empty apartment during my lunch break.

Was sent to a completely different location to chop pickles all afternoon.

And now, I'm stuck here in a part of Boulder I've never been to.

I sit in a seat next to the huge glass windows. The Tasty Mango is a cute deli, all pinks and oranges with a bright, modern design.

Everyone was great to work with. Many of the dishes have funny or scandalous names, like the "Love Relish," a sweet and spicy condiment, and the "Ho for Dill Dough," which is a hoagie on pickle bread.

Anthony Pickle slides into the booth across from me, his boyish looks and messy hair a perfect match for the swirly pink and orange apron he wears. "That was a day," he says. "I was glad to have you."

"I'm not sure I was much help."

"You were a big one." He unties the apron and folds it on the table. It's quiet inside the deli in the break between lunch and dinner, like the lull at the hotel between check-out and check-in. "Magnolia left the moment she heard her sister was in labor, and then magically, you appeared."

"Have you heard anything?"

"She's still at it. Took over twenty hours with Rebel, so it will probably be an all-nighter."

"Are you going up there?"

"Definitely. I'll let Sharlene close. Tomorrow, we'll have our usual manager. This was her day off, so we ended up short when Magnolia left."

"Are you usually here?"

"No. I came the minute Magnolia called. I knew they'd need help."

I glance around the restaurant. "I like it."

He fiddles with the "Tasty Mango" patch on the apron. "Do you know how long you're here for?"

"Nope. Raya stuck me on a shuttle bus. It was supposed to pick me up half an hour ago, but I might be forgotten."

"I can give you a ride back to the hotel on my way to the hospital."

"Sebastian is going to pick me up."

"The general manager?"

I nod. It's too much to explain, and I don't want to.

"I always liked Sebastian. How's he doing?"

"Good."

Anthony stares out the window. "Interesting that they put you out here. Was it Sebastian's idea?"

"No. Raya's. I'm an intern. She's in charge of what I do."

"Still."

"There are some…complicated dynamics at the hotel."

This makes Anthony's eyebrows lift. "Havannah doesn't like complicated dynamics. That's why Sebastian has always been such a good fit." He sits back against the shiny orange booth. "I sense this was Raya, then."

"I'm not sure who all was part of the decision to banish me from the hotel, but I still live on site, so I guess that's something."

"You want me to check in with Havannah about this?"

"While she's in labor? Oh, no. I'll be here tomorrow and happy to chop." It's my punishment. Might as well see how all this plays out. "It's a good place. I learned a lot. They don't let us do much of anything in the hotel kitchen."

"Chef Monique is a bit territorial."

Lights flash against the windows. It's Sebastian's SUV.

I jump up. "That's him. Thank you for a good day. It was nice to meet you, Anthony. I hope to meet Magnolia soon."

He lifts a hand to wave goodbye as I rush out to Sebastian's car.

Arya opens the passenger door. "Switch!" she says.

I halt. That's interesting. "You sure?"

"Totally. We're headed home." She moves to the back.

I step into the car and plop down on the passenger seat.

Sebastian envelopes me in a hug, and we sit there a while, holding onto each other.

"Geez, y'all, it's not like you survived a hurricane," Anya says, but her voice is gentle.

Sebastian pulls away. "It's been a day." He laughs. "You smell like pickles."

I sniff my hands. "I washed them so many times!"

"It gets in your pores," he says. "Don't worry. I like the smell."

"So what happened?" I ask. "Why did they send you home?"

"Apparently so they could cut off my access to the hotel. My badge doesn't work."

My belly quakes. "Are they going to fire you?"

"I can't imagine so." He reaches out to squeeze my hand as we back out of the parking spot. "But remember what I said. We go on. It will be fine."

But will it? Him with that huge house and a sister to support? Me, gosh, do I move in with someone I've been dating for two months? Because of the secrecy, I haven't even told my parents about him. They would want to fly out, meet him, ask questions.

Only Camille knows.

Arya leans forward. "The news seems to be out. We saw Maverick, and he had already heard."

"Maybe it's good that I'm elsewhere, then," I say.

We're almost at Sebastian's house when Brooklyn starts messaging.

Brooklyn: I heard you got caught with Sebastian! Where are you?

Before I can respond, she writes again.

Brooklyn: Answer your door!

Brooklyn: Are you not here?

Me: I got sent to work off site. I was at Havannah's deli.

Brooklyn: You're not at the hotel? Did they kick you out of your apartment?

Me: No. But I lost access to the rest of the hotel.

Brooklyn: This is terrible!

Me: How did you find out?

Brooklyn: Owen and I worked housekeeping. When we got to laundry, everybody knew. Apparently Martina went with Raya to prep the empty apartment for the new guy coming, and you were in there????

Me: So Martina told?

Brooklyn: She didn't know anything, but was asking who it could be. Then Ilsa said she saw you in HR. Then Aisha said she saw Raya put you on a shuttle. Then Sebastian disappeared, too, and it seemed everyone knew. I didn't say a word.

Me: I believe you.

Brooklyn: Are you coming back?

Me: I'll have to get clothes. But I'm working at the deli until who knows when.

We arrive at Sebastian's. I type a quick *gotta go*, and we pile out of the car.

"Everything okay?" Sebastian asks.

"Everyone knows. All the pieces came together with us both meeting with Jessie."

Sebastian's face is grim as he unlocks the front door. "I think tonight calls for booze and takeout."

"I'll call for Chinese," Arya says.

"I'll get the glasses out," I offer.

We all trudge into the house for a night of commiserating, since none of us know where we're headed next.

42

SEBASTIAN

We all wake up with mild hangovers.

I drive Mila over to the hotel to shower and change for another day at the deli.

After she's gone, I feel adrift. I circle the exterior of the hotel, knowing I have no access to any of the places I've become accustomed to. It's surreal.

I drive to the outskirts of Boulder and hike a trail I used to love taking with Uncle Roger as a kid. It's an easy one, not too taxing, and I appreciate the chill, the scattering of leaves, and the clean, crisp air.

When I get back, Arya is painting on the back porch, something abstract in blues.

"Good hike?" she asks.

"It was."

"I hate exercise."

I laugh. "I know. What are you painting?"

"My feelings about your predicament." She dabs another petal-shape onto the canvas.

"All blue?"

"Kind of on the nose, huh?" She brushes a piece of hair back, getting blue on her forehead.

I look it over. "Well, it's an abstract, so I'm not sure anything else about it could be called on the nose."

"I'm mad."

"But blue and not red?"

She sighs. "I don't do much red."

That's true. Even when Arya packed up and spent her nights wherever anyone would have her, she never got angry about the situation. I think she gets her quiet strength from our mother.

Mila texts me around midday. *Havannah had a girl. Big party here at her deli.*

I wonder if they're doing anything at the hotel. That's something I would have organized. Jessie will probably do it.

Mila: You should come here.

I turn to Arya, who has given up on the painting for the day and is reading on the sofa with Alfalfa. "You want to head up to the deli?"

She lowers the book. "To see Mila?"

"Havannah had her baby. They're celebrating."

She shakes her head. "Nah. Go kiss your girl."

I change into jeans and a sweater before driving to the Tasty Mango. If not for Mila, I wouldn't have even known about the baby. Nobody at the hotel thought to tell me.

It's strange how quickly you can be forgotten, or maybe they don't want to associate with me while I'm on the outs.

That familiar feeling of displacement comes over

me, one I grappled with in the days after Dad left. Maybe that's why I felt the urge to do Uncle Roger's hike. It was one of the things that helped back then.

When I arrive at the deli, there's clearly a party going on inside. I hear the music the moment I open my door. Inside, the employees are all dancing.

Customers sit at tables, amused by the antics.

I spot Mila, wearing a pink and orange apron, swaying back and forth with her hands in the air. She's making the most of this strange ostracism.

When I open the door, I'm flooded with noise and food smells and warmth. Mila dances her way to me and draws me in.

There's no way the hotel is celebrating quite this hard. Probably there were colored decorations and a cake for the employees in the staff room.

But here, one song flows into the next. As customers arrive, they are served, but the party goes on.

A cake shows up and everyone eats, employees and customers. The dancing is still going on as the shift changes between lunch and dinner, and the new employees are eager to take part.

Magnolia and Anthony arrive right as Mila is about to get off work. They have pictures of Havannah and the baby. As their phones get passed around, Magnolia dances over to me.

"Your situation has been noted by my sister," she says. "Anthony spilled the beans when things settled down. Havannah is really mad. Expect a call as soon as she can manage."

I nod. Mila and I hug each other. Hopefully, we'll be

back at the hotel soon. Until then, we stay at the deli, where things feel good and right. We dance and eat cake.

The call comes four days later, on a Sunday. Mila and I are sitting on the back deck in the afternoon sun when Havannah's name pops up on my cell phone.

I put it on speaker. "New mom! How are mother and baby?"

"We're all right. She's still in the sleepy stage."

"I have Mila here with me."

"Good. That saves me a call. Hello, Mila."

"What did you name her?" Mila asks.

"Serenity."

Mila and I glance at each other. Havannah's child names are always unusual.

"Rebel and Serenity," I say. "You're going for yin and yang."

"I'm hoping for yin and yang," Havannah says. "Rebel is a tyrant."

I'm fully aware, having seen the kid race around the hotel all the years I've worked there.

"I hear you two have been at my deli."

"I went for the party," I say. "But Mila was sent there to work."

"Well, this conversation is coming after several others," Havannah says. "I spoke with Jessie and Raya this morning, then just Jessie. I hate to say it, but as of two hours ago, Raya is no longer with the Castle Hotel."

Mila and I exchange another glance.

"What prompted this decision?" I ask.

"Abuse of authority. Big time. Jessie hasn't wanted to bother me, and was trying to stem the damage. Raya fired Maverick, Chef Monique, Hank, and a third of laundry. Jessie has been in contact with all of them to let them know Raya's decision wasn't final and they would be paid for the days of leave."

Holy shit.

"What was she trying to do?"

"According to her, we had a cancer in the hotel — her words, not mine. She was going to cut it out and I would return to a healthier, more streamlined business."

"Why Hank? He didn't do anything."

"She was sure he had security footage of everyone's evil doings and was deleting it."

I reach for Mila's hand. "I have zero access to the hotel. And if she cut out Hank, she had all the authorization."

"Now I have it. I'll have Hank back tomorrow. And you? I presume? You're not too angry that this coup was attempted and you were caught up in it?"

"No, of course not."

"And Mila, I hear you were a delight at my deli, but I assume you want to return to the hotel."

"It was a fun break," she says. "But yes, I'd love to go back."

"I figured." Havannah sighs. "I'll do everything I can from here. For the moment, I have given Jessie my authorization power so she can restore you and Hank and whoever else Raya tampered with. I have a tech guy going through the logs."

"Is Jessie going to start the search for a new assistant manager?"

"Maybe. We might hire from within. I was looking at Sasha. You and I can talk about that in a couple of weeks. She will be acting assistant manager in the interim. Think about who might move into an acting front desk lead position. We have several possibilities, right?"

"We do."

"Excellent. Get me a list of names in the next couple of days. And forgive me if I email you at two a.m. I won't be expecting a prompt reply. Sometimes I have to look outside to know if it's afternoon or the middle of the night."

"I understand," I tell her. I hesitate, then say, "Should I file relationship paperwork for me and Mila?"

"Already done," she says. "Jessie will have your official report of a relationship to sign tomorrow morning when she reinstates your ID. I assumed you wanted that."

"Yes," we both say simultaneously.

She laughs. "I figured."

A small, jagged cry comes through the phone. "That's my cue," Havannah says. "I'll see you all real soon."

The phone goes dark.

I draw Mila close. "It worked out."

"Except for Raya. What got into her?"

I shake my head. "I feel like she never got over me

being hired over her being promoted. It's why we should really look at who we have before we replace her. Be sure."

"She went off the rails."

"I think she had to work to stay on them in the first place."

Mila rests her head on my shoulder. "What will happen to her?"

"She'll go work somewhere else. Terrorize some other staff."

"But you won't give her a reference."

"Hell, no."

I draw her close against me as the sun peeks through the evergreens, its light breaking apart in a starburst.

I live in the most perfect place, working a job I love.

And with Mila here, this completes the picture I always imagined.

43

MILA

Two months later.
The night before Christmas.

The chorus of donkey laughter keeps all of us awake.

It's dim in the barn other than a glow of light over Tinsel's pen. She's the last of the pregnant donkeys to give birth, and all the interns are out in the barn, other than Ilsa, who had the good sense to leave town and parents who bought her a ticket.

"Well, this isn't how I expected to spend the night," Brooklyn says, shifting on the blanket she's spread over a mound of hay.

"We knew this day was coming," Owen says.

"But Christmas Eve?" Brooklyn throws an arm over her forehead. "Is it my turn to sleep?"

I stand up to check on Tinsel. Only a small part of the white amniotic sac is visible. She's got a ways to go.

We're experts, having sat through three miniature donkey births already.

"How is she?" Owen asks.

"Barely started."

Tinsel is quiet, lying on her side, her belly heaving. It's the rest of the donkeys carrying on.

"You think they're cheering or jeering?" Brooklyn asks.

I sit down beside her. "Probably a little of both."

Maverick wanders up. I don't miss how Brooklyn adjusts her hair. Yeah, the two of them are still going at it.

Not that he's slowed down. It's common knowledge that several women from laundry and a couple from the kitchen make frequent visits out to the barn. Olive, our new assistant manager, has nicknamed the hay and feed room the "Hey, Girl, Hey" room.

Sebastian says Maverick is careful to do his deeds on his own time, not working hours, so they've left it. Nobody has complained about him since the Raya days, and we later learned Raya was stirring the pot anyway, offering better shifts to people who reported him.

She was a real piece of work. No one has heard from her since she left.

Maverick leans over the rail. He prefers to be out here. He and Jed, the animal husbandry guy, get along fine. We figure that when our permanent positions are announced in March, he'll be placed out here.

The rest of us have no idea. We still go through rotations, although we no longer clean rooms or work in the kitchen.

"She's going slower than the others," Maverick says. "It's her first pregnancy."

Brooklyn leaps up at that. "Is she in danger?"

Maverick shrugs. "Not right now."

"Why do we all have to be out here?" Owen asks. "Can't we take shifts and wait in our own beds?"

Maverick sticks a piece of hay into his mouth and chews on it. With his flannel shirt, black vest, and boots, he's changed his look. Brooklyn can't take her eyes off him.

"It's team building," I say. "We're supposed to be bonding."

"I could stand for some bonding," Maverick says. He glances at Brooklyn and pushes away from the pen. "I'm going to get some fresh straw to put down." He heads for Hey, Girl, Hey.

I count how many seconds pass before Brooklyn follows him.

It's thirteen.

"I'm going to stretch my legs," she says.

Right. Her legs.

Now it's just me and Owen. He joins me at the pen wall, looking down at Tinsel. "She's never going to quit running after him, even if he's bad news, is she?"

I wrap my arm around his shoulders. "It's been four months. I can't talk her out of it."

"I can't either."

Tinsel makes another big push, and the first small hoof appears.

"Wild how they come out feet first," Owen says.

"It won't be long now. Less than an hour, I bet."

Owen walks around the pen to check her from a different angle. At the end of the barn, a door opens, and a shadowy figure heads our way.

It might be Jed. He's checked on us a time or two.

But as it gets closer, I recognize the walk and the shape.

I hurry over. "Sebastian! What are you doing here?"

"Celebrating Christmas Eve with my lady." He has a straw basket in his arms. He pops the lid on one side. "I have hot chocolate and Christmas cookies."

"This is terrific." I pull a mug out of the basket and pour hot chocolate into it. "Owen, we have treats!"

"Where are the others?" Sebastian asks. "Isn't Maverick supposed to be out here while Tinsel is in active labor?"

"He is. He's in the hay room."

Sebastian takes in the barn. "With Brooklyn, I'm guessing."

"Yep. You called it." I sip the velvety hot chocolate. It's heaven.

Owen sidles up. "I heard treats."

Sebastian sets the basket down. "Help yourself."

We wander over to the pen to check on Tinsel.

"It's very nativity," Sebastian says. "The birth in the manger on Christmas Eve."

"At least it's the donkey this time."

Sebastian drapes an arm around me. "This will be a Christmas we remember."

"Because we spent it in a barn?"

He leans in close. "Because we spent it together."

His lips are cool against my warm ones from the

drink. We take a moment to relax into each other until the chorus of donkey laughter gets louder.

"I see a snout!" Owen says. "Isn't this when we have to decide if she needs help?"

I break away from Sebastian. "Donkey births often need help."

We watch a moment as Tinsel labors.

"I think the other donkeys are telling us to help," Owen says. He opens the side door of the pen to go inside.

"He's not going to get kicked, is he?" Sebastian asks.

"We went in for the others, too," I say. "It wasn't a problem."

Owen puts on a pair of gloves and starts pulling at the sac to expose the foal's snout.

"Is it breathing?" I ask.

"I think so," Owen says.

I can't stand it anymore and head inside the pen to kneel with him. "Tinsel looks awfully tired."

The donkey drops her head to the hay, wheezing.

"Call Jed," I tell Sebastian. "Tell him we're worried about Tinsel."

Sebastian whips out his phone.

I crawl to Tinsel's head. "You're a good girl," I tell her. "You're doing so great."

She rolls back and forth, tossing her head.

"I'm going to pull," Owen says. "My gut is telling me to pull."

When he grasps the foal's hooves, Tinsel lets out an unhappy squeal.

"Shh, girl," I say. "We're trying to help."

Maverick arrives, not bothering with the gate, but vaulting over the pen wall. "She's in distress. Did you call Jed?"

"He's on the way," Sebastian says. "He said to slowly pull the foal out if you need to. Not too fast."

Owen and Maverick take positions on each side of the baby.

I put Tinsel's head in my lap and stroke it. "You're all right, girl."

She seems spent and doesn't fight or cry. Maverick and Owen pull on the foal with smooth, easy pressure until it flops into the hay.

Tinsel makes a long sigh.

I hug her neck. "You did it, girl. You did it!"

The foal wiggles and rolls as Maverick and Owen pull the sac away and use a towel to clear its nose and mouth.

Tinsel lies quietly for another moment, then seems to realize her foal is out and stands up to check on it.

"Let her do her job," Maverick says, backing away. "It will be instinct for her."

We retreat to the pen walls as Tinsel tends to her foal, nudging it to stand up.

The baby attempts to rise on wobbly legs, but falls on its snout.

I check on Sebastian. He and Brooklyn watch from the rail. She has a glow about her. I know all about that. It's why she goes back. She doesn't expect Maverick to be hers. But she does expect him to perform.

And apparently, he's spectacular.

The side door opens and Jed runs in, his gray hair

flapping with his jaunty steps. "How's she doing?" He stops at the rail. "Ahh, there she goes. Our Christmas girl has a Christmas foal."

"Is that why she's called Tinsel?" Brooklyn asks.

"It is," Jed says. "Three years ago this week."

The foal makes another valiant attempt to stand, then collapses into a heap. It might take an hour for it to succeed. We've been through this before.

But now all the babies are born.

"I'll stay with her," Jed says. "You all have done your duty. Have your Christmas Eve." He winks at us. "Only a short while until midnight. You don't want Santa to see you all afoot while he's doing his business."

We laugh at that. Owen and I file out of the pen, but Maverick stays behind. "I think I'll hang out," he says. "Keep Jed company."

We collect our blankets and Sebastian's basket.

Brooklyn snags a cookie. "Where did these come from?"

"The party in the secret restaurant," Sebastian says. "Just a few close friends of Havannah and Donovan."

"I've still never seen it," Brooklyn says.

"Me neither," Owen says.

I keep quiet. Sebastian let me into the restaurant ages ago. It's a beautiful open space with an incredible view of the mountains.

"Soon enough," Sebastian says. "Now that Havannah's here full time again, we'll be back to normal."

We reach the rear door of the hotel. Owen and Brooklyn go inside, but I hang back.

"You going home with me?" Sebastian whispers in my ear.

"I was hoping so."

Brooklyn realizes I'm not coming in and retreats for a fierce hug. "Merry Christmas, Mila. Have a great day tomorrow."

"What are you two going to do?" I ask.

"We're working," Owen says. "Thought we could take other people's shifts since we couldn't go home."

"That's nice of you both," I say. "Hotel work is never done."

Sebastian looks up at the tower. Quite a few of the windows are dotted with light. "It's always busy around the holidays."

Owen and Brooklyn head inside, and I walk with Sebastian back to his car.

Snow starts falling, a white sparkle in the light of the lamps.

"It's sure beautiful in Colorado at Christmas," I tell him. "I never had a white Christmas in Houston. Not once."

"They're all white here," Sebastian says. He draws me close to him. "And I believe it just turned to midnight."

I check my phone. He's right.

"Merry Christmas, Mila," he says.

"Merry Christmas, Sebastian. I love you."

He pulls back. "You do?"

"You know I do."

"And you finally said it."

"Finally."

"I love you, too, Mila." His hand slides beneath my hair. As he closes in for a kiss, I feel the whisper of snow on my forehead and the warmth of him in front of me.

I've found a new home here. A place I love to work. A man I love, who loved me long before I could bring myself to say it back.

And a confidence I didn't know I would ever feel.

Maybe I did have a hard time finding someone to appreciate me. Maybe I was awkward and a late bloomer.

But I got here.

And kissing him on Christmas, beneath the fall of snow outside the place we both love, I believe with my whole heart that Sebastian was absolutely worth the wait.

EPILOGUE: MILA

March.

I pause by the front window of the hotel to look out on the madhouse that is the parking lot.

Bertie rushes by with a wry grin. "You interns outdid yourselves. We've never had a crowd like this."

Brooklyn hurries forward. "Mila, you need to go out to the gardens. Nobody knows the boundaries of your egg hunt to place the eggs."

Really? I drew a map. "Thanks. I'll go now."

"May the best intern win!" she calls.

"Exactly!" I volley back as I head through the lobby to cut to the side yard.

The five of us are at the end of our internship period. Maverick took himself out of the running for event manager and accepted a position Jed created for him as his assistant with the animals.

For our final assignment, the four of us left were

each given the same budget to create our own event for the hotel's Spring Spectacular.

I'm heading up the Easter egg hunt, which involves ten thousand stuffed eggs in the garden. To make it more interesting, there is an adult version with discounts and gift cards to dozens of local stores.

Owen is using the western ballroom for a massive craft event where kids can make bunny ears and decorate baskets.

Ilsa has taken over the restaurant for a five-course spring menu crafted by Chef Monique.

But it's Brooklyn who has outdone herself with a flower princess ball. She has set up the main ballroom as a pageant for hundreds of boys and girls wearing all manner of flowers and greenery. Most everyone who arrives comes in costume for her event because the winners get miniature motorized cars, which she got donated by a toy company.

She has proven scrappy with her budget, and when I walked through the ballroom with Owen earlier this morning, agog at the flowers and archways and a zillion Instagram-worthy photo spots, we both agreed that Brooklyn might have the event manager position in the bag.

But I'm impressed with myself as I push out the side door to enter the garden. Music from the DJ provides a festive, happy atmosphere for the bright, sunshiny day.

Already, hundreds of children are waiting outside the gates with their Easter baskets. Some of them wear the bunny ears from Owen's event. Others dance in front of a long line of motorized bubble machines I rented.

I chose an outdoor space to spend the majority of my budget on the takeaways, a definite gamble with the weather. Ten thousand eggs didn't come cheap. I contacted hundreds of businesses for the gift cards. I figured this would showcase my ability to network.

Chef Monique's kitchen crew was too busy with Ilsa's culinary event to spare anyone to put out eggs, so most of the staff in the garden wear laundry blues or custodial gray. I hope they don't mind the extra work.

Trey approaches. "We're not clear on where the under fives end and the bigger kids begin." He holds out the map printed on a clipboard.

I turn it around. "If you look at it this way, it makes more sense."

"Oooh, here's the castle. And this is the path. And the tulips are the boundary." He laughs. "I never said I was spatially gifted."

"We put up the temporary fence to protect the flowers and to keep the little ones from straying into the big ones' territory, or vice versa."

"Got it." He waves at the workers. "More over here!"

Egg hunts are fierce where I come from. In fact, some egg hunts back home host the youngest kids at a completely different time of day to avoid them getting trampled by the exuberant older ones.

I've separated them by only twenty minutes to avoid losing half my crowd if a family has children in both age brackets. I have a feeling once they go inside to Brooklyn's ball, they are never coming out again.

The adult version is well after the kids' hunt, timed to be between shifts of Ilsa's culinary event. I hope to catch them after the one o'clock but before the two-thirty seating.

Ilsa's is the only event with tickets. It sold out within a couple of weeks, which was a big win for her. The rest of us have a free-for-all, and we had to wildly guess at turnout.

I spot Cristal from laundry and her boyfriend from Bertie's crew spreading eggs. I'm glad at least one of Maverick's angry exes has moved on. Sometimes there are flare-ups among the women he sees. After six months, you'd think they would know his reputation, but he's got something they want.

Brooklyn still sees him off and on. She's dated a few Boulder locals outside of the hotel, but none of them have lived up to Maverick despite his flaws. She's drunk the Kool-Aid for sure.

Ten minutes until the littles will go. I head for the sound system and pick up the microphone. The DJ running the music turns it low so I can speak.

"Hello and welcome to the Castle Hotel egg hunt. Are you all excited?"

A chorus of cheers and high-pitched screams erupts.

"That's great! The first group to go will be children under the age of five. If you are already this many…" I hold up my hand with five fingers spread, "you will go when I call you in about half an hour! Families with children both over and under five, please separate them into their age groups. Thank you!"

I click off the mic and the music gets loud again. I wander the crowd, exclaiming over costumes and joining in a dance party in front of the bubble machines.

Havannah appears, baby Serenity strapped to her front. Donovan follows behind, trying to corral Rebel as he darts through the bubbles, waving his hands to maximize how many he can pop.

"It's lovely, Mila," Havannah says. "The weather cooperated and everyone is having a good time." She snags Rebel's shirt. "Bring it down, love. You're going to smack someone."

Rebel pulls away and takes off.

"I'll follow him," Donovan says.

"Boys," Havannah says. She peers down at the baby. "Please be a calm one."

The music drops low, and the DJ calls out, "Five minutes until the under-five-year-olds!"

Families move toward the garden gates.

"We'll be back for Rebel's age group," Havannah says. "I'll see you in the staff room at six for dinner and the big announcement!"

"I can't wait!"

I slip through the crowd and enter the main gate, careful to close it behind me. This is the scariest moment of a hunt. If I didn't plan well, people will trip and fall and there will be a disaster.

I take the mic. "Hello! Parents of the under fives, please direct your attention to the yellow balloons!" I point to my right. "There are three gates that will open.

If you encounter a fence, that's the boundary of your hunt!"

All sorts of catastrophes break across my vision. Trampling. Gates falling over. Fences jumped and no eggs left for the older kids.

I draw in a deep breath and check that staff members stand at each yellow gate. Everyone is ready. "Let's count it down! Ten, nine, eight…"

I let them keep going.

A hand lightly touches my waist. I sense Sebastian behind me. "It's going to be great," he says.

I nod.

"One!"

The gates swing wide.

I hold my breath.

The gates were a good idea. The crowd enters slowly, parents holding the hands of their little ones. The oldest of this age group dash ahead once inside, picking up eggs as they go and dropping them into baskets.

Within seconds, everyone is on the hunt and the eggs quickly disappear. I reach beneath the DJ table and pull out two enormous baskets of eggs. "You want to help me distribute to any sad kids who were too shy to run and grab?" I ask.

"Absolutely."

He takes one of the baskets, and we head for the gates. Everyone will have to leave the way they came. As we wait for people to walk by, I take Sebastian in, tall and handsome in his suit, his wavy black hair glinting in the sunlight.

Looking at him and realizing he's mine — it never gets old.

The eggs are all gone. The fences have held. I check my watch. Three minutes. It's amazing how fast they get snatched.

Parents lead their children out of the garden.

"You look like you could use a few extra," I say to a little girl who only has three eggs. I drop a handful into her basket. "Make sure you go inside to make bunny ears or dance at the ball!"

A band of kids with baskets filled to the brim walk out, and I smile and wave as they go.

One small girl in her father's arms is crying. "I didn't get any!" she sobs.

"Let me see your basket," I say. It's empty. I pour a good dozen eggs into it. "All better!"

She reaches a hand into them. "Look at all my eggs!" She holds a pink one up to show her father.

The mom mouths, "Thank you."

When everyone has passed, I still have a decent amount of eggs in my basket.

Sebastian walks over. "I used all mine."

"That's good. I have more for the next round."

"Such a brilliant idea. Nobody goes home sad."

I take his basket. "Exactly."

I dump my leftovers into the baskets I've prepared for the older kids. There will be fewer tears in that group, but I will still try to even out the distribution.

A happy cry goes up from the group. I turn to see what is happening, and spot Maverick leading Tinsel and her foal through the crowd.

People stop to pet them both.

"Did you know he was going to do that?" I ask Sebastian.

He shakes his head. "Maverick is full of surprises."

Maverick kneels down to tell the kids about the special donkeys from Avalonia. "Tell her a joke," he says to a kid near him.

The boy is shy, but the one next to him says, "What kind of jokes make a baby chick laugh? Practical yolks!"

Maverick lets out a deep, loud laugh. Within seconds, Tinsel is laughing with him in a high-pitched *hee hee haw haw haw.*

The baby looks up at Tinsel and adds her tiny *hee hee haw haw.*

"Do all donkeys sound like that?" I ask Sebastian.

"Nope. Havannah brought these from Avalonia. It's their special breed."

"Adorable."

The older kid hunt goes as smoothly. We get lucky that Brooklyn's ball has scheduled the fashion show for costumes at the same time as our adult event, so we don't have to contend with children trying to break into the hunt meant for grown-ups.

Then I'm done. I help break down the gates and give away all the balloons. I spot Sebastian in the lobby as I catch the tail end of Brooklyn's ball. An adorable girl is crowned the spring princess, and she waves like royalty from the stage.

Owen comes up beside me. "I think we may have left a lot of crayon marks on the floor of the western ballroom."

I laugh. "Housekeeping is going to hate us."

"Not as much as they would have if I had bought glitter."

"Good call."

Brooklyn hugs the princess and the music swells as tired kids and parents file out of the ballroom to the parking lot.

Owen and I keep to the wall to let them pass.

When the space is mostly empty, we approach Brooklyn to help break down the archways. Havannah appears, free of children for the moment. "Let's get some help for you," she says. "Always schedule extra workers at the end of an event." She gets on her phone.

Brooklyn grimaces. She hates it when she gets criticism, especially right before the big announcement.

Havannah waves us through the back doors. "You've all done enough. Let the staff handle the cleanup. I'll see you in the staff room shortly."

"Oh, gosh, it's time," Brooklyn says. She takes Owen's hand, then mine. "No matter what happens, I love both of you."

I squeeze her fingers. When we enter the staff room, most of the professional employees are there. Jessie, Suze, Olive, Chef Monique, Chef Filo, Hank. I spot Sebastian by the food table. He's talking to Maverick.

Ilsa sits alone at the end of the front row. None of us have gotten to know her, but I decide to plunk down on a chair beside her. "How did your foodie event go?"

"Flawless," she says. "I had a net profit of fourteen thousand dollars."

Dang. The rest of us *spent* our budgets. "That's fantastic."

"If I'm not named event manager, it will be because this place doesn't care about the bottom line."

"I see." I glance over at the food table, where Owen and Brooklyn are watching. Brooklyn hides a laugh behind a cup.

Owen saves me. "Mila, Ilsa, come get refreshments. The punch is good. I think it's spiked."

"Okay!" I jump out of my seat.

Sasha dashes inside from the front desk. She opted to stay there as lead, which is how we got Olive for assistant manager, but she's dying to know where the rest of us are going.

Our CFO Everett strides in, tall and imposing in his business suit. His eyes dart to Ilsa, then away, but I don't miss how she sits taller.

Interesting. I wonder what's going on there. Everett is another elusive figure at the hotel, always holed up in his office with the accounting team.

He approaches Sebastian and they shake hands.

Havannah breezes in with a flutter of scarves. "Okay, everyone, I have exactly twenty minutes before Serenity will insist on a feeding, so let's get to it!"

We all settle in the chairs. I sit by Ilsa again, and Owen and Brooklyn finish the row. Maverick stands by the door, shoving food in his mouth and ogling all the women.

Some things never change.

Havannah clasps her hands together. "This is an after party for our spring event, which went so fantastically. I couldn't be more proud, especially since I didn't have to plan one minute of it!"

Everyone laughs.

"Let's give it up for our four interns who made this day so spectacular."

Brooklyn and I squeeze hands as the rest of the staff applauds.

Havannah walks closer to us. "I want to tell you how proud I am. It's been beautiful to watch you all grow from new college graduates into important partners in running this hotel." She turns to the door where Maverick stands. "That includes you, Maverick! What a delight to bring Tinsel and her baby out to the children. You won't even believe the social media attention the hotel got today."

Maverick lifts his cup in acknowledgment.

"The professional staff has all given their input on where to place each of you. No matter where you end up, I hope you love your new role at the Castle Hotel."

She returns to the front of the room, where Sebastian passes her a set of cards.

Ohhhh, so he has known all this time!

I send him a look of *HEY!* and he shrugs.

But of course, I get it. This was a professional secret.

Havannah holds the cards against her chest. "I'm going to talk about Owen first. Owen, you have proven your reliability, your easygoing nature, and your absolute brilliance in handling difficult guests. Sasha and Olive both noted during your rotations with the front desk that you were exceptional in de-escalating tough situations, meaning that the managers were called significantly less when you were on shift."

She smiles at Owen. "So as of Monday morning, you will be promoted to chief guest relations officer. You will work with the front desk, the managers, and security to help handle any complications that occur with our guests. Congratulations." She waves Owen forward for a hug, then shows off his card, which bears a shiny gold pin with his new title.

Everyone claps. Brooklyn whistles.

When the room quiets, Havannah looks down at her next card. "Ilsa, we are all in awe at the incredible event you put on today and how it was marketed and executed. It was a highly profitable part of our Spring Spectacular when I didn't even ask for profit. Our CFO, Everett, has noted your attention to detail during your rotations in accounting, and because of his recommendation, plus your dual major in business, you have been named the marketing liaison with finance. We look forward to great things from your brilliant mind."

Ilsa stands up. Havannah must realize Ilsa is tensing for the hug, so she extends a hand instead. "Congratulations."

Brooklyn and I hold hands. I can see there will be no loser here. One of us will be event manager, and the other will be something amazing, too. Of course, with the way they are creating new roles, it may be that there is no event manager. Maybe the position will be split. Maybe none of us could handle such a big title.

"Brooklyn," Havannah says. "We have been impressed by your all-around ability to work in every aspect of the hotel, and your princess ball today was the crown jewel of your abilities. I have had the pleasure of working beside you on several events, but many of us have noticed you love princesses above all things."

The room laughs.

"It's true!" Brooklyn says, prompting another round of laughter.

"Because of this, we have created a position devoted to everything princess, including all upgrades to our princess wing, all choices about decor in the rooms and the tower, all parties and events involving the princess themes, and are naming you, until you come up with a better title, chief princess of the Castle Hotel."

Brooklyn jumps to her feet, tossing her long blonde hair, and giving a queenly wave. "I accept this honor, all ye peasants."

Havannah laughs, handing her a card with a gold crown pin. The two embrace in a long, happy hug.

I steal a glance at Maverick. He has set down his food and claps exuberantly, letting out a loud whoop.

He's proud.

He likes her.

I wonder what it will take for him to actually admit it. To choose her.

Maybe it's not in him.

I glance at Sebastian. His grin is big.

It's down to me.

Havannah gives Brooklyn a moment to sit down, then says, "Mila. I remember well when I saw your application. I thought, hospitality plus interior design. I can't wait for that. But you have been so much more.

You're strategic. You're a team player. You adjust to whatever task you're given. You can fix a toilet, smile through a long day of laundry folding, and watch hours of security footage without complaint. You showed today that you can pull off a tricky event for all ages, and you consider budget, safety, and a good time. I am more than thrilled to turn over much of my personal control to you as our event manager. Congratulations."

Tears smart my eyes as I stand up. I can barely hear the applause and cheers. Havannah holds out her arms and I walk into them in a daze.

As she pulls me in, I see Sebastian clapping loudly. He beams at me.

I did it. I pulled it off.

I got everything I wanted.

The job.

The man.

Friends.

A life I love.

As Havannah takes a moment to pin the gold bar to my hotel vest, I want time to slow down. To let me take this in.

It doesn't matter if I'm not as beautiful as Brooklyn, or as business savvy as Ilsa, or as powerful as Havannah.

I can work hard. I can love hard.

I can reach for what I want.

And get it.

Sebastian moves close, his arm around me. "I knew you could do it."

"You already knew I *had* done it!"

He kisses my hair. "Toughest secret I had to keep."

I finger the pin. "How many weeks ago did you order these?"

"Two."

"Sebastian!"

"It was hard."

"I guess we're legit. No more gap in the chain of command."

He leans in close to my ear. "Exactly."

I shake hands with several staff members before we get another break.

Then he leans in again. "I've already reconfigured your ID. Meet me in the secret suite in ten minutes?"

I glance around to make sure nobody overheard him.

Then I whisper back, "Make it five."

I hope you loved Mila and Sebastian! The Tasty Trilogy is complete! You can get a signed copy of Tasty Cherry or all three books in a gorgeous gift box at JJ's direct store LoveStoryBox.com.

If you love the Castle Hotel, learn how it began by going back to Havannah and Donovan on their first date, where she goes into labor at a restaurant and tries to hide it, in *Tasty Mango*.

Want to learn more about Anthony and Magnolia's

rivalry that leads to the creation of the Tasty Mango? Read *Spicy Pickle*.

Want to start at the very beginning? Meet brothers Dell and Donovan in JJ's original romantic comedies *Single Dad on Top* and *Single Dad Plus One*.

There will be another trilogy at the hotel! Look for *Tasty Banana* in 2025. Join JJ Knight's email or text list at JJKnight.com/news to be notified when it's out!

Or take a step further and VOTE on which member of the Castle Hotel staff needs a happily ever after. Is it Maverick and Brooklyn? Brooklyn and Owen? Some other combination? Someone new? Fans will decide on JJ Knight's Great Pickle Patreon, where you can join for free. (Hint: We play Pickle Bingo, too!)

BOOKS BY JJ KNIGHT

Romantic Comedies

Big Pickle ~ Hot Pickle ~ Spicy Pickle

Tasty Mango ~ Tasty Pickle ~ Tasty Cherry

Royal Pickle ~ Royal Rebel ~ Royal Escape

Juicy Pickle

Second Chance Santa

The Wedding Confession

The Wedding Shake-up

Single Dad on Top ~ The Accidental Harem

MMA Fighters

Uncaged Love ~ Fight for Her ~ Reckless Attraction

Get emails or texts from JJ about her new releases:

JJKnight.com/news

ABOUT JJ KNIGHT

JJ Knight is one of the pen names of six-time *USA Today* bestselling author Deanna Roy. She lives in Austin, Texas, with her family.

Visit her at jjknight.com.

facebook.com/jjknightauthor

instagram.com/deannaroyauthor

bookbub.com/profile/jj-knight